Night
of the
Fête

Night
of the
Fête

V S Rose

Matador
9 Priory Business Park
Kibworth Beauchamp
Leicestershire LE8 0RX, UK
Tel: (+44) 116 279 2299
Fax: (+44) 116 279 2277
Email: books@troubador.co.uk
Web: www.troubador.co.uk/matador

ISBN 978 1780884 424

British Library Cataloguing in Publication Data.
A catalogue record for this book is available from the British Library.

Typeset by Troubador Publishing Ltd, Leicester, UK

Matador is an imprint of Troubador Publishing Ltd

Printed and bound in the UK by TJ International, Padstow, Cornwall

For
Han and Wendy

1

At a home in the backstreets of Lower Riverend...

'Shit, only two As and a B. Perfection failed.'

'Well done son, don't be hard on yourself. Your mother and I are very proud of your A-level exam results. You've done well son, better than me or your mother managed. I know you'd like to go to university, Rick, but I'm sorry, you know that there is no way we can support you for another three years, especially now it looks like they're going to close the factory, so I'll be out of work soon. Getting a job is not so bad you know and just think how nice it will be to have your own income and some independence. You won't have to come running to me to borrow a fiver to go to the pub or to buy your mother a nice birthday present. I'm sure you'll find a good job with exam results like that; any employer would be pleased to have a bright boy like you on their payroll. Tell you what, let's go down the pub. I'll buy us both a pint to celebrate. You coming too, dear? Fancy joining us at the Bell and Beagle to celebrate our clever son's exam results?'

Rick Johnston was tall and relatively good-looking; not strikingly so, but handsome in a "boy-next-door" way. He had dark-brown wavy hair that curled over his shirt collar and twinkling grey eyes flecked with green. He had a happy disposition and a wry smile usually sat on his lips. He took care of his looks, but was not vain like his friend Niall. He enjoyed sport and had a good physique. He kept trim and fit by swimming two or three times a week at the public swimming pool and enjoyed playing in the school football and athletics teams. Rick was intelligent and interested in science and technology; he had a passion for finding out how things worked and why they went wrong. He cared for people and his environment and genuinely wanted to contribute something significant to improve the lot of people living in poverty in the Third World. A career in banking or insurance was not for him, he wanted to become a scientist and invent something new that would have a positive impact on improving the lives of people living in difficult remote villages in Africa or Asia. Rick was a nice guy.

He lived with his parents in a small two-bedroom 1930s terraced house in Lower Riverend, a suburb of Sevenoaks in the county of Kent. Lower Riverend was a scruffy, uninspiring village built in the early thirties, with a small run-down industrial estate and a few local shops in the centre. These were not designer boutiques, bio-greengrocers or Italian delicatessens, but an "Everything for One Pound" shop, a small Co-op supermarket and two charity shops. The architecture and houses here had not aged gracefully; it was very different from its upmarket neighbour, Sevenoaks. The relentless noise from the traffic on the nearby M25 motorway infiltrated every house and garden. The traffic was invariably stationary and toxic during the day, and went roaring past during the night, disturbing the sleep of the inhabitants and invading their dreams with visions of car crashes and endless traffic jams.

Rick was an only child and had achieved a lot in his exams. His parents, Olive and Cyril, were caring, but poorly-educated, people who had not had much success or luck in life. They were a very close family and the parents had a high moral attitude. Life had taken its toll on his parents and they had aged prematurely. Cyril was tall and lean with thinning straight grey hair. He worked in the local factory which produced tinned jams, mustards and pickles. Olive was short and rotund with pink cheeks and short grey curly hair. She worked part-time on the checkout tills in the local Co-op to supplement the family's income. She took pride in the fact that their house was always spotlessly clean and dinner was always on the table at 6:00 pm every evening when Cyril got home from work. Olive and Cyril earned enough money to survive without receiving any government benefits and had even managed to pay off their mortgage by saving hard when they were younger, but there was not much money to spare for treats and certainly not enough to support their son through university. They knew that Rick deserved to have the opportunity for further education and he was certainly intelligent and conscientious enough to make a successful student. It hurt them deeply that they were just not able to offer him this chance when so many of his school friends would be leaving home to start university in September and he was certainly more deserving than many of his friends. Cyril's job was now under threat and there was not much factory work in the region for someone aged over forty and he was well short of retirement age.

Rick had attended the local comprehensive school and somehow had managed not to fall in with the wrong crowd, but had nurtured a small close group of friends who had all supported each other. Andy, Niall and Stan were his closest friends and he wondered how they had fared in their exams. He was obviously upset that he could not go directly to university, but he loved his parents and did not blame them for their lifestyle. They had desperately wanted to help him pursue his studies and had offered to remortgage their house to raise some finance to fund him to attend university, but because his father was almost certainly going to lose his job in the near future, this was not a realistic proposition. Rick was loath to get a student loan to fund his university studies and accommodation, because he dreaded building up vast debts at such a young age and having repayments hanging over his head for years to come. He knew he would find a way of making a success of his life. It was important to him to make the most of his talents, even if he could not take the quickest, most direct route to academic success. He would become self-sufficient and make his parents and teachers proud of his achievements. There was always the option of furthering his education through Open University courses or studying part-time at college while working.

While in an affluent family home in nearby Sevenoaks...
    'Darling you passed home economics and English

3

literature A-levels with D grades, that's tremendous. Well done, sweetheart. Let's have a bottle of champagne to celebrate. Perhaps we should investigate the possibility of sending you abroad for a year to complete your education. Maybe Switzerland would be nice. How about attending a Swiss finishing school where you can improve your deportment and learn some French language and cordon bleu skills? Would you like that? I'll talk to your father about it.'

I'd be happy just to find a handsome, rich guy with a pad in Chelsea, who'd cosset me with jewellery from Hatton Garden, kitten-heel shoes from Manolo Blahnik, sexy lingerie from Princess Tam Tam and perfume from Chanel, mused Juliet. *Oh, and a weekly trip to the Oasis Spa to chill out and be pampered with my girl friends. No, I don't know what I want really. Certainly, that scenario would well suit some of my girlfriends, but is it really for me? I don't think so. Perhaps a gentleman farmer would suit me better, so I can live on a pleasant farm in the country; oh, providing it didn't smell too much. I'm not sure I want my Wellington boots to always be muddy and smelling of cow poo. A fruit and vegetable farm would be ideal, with trees covered in blossom in spring and full of fruit ripe for picking in summer and autumn. Yes, that's what I would like; an idyllic rural retreat, not too far from mummy and daddy. Definitely not a posh pad in London. Yes, and I'd also like a stable-block for two horses.*

Juliet Morgan was tall with long slender limbs and a rather boyish physique; no generous curves, just small buttocks and small firm breasts. She had long straight hair, naturally dark-blonde, but highlighted with gold and silver streaks. Her eyes were hazel, capped by strong eyebrows that needed to be kept under control. She was fun, sporty and well liked at school. She was inherently good, always doing as she was asked. She looked like her mother had when she was young, but did not have her mother's intellect or wild streak. She loved her parents and was a good caring daughter.

Juliet lived with her parents, Robert and Kathleen, in a large detached house in Sevenoaks set well back from the road in a mature garden of about one acre. The house was modern, but had been designed in the classic style of the county with a timber-framed construction, a half-tiled facade and tall elegant chimneys. Tasteful, but fully functional, with all the trimmings: an enormous farmhouse kitchen overlooking the garden, a separate laundry room, two master bedroom suites with a dressing room and en suite bathroom with power shower, two additional bedrooms with a shared bathroom, a sauna, a study, a formal dining room, a vast lounge and a double garage with a wine cellar. They also had a swimming pool in the garden, electrically heated, but with backup of solar power, and with a sliding glass cover so they could swim all year round.

Robert, Kathleen and Juliet all enjoyed swimming and relaxing by the pool, taking pleasure in their private well-tended garden. They were all quite sporty and looked after their health by exercising regularly and eating well. Robert was tall and slim, with a serious personality and a deep voice that commanded respect. He was handsome, with tousled black hair, streaked with grey, and dark brown eyes. He took an interest in his clothes and favoured a smart style with clean lines. Hugo Boss was his preferred designer. Kathleen was more bohemian and fun-loving in character than Robert. She favoured a smart-casual style of dressing, always looking elegant, but understated, in clothes made from natural fibres; cotton, linen and cashmere. She was very attractive with clear blue-grey eyes and shoulder-length dark-blond hair with highlights. She wore her hair with a side-parting and it was expertly styled and conditioned to give a full, bouncy appearance. Her make-up was discreet, she preferred a natural look, and she had always looked after her skin, which was radiant, so she rarely wore foundation. Kathleen favoured a Mediterranean diet with lots of tomatoes, vegetables, fruit and fish. She enjoyed cooking quality food for her family and they ate outside in the garden whenever the opportunity arose.

Robert was a successful investment manager in the City and had always invested his annual bonuses wisely in property and shares. He was not the frivolous sort like so many of his colleagues who regularly blew their bonuses on boys' toys for Christmas; Ferraris, power boats or Harley-Davidsons. Robert's only concession to this materialistic "I'm faster than you attitude" was his 600cc ride-on mower that he had treated himself to last Christmas. His car was a practical BMW 5 Series estate. He had aged prematurely. Immediately after Juliet was born he changed overnight from being a wild boy to being a very caring serious father. This was not entirely to Kathleen's liking. She had loved him because he was a rebel when he was younger and she still strove to retain her rebellious streak, despite all the trappings associated with life among the affluent upper middle classes in Sevenoaks. She wished Robert would sometimes do something irresponsible again.

Juliet had had a sheltered upbringing and had attended the local private girls' school. This was not a school noted for its academic record, but a school where Juliet had obtained a reasonably diverse and solid education, in a non-confrontational environment. She had been able to study some valuable life skills including needlework, household budget management, flower arranging and cookery as well as history, geography, mathematics, media studies and English. She regularly participated in sports activities after school. She was a keen horse rider and played in the school hockey and tennis teams. She had a small group of like-minded girl friends, which her parents approved of. Like Rick, she was an only child, but unlike Rick, her parents were both well educated and gave her plenty of support in everything she did. They wished she was slightly more academically inclined, but that was just not the case, and the important thing was that she was a kind loving daughter which more than made up for her lack of academic achievement.

Sevenoaks was an affluent market town with fast train links to London, highly favoured by bankers and investment managers who did their daily commute to the City of London, but could enjoy walks in the countryside at the weekend. It had a weekly market on Saturday mornings which sold fresh fish, olives, cheese and many other exclusive foodstuffs, flowers and artisan pottery. The market was a favourite haunt for the locals, and selecting the olives for the evening's aperitifs was generally followed by a coffee and muffin in Caffè Nero. The shops in the High Street had mostly been restored and their windows were dressed with an artistic display of exclusive and expensive wares. There was a small region of narrow back streets known as "The Shambles", which dated from medieval times and contributed to the charm of the town.

The magnificent National Trust estate of Knole Park stood near the town centre. The Knole estate was comprised of a Tudor manor house surrounded by an extensive deer park which was an outstanding attraction for the town and the park was well frequented by the locals at weekends. The park was first surrounded by a fence in the 15th century and originally had been used by the nobility for hunting. The park today retained a very natural look, which was typical of the local Kent countryside, with swathes of bracken and woodland including beech, hawthorn, oak, yew and silver birch trees. It was the perfect location for a gentle family stroll after lunch on a Sunday and was also an ideal training ground for serious joggers who enjoyed exercising in nature. As well as the usual squirrels, moles and rabbits one would expect to find in a country park, native fallow deer and Japanese Sika deer could also be found grazing quietly in the grounds. They were quite tame and remained relatively unperturbed by the large numbers of visitors to the park. In fact they positively enjoyed being hand-fed bread and carrots by fearless children, who defied the many "Do not Feed the Deer" notices.

The great storm of 1987 had caused much devastation and the park was still littered with fallen trees, which were slowly decaying and creating an interesting component to the undergrowth and a habitat for insects. A replanting programme had been instigated to restore the woodland that was devastated eighteen years ago and numerous plantations of young trees had sprung up around the park to replace the lost oaks and beeches. There were also some formal boulevards in the park lined by ancient trees, which attracted young mothers with prams or buggies to push. In spring the park was painted with fresh greens of every hue, but it was in autumn that the colours were particularly spectacular, when the beech leaves turned to vibrant copper.

The manor house was a hotchpotch of ages and styles as various earls, lords and archbishops had extended the original house during the seventeenth and eighteenth centuries. It contained a magnificent art gallery of Old Masters and portraits by top English artists including Reynolds and Gainsborough. The majority of the house was open to visitors from Easter through to the end of October, while the extensive deer park surrounding the house remained open all year round. The owners, unable to meet the huge costs of upkeep, had bequeathed the house to the National Trust and now occupied a few private apartments within the house which opened onto a walled garden, where they could sit, sheltered from the prying eyes of the visitors.

So, Sevenoaks benefitted from affluent inhabitants, stylish detached houses, good schools, small exclusive shops, an artisan market and a magnificent deer park and manor house. Basically, it was a nice civilised place to live, convenient for London and the rolling Kent countryside.

Some fairies lived there too, because they also liked it a lot.

****** SPECIAL ANNOUNCEMENT ******

Fairies' 205th Grand Fête
Saturday 3rd September

Fancy dress parade – Prizes galore
Blueberry punch
Candyfloss
Tombola
Face-painting
Fawn racing
Frog baiting

*** Sumptuous feast ***

Music and dancing till dawn

Starts at 7:30pm
Be there or be square

Contact Coralie for more information or with offers to
help with the organisation

The fairies were friendly with another type of being, the Pevi. But there was trouble afoot in Sevenoaks for the Pevi and this had recently been reported in their weekly newspaper:

THE PEVI WEEKLY
13 August 2005

This Week's Headline News Stories
Brought to you by Edmund, Chief Pevi
Sevenoaks, UK

Positive-Ion Decrease in Sevenoaks – A Crisis Waiting to Happen?
 Atmospheric monitoring shows that the concentration level of our vital life-giving positive ions is decreasing in Sevenoaks. This reduces the strength of our immune systems and leaves us vulnerable to disease and allergies.

Young Pevi in Sevenoaks are Depressed
 Doctors have observed an increased occurrence of depression in young Pevi in Sevenoaks. Could this be related to the decrease in positive ions in the atmosphere?

2

In Lower Riverend...

Rick was fed up. He knew his parents couldn't afford to support him through university, they had already discussed that several times, but he had achieved good grades and had an offer from Bristol to study molecular biology. He wondered whether it was feasible to contribute to the costs of his fees by working his way through university, but the likelihood of finding a part-time job that paid sufficiently well was miniscule. Perhaps he could try his hand at being a high-class gigolo. He'd have to work hard on improving his diction and do something about his South London accent. He'd also have to buy some smart, expensive-looking gear and get a new hair cut. Rick chuckled to himself. This plan was just not a goer; he could never keep up the pretence of fawning over a woman, however gorgeous she was, who wanted to pay him for sex. He'd rather oblige for free and feel her radiate with passion and happiness. Anyway, his sexual experiences were limited to making love twice to a girl he had met last year on holiday in Wales; he was an amateur, so would have a serious learning curve to climb.

He preferred the alternative approach of getting a job as a laboratory technician in one of the biotechnology companies nearby and studying part-time. His Aunt Sarah had followed this course. She had started work at eighteen and studied hard to obtain a Higher National Certificate in biochemistry; then she had passed her Membership of the Institute of Biology exams, before finally embarking on a PhD in molecular informatics at the ripe old age of thirty-four. Not the easiest route to follow, but it had worked for her. All this was achieved while working in the pharmaceutical industry and getting paid a decent salary. She was now a scientist of international acclaim who gave presentations on her research at conferences all over the world. Science definitely ran in his mother's family's genes, though his own mother had somehow fallen between the cracks when intellect had been distributed. He suspected that, unfortunately, things were probably harder these days. He knew that many employers in the pharmaceutical and biotechnology industry were strapped for cash and were generally looking for cost-cutting solutions, rather than being philanthropic and employing people to work a four-day week and study on the fifth day. However, perhaps he'd give Aunt Sarah a ring tomorrow and ask her advice; he'd like to talk to her about his options and she'd be proud to hear about his academic achievement.

Meanwhile, he wanted to celebrate his two As and a B with his mates in a pub in Sevenoaks; the Greyhound and Ferret was his favourite venue. There were no decent pubs in Lower Riverend. He hoped his friends had also achieved the grades they wanted, though this was doubtful for at least two of them. Maybe the drinks would be on him tonight.

While in nearby Sevenoaks...

Juliet was fed up. She had hoped to pass three A-levels with C grades; home economics, English literature and media studies, but she just hadn't put in the study time for media studies and her D grades in home economics and English literature were hardly exemplary. She felt she'd wasted the opportunity her parents had given her. In retrospect, she realised that she probably hadn't been pushed hard enough by her teachers. Still, she accepted the fact that the reality was that she only had herself to blame. She had set her hopes on being accepted at the Sloane Business School, an exclusive college in London for business and secretarial PA studies, which also ran the legendary PumaWalk courses on image and style. She needed better results to enable her to fulfil her true potential and follow her preferred course. PumaWalk was her dream because they would have taught her correct deportment and given her direct contacts into the modelling world. She knew she was quite stunning. She had known this since she was eleven, but she was still rather ungainly so would need expert tutoring to become a top model. At the very least, a diploma from the Sloane Business School would have given her a firm foundation to get a well-paid job in the City as a personal assistant to some rich banker.

She wanted to be independent and earn a reasonable salary in the short-term. In the long-term, she dreamed of an ideal family life, married to a caring husband and living in a large comfortable farmhouse in the countryside. But she had blown it by not taking her studies seriously enough and now she had to reconsider her options. Maybe she could retake media studies at Christmas and crash revise until then.

Her thoughts were interrupted when the phone rang. It was Juliet's best friend Claire. Claire was ecstatic because she had obtained better grades than predicted and could now choose between offers from two different universities. She was being very irritating and kept screaming and squealing with joy, asking Juliet which university she thought she should choose.

'Let's go to the pub tonight to celebrate and have some fun. I feel like getting seriously drunk and picking up some funky guys. See you at six-thirty down the Greyhound and Ferret in Sevenoaks High Street. I'll call the rest of the gang.' She hung up with a cacophony of cheerful giggling, completely forgetting to ask Juliet about her results. That did not improve Juliet's mood.

Rats, thought Juliet, *I really don't want to go out tonight. I just want to mope about the house and not see anyone or try to shape up and be cheerful.*

Later, however, when she had regained her composure, she realised that she would have to admit her failure at some point, so she decided she might as well get it over with tonight and drown her sorrows with a few large glasses of Pinot Grigio in the company of her best girl friends. After all, they would be sympathetic and she would make herself have fun. She was not someone who got maudlin when she was drunk. She went up to her room to plan what to wear for the evening.

Rick got to the pub early at 6:00 pm, before his mates had arrived. He chose a big oak table in the corner where they couldn't be seen directly from the bar. It was going to be a heavy session, so he reckoned it was best not to draw attention to themselves too early on in the evening. He went to the bar and ordered a pint of Stella Artois. While he was waiting for his mates, he reflected how much he liked the decor of the Greyhound and Ferret which was a mix of old dark beams, wooden furniture and stripped polished floorboards, with a contemporary glass and steel bar, backed by a long mirror and black cubic wine racks. There were bright modern posters advertising various wine and beer producers on the walls. He did not like the landlord much, however, who seemed overtly cocky and opinionated. His red face and fat pock-marked nose, suggested he drank too much and probably had high blood pressure. Not someone who welcomed his customers with a friendly word. Rick told himself that he really should re-explore some of the other pubs in the town centre, especially those that had been renovated recently.

Andy soon arrived, quickly followed by Niall and Stan. Together they formed a motley crew, with a wide diversity of character and appearance. Rick stood six-foot high, with dark wavy hair and a permanent smile. He worshipped his vintage Norton motorbike which had been given to him by his grandfather for his eighteenth birthday. Rick was mature and emotionally well balanced for his age. Andy was taller and thinner than Rick and had even longer hair. He dreamed of becoming a rock musician and playing lead guitar in a heavy metal band. He was rather shy and had a tendency to hide behind his hair when threatened, in a rather girlish way. Like many shy tall men he walked with a slight stoop, embarrassed of his true height. Niall in contrast was small in stature, but dramatically good-looking. He was very sharp and quick to spot any opportunity to get one over on his mates; always ready to play a trick on his friends. And then there was Stan.

Stan just didn't fit with the rest of the gang. He was not particularly bright, but was highly studious, incredibly serious and somewhat old-fashioned. Stan didn't really have any other friends at school and Rick and company had taken pity on him and taken him under their wings. He enjoyed being one of the gang, even if it wasn't his ideal gang, at least he was associated with some really interesting guys at school and he felt protected by them.

After the initial blokeish banter, talk came round to exam results. Rick was delighted to hear that both Andy and Niall had also done well, but it was heartbreaking to hear Stan tell of his disappointment at failing both A-levels. He didn't know what to do with his life now and his parents were embarrassed by his failure to excel. The conversation soon became strained, so Niall went to the bar to get another round, hoping Andy and Rick would sort Stan out before he returned with the drinks. Luckily for him, the pub was busy and there was a melee of people at the bar, so service was slow. The ploy played off and Niall was spared any need to be sympathetic to Stan. He found them all chatting happily when he got back to the table with the drinks. After all, it was an evening for celebration and Stan didn't want to ruin his dear friends' fun. It was more important to keep them as friends and not wallow in his sorrow.

Claire arrived at the pub first of the girls. She was still hyper-excited about her exam results and ready to chat all evening about what the future held for her at university. It was a warm August evening and she was happy to wait outside the pub for Juliet and Susie to arrive; the rest of their girl gang had unexpectedly declined to join the celebrations. Claire wondered if maybe she had been a trifle overwhelming on the phone, and she also realised that she had completely forgotten to ask her friends about their results. This was very bad form, but she would be off to university soon and making a completely new set of interesting intelligent friends, so it didn't really matter too much if she had put her foot in it and upset some of the old gang. Juliet and Susie were the most fun anyway and they would be here soon.

Juliet arrived next, quickly followed by Susie. Susie, like Juliet, was suntanned tall elegant and slim with long straight blond hair. She had a kind demeanour similar to that of Juliet, though she was more academically gifted. Claire, on the other hand, was pure Celtic, with a curvaceous body, porcelain skin and fiery red hair, with a temperament to match. The three girls went into the pub arm in arm and laughing cheerfully together. They were pleased school and, more importantly, exams were over for the summer and they could enjoy the delights of a long relaxing holiday without too much stress. They had been drinking at the Greyhound and Ferret occasionally since they were seventeen and no one had ever questioned their right to be there. They were now all eighteen so could drink perfectly legally and had their ID cards to prove it. Their arrival in the pub caused a few heads to turn. They looked gorgeous and radiated a genuine happiness.

Claire, in a moment of rare generosity, fuelled by her realisation that she had been a trifle self-centred on the phone, offered to get the first round in. She came from the least well off family of the three and had the smallest allowance so often couldn't afford to pay her way, but her mother had given her twenty pounds to spend this evening and that should be enough for two rounds. The Pinot Grigios were quickly downed and Susie went to the bar to refresh their glasses. Susie had achieved what was expected of her and would now go to the Sloane Business School. Juliet was silently seething with jealousy, but knew she only had herself to blame. She would get there next year, or go to Switzerland as her mother wanted. She felt happy for Susie though.

Meanwhile, the guys and especially Niall had noticed the giggling group of girls and were watching and planning their move.

When Juliet went to the bar for the third round of drinks, she was horrified by the treatment she received from the landlord. He turned purple in the face and screamed at her to get out of his pub. He went completely berserk, shouting that he had told her a hundred times before never to set foot in his pub again, and he was going to phone the police immediately. He called her a little whore and a druggie. Juliet was completely perplexed and rather shaken. No one had ever shouted at her in this manner and been so insulting in public.

Rick happened to be waiting to be served at the time and observed the landlord's wild accusations at close quarters. He felt sorry for Juliet who was clearly highly distressed and embarrassed at being shouted at in a crowded pub. She certainly didn't look like a prostitute or drug addict to him. On the contrary, he thought that she looked remarkably sweet and innocent. He felt he should do something to support her. He pushed his way to her side and spoke assertively to the landlord, telling him that she was his friend and he had no right to shout at her and make such insulting and unjustified accusations. Unfortunately, his intervention did not have the effect he had desired and the landlord just turned on him and ordered Rick out of the pub too. Everything was getting completely out of hand.

Rick and Juliet went outside in a shocked but rather bemused state. Rick apologised to her for intervening and hoped that he had not offended her. He proffered his hand and introduced himself. She was still shaking from the shock of being insulted so forcefully and stammered her reply.

'Yes, um, hello Rick. I'm Juliet, Juliet Morgan. Thank you so much for trying to intervene on my behalf. I have absolutely no idea what the landlord was talking about. I haven't been in that pub very often and I certainly won't ever go back now. I was just enjoying a drink with my friends to celebrate our A-level results. Not that I did very well, but both my friends did. I feel very shaky after the way he treated me. Perhaps we could go and sit on that bench over there, while I recover my composure. What a horrible man!'

Rick took her arm and led her to the bench. He told Juliet that she looked a bit like another girl who he had seen sometimes in the pub, who he was sure was dealing in drugs and he suspected that it was a case of mistaken identity. They sat quietly for a few moments waiting for Juliet's heart to stop racing and then noticed that there was a police car parked down a side road, just opposite the pub. Juliet had just about stopped shaking by now and they decided to go and talk to the police about their appalling treatment.

The policeman was sympathetic when he heard their story, but didn't want to get involved and replied, 'Oh no, we're getting out of here. That landlord's a complete loony; he's always calling the police about minor misdemeanours. I'd find another pub to frequent if I were you.' He rejoined his mate in the car and the two policemen promptly drove off at high speed with their blue light flashing.

The two teenagers didn't know whether to laugh or cry. Their evening of celebrations had been ruined by a crazy landlord, but they had recovered sufficiently that they could now see the funny side of things. They looked at each other properly for the first time. Juliet thought Rick had lovely laughing eyes and he thought she looked like an angel, definitely not like a whore. They both smiled and realised that they had made a new friend in each other. They looked at each other in silence for several seconds then started to laugh. A gentle giggle at first, but it was soon superceded by a full belly ache of a laugh that rocked the neighbourhood.

The rest of the girls and boys had watched the events unfold at the bar with first curiosity and then amazement at the landlord's nasty accusations. They decided it was time for them to leave too. Claire told the landlord he was a "tosser" and should be sued for libel, before marching out of the pub arm in arm with Susie. Niall also decided to put his awe in and called the landlord a "pervert" and a "stupid old fart" before walking slowly outside, quickly followed by an embarrassed Andy and Stan.

It was clear that a new plan was needed if they were all to enjoy the evening and Juliet already had an idea what this could be.

3

Juliet had a brilliant plan, cheaper and more fun than sitting in a stuffy pub lounge drinking oneself silly all evening. They could buy some bottles of wine and crisps, take an iPod player and some speakers and have a party in a secluded glade she knew in Knole Park, far away from the prying eyes of the family who lived in the magnificent Elizabethan house at the centre of the park. It was still light, so there would be no problem finding a good place and Juliet knew the park well; she had been playing hide-and-seek there since early childhood with her nanny, and going for walks with her parents after lunch on Sundays. She also knew the location of a secret gate which was hidden by bushes and never locked. They could enter there unobserved and enjoy the still balmy August evening and the intoxicating smell of nature. Juliet thought the park smelt of deer poo and bracken, so decided she should take some scented candles or incense sticks to create a more sensuous atmosphere. She loved nature, but only up to a point.

The guys and girls were all in favour of the plan and agreed to meet up in forty-five minutes' time. The boys went to the off-licence to buy a selection of drinks, while Claire and Susie went to the late-night Tesco to get some cheap wine and easy-to-eat food for the party. Juliet's house was en route to the park, so she ran home to get her iPod and speakers. She hoped her parents would be out for the evening, so she wouldn't have to explain her exploits to them. They might not approve of her plan. She was in luck this time and she managed to find a box of sandalwood-scented candles and three bottles of cheap Spanish Cava at the back of the drinks' cabinet that no one would miss. She wisely decided against taking her parents' vintage Moët & Chandon champagne even though that would have seriously impressed her new friends.

The dire consequences of being exposed as a petty thief at home just weren't worth the brief moment of glory. She also grabbed a warm fleece, not the sexiest garment in her extensive wardrobe, but practical as it would undoubtedly get chilly later. Everything was hurriedly packed into her favourite large patent orange tote bag and she set off down the road smiling broadly and singing a Robbie Williams tune, *Angels*, quietly to herself; happy to have made some new friends. In the short time she had known him, she had found Rick quite attractive and felt a quickening of her heartbeat as she tried to picture his face and lopsided smile again.

The boys and girls all arrived in good time at the agreed meeting point in a narrow country lane, near the secret gate that Juliet had described. The girls came armed with bottles of white wine, crisps and a selection of sandwiches and quiches for the party, while the boys, except for Stan, had bought spirits (with the wicked intention of getting the girls drunk quicker) and beer for themselves, so as not to get too drunk too quickly. Stan had rather unwisely decided to do something original and had bought a bottle of advocaat and lemonade from the off-licence, hoping that his ingenuity would impress the girls. This was his mother's favourite tipple at Christmas, a special treat only to be savoured during the festive season. He always tried hard, but rarely quite got it right. Luckily, practical Rick had thought to buy a cheap combination knife, corkscrew and bottle opener in the off-licence and he had a torch in his pocket because he had planned to walk home along some unlit roads after his evening out.

The new friends squeezed through the secret gate, with the girls chatting excitedly and the boys quietly hoping the evening would turn out as they desired; new packets of condoms pressing gently against their buttocks through the back pockets of their jeans.

Juliet led the way through the wood to a small glen she knew. The glen was about the size of a badminton court and was completely obscured from view by a dense undergrowth of bracken and brambles and mature dark-green fir trees. This had been one of Juliet's favourite hiding places as a child, when she had wanted to be alone to think and didn't want to be found by anyone. She was delighted by her choice of location. It was dark cosy and very secret. Perfect. The earth was dry and hard, and covered by long grass with feathery seeds that the youngsters soon discovered tickled every patch of bare skin that it could find. A few euphorbias with delicate pale-green flowers decorated the boundary between the undergrowth and the grassy carpet. As a child, Juliet had adored these unusual plants with their green flowers and had pestered her parents to allow her to create a small bed of euphorbias at home. It finally grew to contain more than twenty different species that she had been able to source on trips to various garden centres in the region.

'Isn't this just perfect?' declared Juliet and everyone agreed.

And so the party started. The friends believing that they were completely hidden from view and able to let their hair down in complete privacy. However, in reality, they were being silently observed by a few innocent deer in the park, attracted by the smell of potato crisps, and by two not-so-innocent fairies, bored and intent on making mischief.

Keen to get the party going quickly, Niall suggested that the girls might like a large whiskey in a plastic cup, but the teenage girls were unaccustomed to drinking spirits and the offer was unanimously rejected, much to Niall's disappointment. Whiskey was not a popular drink with teenage girls, even if they were having a special celebration. Stan proudly offered his advocaat and lemonade and was met with shrieks of derision. Bad enough when it's on-the-rocks, but undrinkable when warm. Juliet came to the rescue with her Spanish Cava, a perfect drink for a summer's evening, even if unchilled. The bubbles soon made all the girls even more giggly. Boys being boys all elected for beer, including Stan. He could always give the advocaat to his mum as a surprise present tomorrow.

Juliet set up her iPod player and speakers and put on some dance music. She was rather conservative in her taste for a teenager, preferring pop to heavy rock, but it created the right atmosphere for chatting and soon the dancing started. It quickly became clear that the girls were there to have fun, not sex, and before long the boys accepted this status quo and could relax and enjoy the fun. Everyone was laughing a lot and the dancing was getting wilder and wilder as the sun went down. Niall and Susie turned out to be particularly athletic and talented street dancers to everyone's delight. This was especially remarkable considering they were hearing romantic Robbie Williams' songs and giving them a street-dance interpretation. Juliet wished she'd brought her camcorder to record their outlandish exhibition. Stan invited Claire to waltz and she graciously accepted, while Juliet and Rick pogoed badly for a while and laughed a lot. Andy was content to sing along with the music and watch everyone else's antics.

Once it got dark, Juliet lit her scented candles to provide some light and atmosphere in the glade. Everyone hoped that their flickering light would not attract the attention of the owners in the big house, but this did not happen as the glade was well shielded from view by the dense vegetation. It was soon clear that the only two people who had any real attraction for each other were Juliet and Rick, and they chose not to smooch together, but to remain at a respectable distance from each other for the dancing, like everyone else. "Fun" and "celebration of the end of school and exams" were the keywords for the new friends' party. Life would get more serious for everyone later. It was not an evening for falling romantically in love.

The deer and fairies found the dancing exhibition extraordinary, but loved the rhythms of the pop music. The fairies wanted to join the party and were desperate for a drink, so they quietly slipped into the glade and grabbed the first bottle they could find...the advocaat. Juliet turned her head in their direction as she subconsciously felt their presence, but saw nothing. The fairies sat unobserved at the edge of the glade, amused by the dancing, commenting on the teenagers' lack of grace and coordination and drinking warm advocaat out of the bottle. The deer soon bored of the exhibition and went back to care for their young hidden nearby in the bracken and crying for their mothers.

'So any ideas for tricks we can play on these youngsters? They are having a lot of fun; I don't see why we shouldn't have some fun too,' enquired the fairy called Benjie, after his fourth swig of advocaat. 'They can't see us, though I suspect that the pretty girl with the long blond hair probably would have the ability if trained.'

'Let's turn the heat up a degree with this party and spike their drinks with our secret hallucinogenic herb, Partitim, and see how the night progresses,' suggested the other fairy, Zak.

'Good idea. Human teenagers are such an easy target and this will be a great spectator sport.'

Unfortunately for the teenagers, they had become the target for Benjie and Zak's well-known mischief-making. These two fairies were best friends and when together, enjoyed nothing more than playing tricks on unsuspecting fairies, Pevi or humans. Always denying their involvement in any unexplained happening, but every fairy knew the culprits. They were trouble, but funny and essentially good natured.

And so it came about, that the fairies spiked the open bottles of Cava and cans of beer with Partitim and the teenagers drank the spiked alcohol. The fairies laughed and laughed as the antics of the group of friends grew wilder. They were enjoying the free alcohol provided by the teenagers and soon finished the open bottle of advocaat, and set their eyes on the bottle of whiskey that no one wanted. Frantically, they sent out thought messages for Niall to take the top off the whiskey and Niall, being highly susceptible to external mental influences, soon obeyed and opened it for them, then carried on dancing with Susie. So the fairies were happy again and continued drinking and laughing, unheard and unobserved by the teenagers.

At some point during the night, Stan decided to put the bottle of advocaat back in his rucksack to take home for his mother; always the sensible boy. But all he found was an empty bottle and next to it was a nearly empty bottle of whiskey. He was pretty sure no one had drunk either of these drinks, so he wondered what was going on. But he felt a little strange, so supposed that he was mistaken. Perhaps it was time to find a secluded corner and curl up into a ball on the soft bracken and let sleep waft over him till morning. He knew that the girls were not sexually attracted to him, so he would be safe.

The next morning, Stan woke up first to find Niall snuggled in his arms. He surveyed the glade and saw that the girls were all cuddled together on the other side of the glade in "spoons" formation, and Rick and Andy were up a tree, wearing only their underwear and shivering in their sleep. Stan quietly disentangled himself from the sleeping Niall and waited for his friends to wake up. Andy and Rick would certainly have some explaining to do! Stan was unable to see this, but the two fairies were lying on their backs in the centre of the glade playing "dead flies" and laughing uncontrollably, still well under the influence of the human's liquor. Their hangovers hadn't yet started, but when they did, they would be mega and the fairies would wish they had not persuaded Niall to open the bottle of whiskey.

Slowly, all the teenagers woke in the early morning sunlight and regarded each other with mild curiosity and amusement. Initially, Andy and Rick didn't know whether to be embarrassed or laugh. Luckily, they were both wearing designer underwear and had good physiques, so laughing seemed the best ploy. Unfortunately, everyone, including the two fairies, was far too drunk to remember the highlights of the night's partying; no one could recall what had actually happened and when the party had finished. Fortunately, no one was injured and although everyone was a little wonky on their feet, no one was too seriously concerned about the events of the evening, just curious why they had got so drunk so quickly.

24

'Perhaps we'll read about it next week in the Sevenoaks Chronicle,' Juliet joked, while watching Rick climbing into his crumpled trousers out of the corner of her eye.

Everyone was convinced that they had only drunk wine or beer during the party, but when the empties were gathered together, they counted four empty wine bottles, eighteen empty beer cans and an empty bottle of advocaat and a nearly empty bottle of whiskey. The friends were confused and all agreed to sleep in their bracken beds for a couple of hours, to shake off the effects of the alcohol (and the Partitim), before venturing home and facing the wrath of their parents. A good and convincing explanation for their failure to come home would need to be invented and agreed upon. The simplest explanation they could come up with, was that they had spent the night at a friend's house because they were very tired at the end of the evening's celebrations, but were unable to find a taxi home. They wisely decided to phone home before sleeping again as it was already 7:30 am and their parents would be up and about.

Juliet postulated that *Parents always worry too much. They do not trust their offspring to take care of themselves, but there again, perhaps they have good reason.*

When the youngsters turned on their mobiles, they found that they had all missed calls from their parents the night before. They nervously phoned home, apologised profusely and said that they hoped their parents had not been too worried about them. Everyone was told to be more considerate in future and phone home whatever the hour if they were not coming home. They then snuggled down in the long dry grass, with girls on one side of the glade and boys on the other side, before falling asleep again to rid themselves of their hangovers.

The fairies, Benjie and Zak, decided that the iPod and speakers would be useful for their fête in two weeks' time, so took them away to give to their beloved fairy queen, delighted with their new acquisition. The hangover would start in an hour's time and wreck the rest of their day.

4

The fairy community in Knole Park had thrived for several centuries. They lived in close harmony with nature and cared for the sick animals, plants and trees in the park to the best of their ability. There were about sixty fairies in the community. They lived in houses built of bracken and twigs, with a carpet of moss on the floor. The furniture was simple but practical. They spent as much time as possible outdoors, communing with nature, so lavish houses and furnishings were not necessary and not lusted after. Their village was protected by a magical perimeter that hid the houses from the view of humans and also prevented humans approaching too closely. The fairy palace where the queen lived was grander than the village houses and decorated with antique furniture from their ancestors and with exotic presents brought by fairies visiting from foreign countries.

Their world revolved around harmony and having fun, and they enjoyed drinking far too much alcohol on their frequent ritual occasions. Hangovers and minor disputes were a common part of life, but aggression, terrorism and wars were unheard of and completely uncomprehended by them. They lived life for the present and thought little about history, philosophy or any deeper meanings to life.

Despite their alcoholic lifestyle, the fairies usually remained slim and in excellent physical condition because they had a high quality vegetarian diet with lots of fruit, flowers, nuts and vegetables and they greatly enjoyed taking exercise, especially dancing and flying. They averaged about fifty centimetres in height, but they weighed virtually nothing in human terms because the cells in their bodies contained small pockets of helium gas which is lighter than air. Therefore, they only needed a relatively small pair of wings to be able to fly. They were also strong; stronger than their delicate-looking bodies would suggest.

The fairies who lived in Knole Park belonged to the sect of "Earth-bound fairies". This is a sect which lived on the planet Earth, but inhabited a parallel universe to the human race where matter had a lower vibrational frequency. They had learnt the secret of how to cross between these two worlds at will, but they rarely stayed very long in the human world as the higher vibrational frequency of matter did not suit their metabolisms, so the fairies risked premature aging by visiting too frequently or staying too long. If they stayed too long, they also began to transmute and become visible to humans. A small number of humans have a natural talent for fairy vision, if shown how to use their gift, but even those with this ability rarely knew they had such a skill as the fairies avoided too many manifestations in the human world. Sightings of fairies by human beings are very rare and always initiated by the fairies.

Recently, a new fairy queen had been appointed to lead the community. The new fairy queen was outstandingly beautiful, with an ethereal quality. She had a mass of untamed curly hair the colour of ripe chestnuts. Her hair was so light and fine that it floated gently in the breeze, giving a soft-focus appearance to her face. Her skin was unblemished, the colour of white peach flesh, to which her eyes made a striking contrast, being a vivid emerald green. She prized all things quirky colourful and modern and loved to wear the latest creative fashions; many designed by herself, others she had copied from photos she found in glossy magazines left behind in the park by negligent humans. She was an excellent seamstress. Her main passion, however, was sculpture and she was a talented sculptress. She would spend any free time she had working on her latest two artistic projects; a bejewelled bullfrog with a mosaic-encrusted body and enormous ruby eyes that followed you around the room, and a giant erotic orchid flower with petals so sensuous they begged to be caressed and kissed by the beholder. She had been working secretly on these projects in her studio for over a year now, as surprise gifts for her partner, Pablo, on his next birthday.

The queen could be taken for a gentle angel when she smiled and she knew well how to use her allure to enchant strangers and charm her fellow fairies. However, her external sweet demeanour hid a forceful intelligent character. She was after all the Sevenoaks fairies' new democratically-chosen and highly-respected leader. She was fair in dealing with disputes, cared for the weak, and could defuse any potentially explosive situations with her charm and quick wit. She deserved her new status as queen of the Sevenoaks fairies. Her name was Coralie, and she was held in high esteem not just in Sevenoaks but throughout the world of the Earth-bound fairies.

Coralie's lover, Pablo, was a tall Spanish fairy with dark hair and handsome features. He was a talented musician who sang, played gipsy guitar and wrote ballads for the many festivities celebrated by the community. Pablo's artistic temperament meant he was prone to frequent periods of melancholy when something did not go one hundred percent to his liking. He mourned the end of the summer, rainy days, burning the toast and when Coralie travelled without him to visit other fairy communities in the UK or abroad. He also got depressed for absolutely no reason at all, which prompted Coralie occasionally to take even longer absences from him. However, despite his depressive shortcomings, which were sharply in contrast to her enormous positivity and self-confidence, they loved each other deeply and with an overt passion that was the secret envy of their adult community.

Sex was strictly for fun for fairies, while reproduction was a serious matter in which the entire fairy community had a say. When a fairy died, and this was quite a rare event as they usually lived to be about one hundred years' old and rarely got ill, a single tooth would be extracted from the corpse. The community would then discuss at length the merits and faults of the deceased fairy and whether they had made on average a positive or negative contribution to society during their lifetime. Had they cared for the young or the old? Had they supported the fairy ideals of peace, friendship and equality? Had they collected fruits and nuts for the frequent feasts? Or, had they retreated from society and led a selfish existence or, worse, been petty thieves or trouble makers? The detailed mode of asexual reproduction used to create a new baby fairy from the extracted tooth would depend on the community's view of the deceased fairy's worth.

If the outcome of these debates was that the fairy had indeed been a beneficial member of society, then the tooth extracted from the dead fairy would be placed in a gold casket and surrounded by earth collected from a pine forest and which had been soaked with fermented cow's milk. A fresh quail's egg would be broken on top of the earth and ten grams of sage leaves added to the casket. Finally, the casket would be placed in the glowing embers of a bonfire overnight, while the fairies sang, danced, fornicated and got hideously drunk until morning broke. In the morning, the fairy queen had the task of removing the casket from the ashes and opening the casket. If the reproduction had been successful then an embryonic fairy would be found lying in the casket. The sex of the deceased fairy was retained by the embryo using this process.

The baby fairy would be cared for by the elder female fairies until it was strong enough to be completely self-sufficient. This was usually a matter of months, not years as with human babies. The human legend of a tooth fairy is a misinterpretation and bastardisation of this process. These babies reincarnated by this process were called the "pure" fairies. If the fairy queen was too comatose to undertake the meagre task of opening the casket the following morning, then the embryo would perish, and it was deemed that the gods had not agreed with the community's decision on reproduction. Hence the fairy queen was held guiltless, but actually was able to have the final say.

If, on the other hand, it was decided that a deceased fairy had not made a positive contribution to society, then it was necessary to alter the genetic make-up of this fairy to randomise the possibility that upon rebirth it would have an opportunity to be a good citizen; though this was by no means predestined. This randomisation was achieved by pounding the tooth to a fine powder with a diamond-encrusted hammer and then undertaking the same process as described above, with the exception that the casket was left in the embers of a bonfire for two nights, not one. The outcome could be anything from one to three new embryos and yet again the fairy queen had the responsibility of opening (or failing to open) the casket after two nights of partying. These babies were called the "randomised" fairies. The sex of the deceased fairy was not necessarily retained in the new embryos and it was even possible for hermaphrodite fairies to be born using this procedure.

This strange method of reproduction kept the population about constant, but with ever-improving values of community spirit and individual kindness. There was the obvious benefit that fairies could indulge in frequent sexual encounters without the worry of unwanted pregnancies. The reborn fairies had no memory of their past life even though the community knew all about their characters and any failings from their previous incarnation. It was strictly forbidden to talk about any memories from a fairy's previous existence. When this law was disrespected, minor spates of bullying or blackmail often resulted, especially for the randomised fairies who, unlike the pure fairies, were generated from an, arguably, suboptimal bloodstock. This victimisation was seriously discouraged in the Fairy Law Chronicles as it was reasoned that the randomised fairies could not be held responsible for past errors by their ancestors, but in practice, such indiscretions were rarely so cruel that they required any severe form of punishment.

The fairies greatly enjoyed the rebirth festivities, especially the excitement of what would be found when the casket was opened and the baby fairies were cherished and well cared for while they developed into juvenile fairies.

However, there were currently no rebirth celebrations in

the foreseeable future and the next major event in the community's calendar was the annual fête and this year there were rumours of exciting new attractions. Everyone was looking forward to the evening's festivities, and to meeting fairies from communities around the world and getting plastered together. Coralie was busy planning the events of the evening, determined to make it the best fête ever, one that would be talked about for years to come: a five-star party. She hoped the weather would be clement that evening and the punch would be superlative. She also hoped that Pablo would be in a positive frame of mind.

5

Also in Knole Park, one could find a race of Pevi. The Pevi were close friends and allies of the fairies in Sevenoaks. Physically, they resembled small flying squirrels with brilliant auras and they could move with lightning speed among the tree tops. They did not strictly fly, but glided between trees, using the flaps of skin between their front and back legs to steer and keep them airborne. They were invisible to humans who had not been trained to see them, but they could be seen by the fairies, appearing as small patches of flickering light encasing a cherry-wood- or golden-brown-coloured furry squirrel. They did not require much food and could survive on a miniscule diet of assorted nuts and seeds, however, they enjoyed large feasts on special occasions. Their distinctive aura could only be maintained by converting positive ions in the air to energy and light. Their aura was essential to maintain a healthy immune system and general sense of well-being. They also provided a communication channel to other Pevi and warmed their bodies in winter. At dusk, their lemon-yellow daytime auras turned to a gentle azure blue, giving them a natural camouflage and hence protection. The energy channels in their auras enabled the Pevi to undertake thought transference and mind-reading activities among themselves.

Unlike the fairies, they could travel between the parallel universes of the fairies and humans without any negative side-effects. In this way, they were able to keep the fairies informed of everything that happened in both universes without deleterious effects on their health. Although the Pevi were invisible to most humans, the sensitive ones might occasionally catch sight of a light moving out of the corner of their eye and feel a slight breeze as they flew past. Some even registered a feeling of extreme calm in the presence of a Pevi.

The Pevi were a younger race than the fairies in Europe, but their origins lay in South America. Their formal annals of history only dated back to the early seventeenth century when they arrived in the UK, but it is known from their ancient legends that their early ancestors lived in Venezuela in the forests that bordered the banks of the great Orinoco River. Apparently, Paddington Bear was not the only creature to relocate from South America to the South of England. It is further known from their legends that they arrived in Europe from South America by travelling on one of the merchant ships from the third exploration mission of Christopher Columbus at the end of the fifteenth century. At this time, a plague had broken out higher up the Orinoco River that had wiped out about half of the Pevi in that region. The Pevi who lived nearer the delta were scared and decided that it was necessary for some members of their community to escape across the ocean to find a new land far away from the plague-ridden jungle and so ensure the survival of their race.

Those who wished to leave their homeland went down to the harbour together where they discovered Christopher Columbus's ship ready to sail. They hurriedly returned to their community where goodbyes were quickly said and provisions gathered. Then, unbeknown to the sailors, an intrepid group of male, female and child Pevi boarded the ship bound for Europe, carrying supplies of water, nuts and fruit for the voyage.

When they finally arrived in Europe after many months at sea, the Pevi disembarked from Columbus's galleon in the south of Spain and travelled north across the plains of Spain, arriving in the Pyrenees just as winter broke in the mountains. Here, they saw their first ever snowfall and realised that they would need to find shelter to protect themselves from the cold and perils of the deep snow drifts. High in the Pyrenees, they met a mystical hermit who possessed the ability to see the Pevi, much to their surprise. Realising the precarious situation they were in, he offered them warmth, food and shelter in his cave. The hermit had lived most of his adult life in the Priory of Serrabone in the foothills of the French Pyrenees, but had recently decided that he needed to spend a few years in closer contact with nature, and in further isolation from his fellow men, in order to pursue his desired studies of nature. He needed peace and quiet come to terms with what he now saw as the sad finality of death, which conflicted with his religious beliefs. His name was Jean-Marc.

It was Jean-Marc who gave the Pevi their name. Pevi is an acronym for the French description "Petit Écureuil Volant Invisible", which translates as "small invisible flying squirrel". The hermit was to have an enormous impact on the education and development of the Pevi race.

Jean-Marc was a kind, studious man in his early forties. He was creating a beautifully illustrated manuscript, which described the wonders of the Pyrenees' fauna and flora. The book was dedicated to an elderly monk whom he had been very close to in the priory and whom he had loved dearly. The monk had recently died of old age, leaving Jean-Marc feeling very empty and alone without the daily reassurance and friendship of his mentor. The Pevi had never seen anything so magnificent as his illustrations and text. The natives in their jungle in South America had only limited means of verbal communication and no real written language, so Jean-Marc's manuscript opened their eyes to a completely new world. They sat looking at him work in awe. He was pleased to have their company and the glow of their auras filled the dark cave with warmth and a mellow light, casting ever-changing patterns on the walls as they moved around the cave.

Then one day, one of the younger Pevi gestured that he would like to understand the meaning and construction of the words Jean-Marc was writing. Jean-Marc was quick to understand the request and so started to teach the Pevi to read and write in the ancient French language of Occitan, carefully explaining the letters of the alphabet and their pronunciation to his transfixed audience. Although the

34

concept of a sophisticated language and writing were new skills to them, the Pevi were fast and enthusiastic learners. It was far too cold for them to venture outside, so they spent the winter months in the hermit's cave educating themselves. Needless to say, Jean-Marc found his new friends polite and enchanting. And, although he often wondered if perhaps he was possibly going a little crazy by talking to these ethereal squirrels, he was very happy with their charming company during the long dark days and nights. They lifted his spirit.

When spring finally broke after an exceptionally long hard winter, the Pevi bid farewell to their friend and mentor and continued their journey north through France. Jean-Marc had been an inspiration to the Pevi and from that day forth, they loved to learn about the world around them and were inquisitive of all things new or old that they encountered. En route, many of the Pevi decided to leave the main group and set up home in France. One group stayed near the hermit and started a community on the Mediterranean coast, where the Pyrenees descended to the sea, above a village called Collioure. They felt at home in this region and could regularly visit their mentor. Another group travelled further into France with the main expedition and set up home in the deciduous forests of central France. The main contingent continued their journey to England, where they fell in love with the parks in the city of London and settled there. Close to the hustle and bustle of medieval London, yet safe in the high trees in the many parks.

Many UK Pevi to this day still have French names in remembrance of Jean-Marc and their long migration from the parched scrubland in the south of Spain to the temperate, deciduous forests and parks in the north of Europe.

Thus the Pevi became highly dextrous and developed the ability to write. Over the following centuries, they collated a vast archive of historical information and scientific findings based on their experiences and travels. The archives had initially been written using minute hieroglyphics and simple ancient French, but later documents were transcribed in a language very similar to the English that they had picked up from listening to the humans talking in London and Knole Park. In spite of their cute cuddly appearance, a characteristic of the species was their impressive ability to learn new skills and their highly analytical minds. They enjoyed frequent heated intellectual debates that could last for days. Their species had never really expanded on a global scale because of their general disinterest and indifference towards procreation. They now numbered only a few thousand worldwide and the largest communities could be found in the beech forests in the south and Midlands of the UK, central France and on the French Mediterranean coast near the Pyrenees; with smaller groups existing in Sweden, Holland, Poland and in the jungles of Venezuela. Because of their small numbers, they felt a strong sense of community and greatly valued the worth and individuality of each other.

The UK Sevenoaks Pevi were privileged to live in close contact with the local fairy community who they adored. The fairies loved to pet the Pevi and were enchanted by their speed, beauty and ethereal nature. At one stage, about two hundred years ago, the Sevenoaks fairies had tried to domesticate the Pevi and persuade them to become their household pets and move into their homes. Although the Pevi derived great satisfaction from being petted by the fairies, they were far too intelligent and independent to allow themselves to be owned by anyone. They therefore continued to live happily in the vicinity of the fairy clan and enjoyed their company and affections, but retained their own social structure and community.

The most senior and influential Pevi was Edmund. Edmund was considered to be very clever by many of the young Pevi, but in practice, the more intelligent ones knew that he used his authoritative demeanour to conceal his relative intellectual weakness. However, he held on to his power because he was generally liked by most Pevi and was a responsible and honest leader who knew everything that was going on in the Pevi world. His wife, Laura, was well loved and respected. She retained an abundance of energy and enthusiasm at all times and loved to recount the ancient legends and songs to the young Pevi, seated around a bonfire in the evenings, so ensuring their traditions were kept alive.

Edmund had made himself indispensable to the community by becoming the central hub for inter-Pevi communication. He had developed and perfected his extraordinary powers of thought transference, so he was able to communicate with Pevi worldwide at will. He issued a newspaper every week, *The Pevi Weekly*, based on reports and stories conveyed to him by the small worldwide network of Pevi. *The Pevi Weekly* was an electronic newspaper which could be received by Pevi worldwide and which dealt with issues of interest to the Pevi. The paper was not physical in nature. To access it, one merely focussed one's entire thoughts on the colour deep purple (coincidentally, the name of Edmund's favourite rock band) and the transmission would be received automatically by thought transference from Edmund. Indeed, the colour of Edmund's aura had transformed from the normal lemon yellow and azure blue of the Pevi to pale purple during the hours of daylight and virtually black at night due to his constant concentration on sending and receiving purple thoughts.

The Pevi were very worried at the moment because the newspaper headlines this week foretold of impending disaster for their species. Never before in their history had there been such bad news in an edition of *The Pevi Weekly*, it was unheard of. Specifically, there was a report from their top scientist warning of an alarming decrease in the concentration of positive ions in the Sevenoaks region, their "manner from heaven", which was essential to maintain a healthy aura. The changes were almost imperceptible on a human scale, but were sufficient to impact on the Pevi's immune system and leave them vulnerable to disease and allergies. In addition, as if these processes could be subconsciously felt by the younger Pevi, it was reported that there was a growing problem of depression among the Sevenoaks youngsters, especially the more intelligent and sensitive young Pevi. Both these factors coming together led Edmund to predict that their Pevi world was deteriorating quite fast and life for them in their beloved Sevenoaks habitat could become unsustainable within a decade at best or a year at worst.

The observations opened the door for a flood of related questions: Was the Sevenoaks trend also seen in other parts of the UK and the world? How quickly was their atmosphere changing? How permanent were the changes? Could they adapt to live in a new ionic environment? Would the changes also impact on the fairies and the humans? Was the depression in the young caused purely by atmospheric changes? Urgent action was called for.

Edmund decided that the first course of action should be to arrange a meeting of all the Sevenoaks Pevi, where these terrifying revelations could be discussed with their top scientists. The date and venue were set for the Saturday evening two weeks after the fairies' fête in the Twisted Oak tree in the centre of Knole Park. Everyone would be there and the debate would continue as long as there were questions and ideas from the attendees, even if it meant that they slept on the branches of the Twisted Oak and continued the debate all day Sunday, or all week if necessary. Ideas must be generated and solutions proposed quickly, this was not a time for complacency. Even completely "off-the-wall" ideas should be freely aired and given due consideration. There were no obvious solutions, so the unobvious and extraordinary must be sought. Their long-term future now depended heavily on their innovation and scientific expertise. No Pevi was excused from attending, not even the very young, the very old or the sick; everyone had to contribute to discussions as best they could and there would be no strong alcohol allowed until the debate came to an end. Yes, like the fairies and the humans, the Pevi also liked to imbibe a small bevy from time-to-time, especially when depressed and under pressure. Their ancestors had picked up the habit by drinking the juice from fermented berries in the Venezuelan forests.

On hearing the news of the meeting, Dr Cedric, the top scientific Pevi in Sevenoaks, immediately started to delve into his annals of physics and chemistry to be prepared for the big debate. Long-forgotten treatises on quantum mechanics and astrology were resurrected from the archives and eagerly read. Meanwhile, Harry, the senior historian, began his research into the annals of ancient Pevi civilisations to learn from any past catastrophes and discover how the nations had recovered and rebuilt their communities. Eve, the senior geographer, began contacting her counterparts in other countries to compile data from around the world to determine the extent and locations of the most severe ionic changes.

Cedric, Harry and Eve were essentially focussing on three questions. Could they find safer regions for the Pevi to move to in the short term should the situation become intolerable in Sevenoaks? Could they deduce a pattern among the areas that were adversely affected? Could they find a longer-term solution to reverse the worrying trends seen in the Sevenoaks region? Any information that could be gleaned before the big debate would be helpful, but they knew that in practice their task would take much longer than the two weeks currently available before the meeting. They also knew that the Sevenoaks community contained the most experienced scientist, in Dr Cedric, and the other worldwide communities did not have access to the sophisticated positive-ion measurement machines that had been developed in Sevenoaks, so would be unlikely to be in a position to contribute any accurate information on their local atmospheric changes. But, they had to act fast and glean as much information as they could before the big debate.

6

The teenagers spent the next few days after their party planning their future. Andy, Claire and Naill would be leaving home in five weeks times to go to university and needed to shop for clothes, books and practical household items with their parents. Juliet and her mother, Kathleen, were busy researching Swiss finishing schools and Susie was busy improving her comportment and throwing away old clothes to make room for some new ones. She would be going to college, but living at home. Stan would also stay at home and retake his A-level exams.

After a few more lengthy discussions with his parents, Rick came to the conclusion that his best option was to look for a job in a biotechnology company and live at home so, hopefully, he could save enough to put himself through university in a few years' time, or be able to study part-time while working. He phoned his Aunt Sarah for advice. She had worked in the biotechnology and pharmaceutical industry for over thirty years and had many useful contacts. She suggested that he took a look at the website of some local science parks, such as Sittingbourne and Guildford, to see if any of the companies based there were currently recruiting. There were also many small biotech companies in London that could be researched on the web. He followed her advice and found two possible employers who were looking for junior research staff. Sarah helped him smarten up his CV to make it much more professional and together they wrote two upbeat covering letters to emphasize his scientific strengths and enthusiasm for the posts advertised.

Six days after their party in Knole Park, the group of seven new friends met up again in a pub to talk about what the future held for them. This time they met in the Queen's Oak pub on the outskirts of Sevenoaks; the Greyhound and

Ferret in the town centre was no longer an option.

The evening was warm and the friends sat together in the pub garden joking, drinking beer and eating crisps. They chatted happily for a while about the fun they had all had on their first meeting and the party that had ensued in Knole Park with the curious ending. They speculated as to why they had all got so drunk, but found no convincing answer. Yes, there were more empty bottles than anyone remembered opening, but, specifically, no one remembered drinking any spirits or advocaat in the park, just wine and beer. It was all very curious.

They all now knew their fate concerning further education and wanted to share their decisions and fears with their friends. Everyone was at a time in their lives of big change and it didn't take long before the chat became more serious. There was so much to discuss. Starting work, university, school abroad, retaking A-levels; the prospects would be diverse for the friends. What would the future hold now they had finished school? What would it be like working a five-day week with only four- or five-weeks' holiday a year? What would life at university be like? Would they be happy in their chosen career path? Would they make new friends easily? What would they be able to earn in five years' time? A myriad of questions demanded to be answered that evening.

Juliet told her friends that she had decided to accept her mother's suggestion of spending one year in Switzerland at finishing school. She had finally conceded that it would be excellent for her self-confidence. It would provide her with the opportunity to improve her French language, cooking and deportment skills and hopefully, she would meet some sympathetic girls from countries around the world. All these possibilities held interesting potential for the future. She was obviously slightly apprehensive about living abroad with a group of girls she didn't know, but they would all be in the same boat and should be sensitive to each other's concerns.

Next, Rick told everyone about the letters he had written applying for posts in biotechnology companies. He hoped he would receive one or two invitations for an interview in the near future.

The rest of the friends then recounted where they would be studying in September. Andy was going to study music and English literature at Birmingham University. Niall was going to the London School of Economics to study political science and economics. Stan was going back to school to retake his A-levels at Christmas. Claire was going to Bristol University to study law, while Susie was going to the Sloane Business School. Everyone was excited except Stan, who naturally felt rather isolated and contributed little to the evening's musings. Even Rick had come to terms with his decision and was looking on the positive side, though, ideally, he would have preferred to have gone directly to university like Andy and Niall.

Rick asked Juliet if he could walk her home at the end of the evening and she gladly accepted his offer. Although it wasn't far, and Sevenoaks was pretty safe at night, she would feel more secure having Rick for company and he was good company. She was beginning to really like him and relished the opportunity to be alone together.

They avoided the main road and meandered slowly down some of the most affluent backstreets in Sevenoaks, commenting on the style of the architecture and criticising the blatant affluence displayed by some of the homes with their high electric gates, dazzling security lighting, and Ferraris and Bentleys parked ostentatiously in the front drive.

When they arrived at Juliet's gate, Rick kissed her gently on the cheek and said, 'Well, I guess it's goodbye now. Thanks for letting me walk you home.' He turned to go, then stopped, and decided to ask her if she would like to go to the cinema with him tomorrow night to see *Madagascar*.

'It's a cartoon film about four animals who lived happily in Central Park Zoo, but then, much to their horror, they get relocated to Africa,' he explained. 'What do you think? Should be fun.' Juliet happily accepted and went to bed with a warm glow inside, already planning what to wear to the cinema.

Rick now had a long walk home, one that would take at least forty-five minutes if he hurried, but he had a distinctive spring in his step and he was looking forward to his date tomorrow.

The next evening, Rick and Juliet met in front of the cinema and he greeted her with a huge smile and a gentle kiss on her lips. He was effusive in his admiration of her outfit, which pleased her greatly as she had taken a lot of time deciding which skirt, top and jewellery to wear and she was pleased with the result. She looked stylish, but also slightly funky, in her short straight purple leather skirt, black vest with a lace trim and she had bought a silver lion's head necklace and matching earrings that were highly appropriate for this evening's entertainment. She had even borrowed her mother's Prada handbag for the occasion. Kathleen had been delighted to lend it to her as she was pleased that Juliet had found a boyfriend at last.

They went inside and sat near the back, holding hands throughout the film. Both of them were big fans of computer-animated cartoons, especially those produced by DreamWorks. After the film, they went for a glass of wine and then Rick walked Juliet home. It was not far to Juliet's house via the main road, about a fifteen-minute walk, but they again decided to take a longer route and this time made a detour through the park. It was deserted and romantic. The large oaks and beech trees cast dark inviting shadows in the bright moonlight, providing perfect locations for a stolen kiss. They stopped several times en route to admire the stars and make the evening last a little longer. At one point they rounded a sharp bend in the path and startled a few deer that were still grazing on the long grass, enjoying the tranquillity of the park at night. They scattered and Juliet's heart missed a beat and she jumped, wrongly assuming it might be something scary as her mind was still full of zoo animals; lions and hippopotami. Rick laughed and hugged her. As the lovers strolled in the dark park, he kissed her gently at every opportunity that presented itself and she enjoyed his attentions. She loved being cosseted and hugged by him. In between their bouts of kissing, they talked about their time at school, their friends, their hobbies, their home-life and parents. They wanted to know as much as possible about each other. They also reminisced again about the party on the night they had first met, and laughed about Susie and Niall's street-dancing antics to the ballads of Robbie Williams.

When they finally arrived at Juliet's gate, they loitered a little longer, not wanting the evening to end. The evening had gone so well and Rick felt an enormous affection and passion for Juliet that he wanted to express. He took her in his arms, pulled her close to feel her body next to his and gave her the most intense French kiss that he had ever mustered in his life. It felt wonderful and he was expecting her to respond positively to him, but instead she pulled away, shocked, and went inside the house, closing the door without looking back.

Distraught, he waited by her front gate for ten full minutes hoping she would return, but she didn't, so he walked home despondently, kicking himself for having misread the situation, and hoping she would want to see him again. His heart was racing. He was in love. He vowed to send her an SMS tomorrow apologising for his presumptuous behaviour.

7

Juliet had now met Rick three times; twice in a social environment with her and his groups of friends, and once alone, last night. The group got on well and they all had fun together. Rick had walked her home after their evening in the pub with the gang and had kissed her gently when he left her at her gate. It had felt warm and comfortable. She had enjoyed his attentions on their first real date to the cinema, though she thought with a smile that she had never been kissed so much in her life as on their walk home through the park. But when they had arrived at her house and he had kissed her with such great fervour and passion, she had reacted with shock, like a child. This had been her first French kiss and she had felt excited but unsettled by it. It had seemed rather too personal an act at the time, but later as she lay in bed, she had decided that she had liked it and felt guilty that she had probably hurt his feelings with her childish over-reaction. She had felt his warm breath on her face and the soft underside of his tongue in her mouth and it had stimulated something inside her which had previously lain dormant. She had even thought that she had felt the hardness of his penis against her torso as he held her and kissed her.

Juliet knew she liked Rick a lot and that he returned her friendship. He was fun to be around, intelligent and had an optimistic outlook on life. They chatted easily together, shared an interest in sport and both valued their family life. Essentially, they got on very well and laughed a lot when they were together. But, she was not one-hundred percent sure that she felt anything deeper than friendship for him at the moment. Although she was eighteen years' old, surprisingly, and unlike most of her girlfriends, she was still a virgin. She had a great respect for her body and her emotions and was concerned not to rush into a relationship without due contemplation of the outcome. Juliet had seen some of her schoolfriends badly let-down and disillusioned by relationships that became too intense too quickly. She had never loved a boy, nor had a crush on one, like many of her schoolfriends had. After that passionate kiss, she realised that Rick felt a certain amount of lust for her and it made her slightly nervous. She loved his hugs and tender kisses, but she wondered whether she was just scared of sex and of being so uninhibited with another human being.

It was impossible to talk with her mother about her feelings and what had happened last night. She knew she would get lots of understanding and sympathy, but she doubted that she would be able to have a genuinely insightful and deep discussion, which was what she needed. Her mother was very loving and certainly not unintelligent, certainly more intelligent and worldly wise than Juliet was. Kathleen had worked as a scientist in pharmaceutical research prior to Juliet's birth, but nowadays she was a typical Sevenoaks housewife in Juliet's mind, interested in local charity work and caring for her family. Mother and daughter were close, but had never really talked much about emotional topics and certainly not about sexual matters in any depth.

As she was surmising her dilemma, her mother entered the room.

'You look thoughtful dear. Is everything OK?' enquired Kathleen.

'Yes,' replied Juliet hesitantly. But she meant "No" and it showed in her eyes.

Juliet wondered if perhaps she should broach the subject of her feelings for Rick with her mum, after all she was an adult now and had legally been allowed to have sex for two years. Her mother had even tried to talk to her about the pill a few months ago, but Juliet had found it too embarrassing and the conversation had soon floundered when Juliet had changed the subject to planning a new decoration scheme for her bedroom.

Then suddenly she felt brave and blurted out. 'Mum, can

we have a chat? There is something I would like to discuss with you. Can I be frank with you and ask some difficult questions? Maybe even some personal questions about the relationship between you and dad and how it started?'

'Of course my darling, that would be lovely. What's on your mind? I don't have to go to collect your father from the railway station for another two hours, so we have plenty of time to ourselves. Shall I make us a nice cup of tea first and perhaps we should have one of those lovely Jaffa Cakes too? We haven't had a nice girl-to-girl chat for ages; you have been so busy with studying for your exams and going out with your new friends recently. I'm pleased that you seem to have found a nice group of friends to socialise with recently and it's nice that Rick has taken it upon himself to walk you home in the evening.'

Oh shit, thought Juliet. *This isn't starting well.*

Juliet's mum rushed happily off to put the kettle on and make some tea. Juliet followed meekly behind, her bravery rapidly seeping away. When the tea was made, the best cups and saucers put out, and the tea poured, Kathleen looked her daughter fondly in the eyes and said with an expression of great earnest, 'Now, what would you like to talk about darling? What advice do you need from your mother? You have my complete undivided attention.'

Juliet took a deep breath and made a short prayer to any god that happened to be listening. She suddenly felt about six years old, completely tongue-tied and nauseous. She was tempted to excuse herself and go to the bathroom, but her mother looked at her with such intensity and love that she decided to persevere and somehow make this "little chat" work.

Juliet couldn't decide how to start the conversation, so she plumped for something rather vague which would put the ball in her mother's court.

'So, when you and dad met, did you know straight away that he was the one for you? How did you decide whether you loved him or not?'

Although Kathleen often gave Juliet the impression that she was rather a superficial person who was probably more interested in possessions than feelings, this was not deep down her true character. She deeply cared for her daughter and immediately sensed all the angst and internal uncertainty that lay behind this simple question from Juliet. Her perceived superficial persona was a mask she had created to protect herself and was a direct result of the affluent, privileged life she led and her snooty acquaintances in Sevenoaks, rather than an accurate reflection of her true nature. She decided to proceed gently with Juliet's questions, but to try to be genuinely frank and open about her relationship with Juliet's father, Robert. After all, Juliet was at a crucial point in her life and had some difficult and important decisions to make concerning her future career and personal life. She needed to be able to talk openly with her mother and receive some wise advice from someone who had already been there.

Kathleen had noticed how reserved Juliet was physically, compared to her schoolfriends, and had been wondering how to broach the subject with her without causing her too much embarrassment. She was delighted that it had been Juliet who had finally approached her requesting advice and it sounded like very adult advice was probably needed. Maybe Juliet would be a trifle surprised at her mother's sense and sensibility! She greatly wanted them to be closer as mother and daughter, but also as friends by the end of this conversation. She would leave Robert to walk home from the station if necessary, after all, it wasn't raining that hard and Juliet's questions needed to be given sufficient thought and discussion time.

'Well, darling, that's a loaded question. I'll try to remember as best I can. It was a long time ago, but it's rather nice to recall those early feelings. This conversation is just between you and me and I trust you will respect the fact that some of the things I'm about to tell you may not be known by your father and I would like it to remain that way. You are at an important stage in your life and it is time you asked yourself some questions about relationships and sex. I will try to help by telling you about my feelings and experiences, but you are very different to me and must make up your own mind about how far a relationship should go. Just because some of your friends are experimenting with sex, doesn't mean you should feel under any pressure. Trust your own feelings.'

Juliet was beginning to feel more reassured that she was going to have a meaningful and helpful discussion with her mother, despite her initial concerns.

Kathleen openly admitted to Juliet that she had been more promiscuous than her daughter, but felt Juliet needed to understand that a loving sexual relationship was what was important and Kathleen had definitely made a few mistakes in the past by rushing into relationships too quickly, often due to a lack of self-esteem, but also due to peer pressure. She knew Juliet would be surprised by the story of her mother's love affairs, which started at the age of fifteen, but she did not intend to lie to her daughter and water down her experiences.

And so Kathleen began the story of her early romances, ending with Robert, and Juliet's eyes grew wider and wider, while the tea was left untouched, getting colder and colder.

So it turned out that Kathleen had been quite promiscuous in her youth. This was partly due to the bad influence of her elder brother, whom she adored, and some of his unsavoury friends. Robert was certainly not her first and only lover. The pill was freely available to anyone over sixteen and no one wanted to be square in the late nineteen-seventies. Free love, easy access to dope and three-day rock concerts reigned supreme and Kathleen was not about to miss out on any of the fun. She was far too independent to settle down with someone too soon. She wanted to taste freedom and to be her own boss. Babies, a rich husband and a detached house in Sevenoaks could wait a decade.

Kathleen's first boyfriend, at the age of fifteen, was Paul.

He was also fifteen, was rather ugly with a piggy nose, and suffered from severe juvenile skin problems, but she needed to start somewhere and grow her confidence. No one else seemed to be too interested in her. Her best friend, Helen, attracted much more attention. Kathleen decided that was due to Helen's 32D bra cup size, which definitely outranked her own paltry 32B at that age; she was convinced it was nothing to do with her looks or personality.

Kathleen remarked, 'Boys could be so, so obvious at that age,' and Juliet enthusiastically agreed with that observation.

Paul and Kathleen's relationship (if it could be called that) only lasted a couple of weeks and they never made love. It never really worked for either of them. The first kiss was slobbery and full of saliva, both of them choking uncomfortably on each other's tongues. Memorable yes, but for all the wrong reasons. The petting stopped well short of heavy petting, as it was quaintly called then, due to excruciating embarrassment on both of their parts. Kathleen was relieved when Paul stopped phoning her.

After Paul, came Steve, a friend of her brother's, with whom she felt less inhibited. He was about four years older than her, so was relatively experienced at sex compared with the disastrous and naïve Paul. He had average looks and a strange fashion sense for the time, preferring to wear round-necked pullovers with suit trousers, whatever the occasion. He didn't possess a pair of jeans. He lived at home with his parents. Steve and Kathleen enjoyed frantic grappling sex in front of the television whenever his parents went out for the evening. He always liked to keep an eye on the television, even when on the verge of ejaculation. Kathleen was slightly put out by this habit, but didn't like to mention her feelings about this. Steve worked as an engineer for British Telecom, so received a reasonably good pay packet every week, much of which was immediately blown on pints of cider (for him) and glasses of vodka and lime (for her) in the Red Lion in Beckenham High Street on Friday night. Having a boyfriend with a job and an income earned her great respect at school.

Kathleen worshipped Steve for six months, until she met his friend, Chas.

Chas was an artist with a small flat in Penge, South London, above a greengrocer's shop. It had an orange front door on which he had painted a large yellow sun and purple moon. The first time she met him round at Steve's house she felt an enormous desire and attraction to him. She desperately wanted to sleep with him and be his girlfriend. She dropped Steve the next day, without hesitation, convinced that Chas would see in her what everyone else had missed, a passionate sensitive charming young woman waiting to be nurtured by a loving creative man.

Sadly for Kathleen, Chas was far too kind and nice to seduce a sixteen-year-old girl. He felt she was too young and innocent (not quite true). He only wanted to befriend her and show her his latest paintings. Chas was heartbreakingly gorgeous and unconventional. She didn't know how to persuade him to see her as a sexually-mature female (which she wasn't). In desperation, she would spend hours walking up and down his road hoping to bump into him, as he came back from shopping or from work, and then be invited up for coffee, a chat and then perhaps something more. She lost weight, became very intense and desperately yearned to seduce him. She even dreamed of having his children and living together in a cottage in Dorset. All very happy families and picture-book perfect. Sadly, Chas had a beautiful bohemian girlfriend who was older, richer and much more fun to be with than Kathleen. Ultimately, Kathleen had to admit defeat and reluctantly move on.

So, Kathleen explained to Juliet, that after two boyfriends and one instance of unrequited love, she had still not met her soulmate. Juliet liked the sound of Chas and felt sorry that her mother's love for him had been unrequited.

The next boyfriend, Spike, was almost the last. He was a Hell's Angel, well, probably more of an apprentice Hell's Angel as he lacked true conviction and a genuinely nasty streak. However, he had a motorbike and a leather jacket with studs in the shape of a skull. He also knew a few Hell's Angels quite well, though in practice he preferred to hang out with hippies and rockers. In fact, he was rather sweet and probably nearly as wary of Hell's Angels as Kathleen was at the time. She enjoyed being with him, especially because his appearance outside her school caused consternation among the teachers and the parents waiting to pick up their daughters. How she loved leaping on the back of his Triumph motorbike after school. Boater swiftly replaced by crash helmet and her school skirt hitched up around her waist. Spike was kind with a good sense of humour and a nice set of friends, who soon also became Kathleen's friends. Kathleen wondered how this gang compared to the set of friends whom Juliet had recently fallen in with; *Probably not too dissimilar,* she surmised.

Kathleen and Spike learnt about sex in his double bed in his parents' terraced house in Brixton. They read magazines together and experimented with new techniques claimed to maximise the enjoyment of the male or female orgasm. They were at ease with their bodies and often ended up laughing about their antics. His parents were broad-minded and didn't seem to mind his sexual antics, though Kathleen always blushed when they came downstairs after a particularly experimental session. They liked Kathleen and secretly hoped that she and Spike would end up married. Indeed, Kathleen could happily have married Spike except for his diet. He lived on fried eggs, chips and mushy peas which he cooked for her most evenings with much relish, never suggesting that she should reciprocate and cook something for him. It was a treat to be looked after and cooked for, but after two years of this unchanging diet Kathleen realised that the marriage could never last a lifetime. She would soon become fat, spotty and worst of all bored. It was time to break his kind heart and move on to university and pastures new.

Kathleen spent three years at university studying chemistry and enjoyed a promiscuous time with several casual boyfriends, but no one serious. She rather enjoyed the lack of commitment after her close relationship with Spike. She returned home after completing her degree with no one special on her arm.

And so we come to Robert. To say Robert was wild was an understatement. He was extremely fearless and highly imaginative in his youth; a combination of characteristics that Kathleen found highly compelling. They met when she knocked him off his motorbike in a country lane while driving home without taking due care and attention of her surroundings. She was horrified by her action, but Robert seemed quite cool about the whole event. He wasn't badly hurt, but the bike was damaged and undriveable. Kathleen phoned her dad's garage and they offered to send a truck to pick up the bike. Kathleen and Robert sat by the side of the road in the soft afternoon sunshine waiting for the pickup truck to arrive. Kathleen was shaking; traumatised and embarrassed by her stupidity. Robert was chatting away, trying not to notice her private trauma. After the motorbike had been taken away, Robert ended up driving Kathleen home in her car because she was still shaking too much to drive herself. And so their love affair started.

Kathleen had graduated from university with a 2.1 BSc degree in Chemistry and now wanted to have some fun and freedom before starting work. She had not taken a gap year before starting university, so felt she needed a good long holiday to expand her horizons. Robert had an offer of a job as a trainee investment manager in the City of London and had negotiated a start date in October, so he was free for a few months. Kathleen and Robert spent the summer together, travelling around Europe on his newly repaired motorbike. They slept in a tiny two-person tent and mostly survived by stealing fruit from trees and operating an elementary shoplifting scam. Kathleen would flirt with the shopkeeper, exposing a bit too much flesh so as to distract his attention, while Robert pocketed anything that would neatly fit into his pockets or rucksack. She would then purchase a cheap item of food and they would leave quickly before the shopkeeper had time to notice anything was amiss. This worked well enough for them to survive on very little money for a couple of months, but Kathleen finally called a stop to the practice because she did not like living on stolen goods, so after that they started paying for their food. They travelled through France, Switzerland, Italy, and Greece. The scenery was superb; they fell in love with the Mediterranean vistas. Every night they set up camp in a quiet field or wood, far away from any buildings, and at nightfall they happily crawled into their little tent for an hour of passion and then deep sleep. Robert was a skilled and powerful lover, who left Kathleen exhausted and bathed in sweat after every encounter. Going to bed in the evening was the highlight of their day.

They married in a registry office when they returned home, with just two friends present as witnesses. Then they set up home in a small terraced house in Sevenoaks. He worked in the City of London, while she got a position as a research chemist for a pharmaceutical company. Their plan was to get rich as quickly as feasibly possible, so they could ultimately spend more time in the Mediterranean. Robert was highly motivated and worked long hours to make huge profits for his clients, but Kathleen was not as motivated at work as her husband. After five years working in a laboratory, she became unhappy about being constantly exposed to so many solvents and obnoxious chemicals and when she fell pregnant with Juliet she was relieved to leave work to care for her daughter and improve her daily environment.

They never returned to live in the Mediterranean region, as they had originally intended, because Robert became highly successful at his job and refused to relinquish his affluent lifestyle for a more bohemian existence. He was proud to have a lovely wife and baby daughter and to provide for them. He thought only about improving their physical environment and buying a larger and larger house for his family.

So here they all were today, living in affluence in Sevenoaks. Kathleen explained that she still loved Robert a lot, but did occasionally regret the rather sedentary lifestyle she had ended up living. She still had a wonder-lust for travel and experiencing life and traditions in foreign countries, but Robert's commitment to his work and clients and his limited number of days' holiday per annum restricted their ability to take long holidays abroad. They had been happy together and still were, but Kathleen told Juliet to make sure she lived the type of life she wanted, not the one that was expected of her.

'Only you can decide how far and how quickly you want to progress a relationship. I certainly made many mistakes when I was young. You are eighteen now and sensible enough to make your own decisions and I'm sure they will be the right decisions. Just remember that life is not a dress rehearsal,' she explained. 'Make sure you know what you want to achieve and go for it. Never look back and regret past decisions, Juliet, but learn from your past, move on, and try not to repeat your mistakes too often.'

They both sat in complete silence at the end of the monologue. Kathleen was silently reminiscing about the past and Juliet reconsidering her opinion of her mother and father.

'So dad really was quite a wild child when he was younger,' Juliet commented. 'He has changed a bit hasn't he? I guess when you were young it was great fun to be promiscuous and you rushed at life seeking to make the most of the new freedom girls had because of the advent of the pill, but do you think you were mature enough to do what you wanted or did you tend to do what your peers pressurised you into doing, what you felt was expected of you?'

'That's a probing question darling. It's true I was hurt occasionally by thinking I could handle sexual freedom and that I was in control of my emotions. Girls were trying to look at life through a boy's eyes at that time, rather than being honest with themselves. They thought they wanted what boys wanted, but sometimes ended up being boys' toys if they weren't careful. I was happy most of the time because I had a positive outlook on life and didn't dwell too much on past mistakes. I certainly had crushes on boys which are an enormous waste of energy and emotion, but I don't think I was really in love with anyone except your father and possibly Spike. So darling, how do you feel about Rick? Do you want to talk about him?'

'Thanks mum, for this discussion. It's been really useful hearing about your love life when you were younger and about your emotions. I am very fond of Rick. He's certainly the only boy I have ever felt anything for. But I need to question my feelings at the moment; I find my mind goes all fuzzy when I'm with him. Is that love? No don't answer that,' she giggled. 'You know, a lot of my friends first had sex at sixteen, or even earlier, I'm the last virgin in my group of girlfriends.'

Kathleen was highly interested to meet Rick, because she had only seen him through the lounge window, as he left Juliet at the garden gate after an evening out. However, she knew how shy Juliet would be about introducing him to her parents, so she decided to let that lie for the moment. If they were serious about each other, and it seemed they were, then there would be plenty of opportunities for her to meet Rick in the future.

Finally, Kathleen proposed that Juliet was always welcome to ask her personal questions if it helped her resolve her own dilemmas and emotions. She wanted to help and be involved with Juliet's life, but didn't want to pry. She walked over to Juliet and gave her a big motherly hug.

'I'm off to pick up your father now from the station,' she declared.

Juliet sat quietly gazing out of the window, trying to come to terms with all the revelations and difficult emotions of today. There had been far too much unexpected information to digest. She had not realised that her mother had been so sexually active in her teenage years. She needed to better understand her own emotions and what she wanted from her relationship with Rick.

8

A few days after Kathleen's revelations to Juliet about her past boyfriends, Rick and Juliet met up again for another date. Rick had sent her an SMS apologising for his behaviour and asking if he might phone her to arrange to see each other again. She had then taken the initiative to phone him and suggest they meet up, just the two of them, with no friends present. He was delighted because he was worried that he might have frightened her when he had kissed her so passionately the other evening. It had felt completely natural to him, but she had seemed rather shocked. He was incredibly attracted to Juliet and found her fun to be with. He was keen that they should become an "item", a proper boyfriend and girlfriend, and was pleased that they had had a few of days to re-examine their emotions of the other night before meeting up again.

They had arranged to meet at 6:30 pm in the evening outside a pub in Sevenoaks town centre. The weather was balmy and the evening would be light till quite late. This summer had been exceptionally warm and sunny and many of the local residents were out and about with their children, making the most of the late August evenings, before the autumn took hold and night fell earlier. Understandably, Rick and Juliet were both apprehensive about how things would work out this evening after the disastrous conclusion to their previous date, but they were also somewhat overwhelmed with excitement that they had a second chance tonight. They both wanted tonight to be a success and there would be no Andy, Niall, Stan, Susie or Claire to give support and keep the conversation lively and amusing.

Their nervousness led them to question several minor issues about themselves as they walked independently to the pub. Juliet questioned whether she looked cool and sexy in her outfit. She was annoyed that a spot on her chin had appeared today of all days, since she had had a clear complexion all summer after the exams had finished. She had wrongly decided not to have her highlights retouched this morning, even though her mother had offered to pay. Rick asked himself why he hadn't noticed the jam stain on his Hugo Boss jeans before he left home. He had decided not to shave that evening because he liked the look of the shadow of stubble, but he was now wondering whether that was such a good idea if he wanted to kiss Juliet again.

And more importantly they both wondered if they would still enjoy each other's company and be able to move forward after the disastrous ending to their last date.

And of course, the really big question they were both pondering was whether or not they would actually have sex for the first time tonight.

Juliet had pondered the last question long and hard after hearing all about her mother's exploits when she was even younger than Juliet was. Juliet had also re-evaluated her experience of being kissed by Rick the other night and had decided that she had greatly enjoyed it, once she had recovered from her initial shock. She felt that she was mature enough to handle a real relationship and Rick seemed a highly suitable partner for her; kind, happy, amusing, intelligent and pretty good-looking. She found the idea of having a "proper" boyfriend, in every sense, an attractive proposition. It was the right time to explore her body's desires and understand what being a woman meant...and she wanted to make these discoveries with Rick. She felt safe with him and trusted him.

Rick had also been pondering whether he should make any sexual approaches at all to Juliet this evening. He didn't want to shock her again and scare her away by moving too quickly. He would be perfectly happy to spend a nice evening in each other's company, finding out more about Juliet's past, her family and herself. He was now also nervous and unsure about how exactly he could make a sexual advance without appearing to be only interested in Juliet's body, and it was definitely a lovely body. He had decided not to make any advances, but had put a condom in his back pocket, just in case.

Both managed a nervous, 'Hi' when they met outside the pub.

'Would you like a drink?' inquired Rick.

'Yes, but let's find an empty table outside in the garden first,' replied Juliet.

Juliet installed herself on a vacant table in the evening sun while Rick went inside for the drinks. When he returned, she was already feeling a little more relaxed and managed a natural smile. The pub garden was busy and lively; full of couples and families soaking up the warm evening sun; children squabbling over packets of crisps and peanuts.

Rick was first to bring up the subject of their previous meeting. 'I'm so sorry about the other night. I didn't mean to insult you. Will you forgive me?'

'No, it's me who should apologise. What you did was quite natural, I just wasn't prepared. Please don't think I'm frigid, I was just surprised. It's the first time I have ever been kissed like that. Actually, in retrospect, I decided how sensual it was. I really enjoyed the evening.'

'Yes, so did I. What would you like to do tonight?' asked Rick. He wanted Juliet to decide.

'Well, the evening is so lovely it seems a shame to spend all of it in a town pub, even though the garden here is OK. Shall we buy some cans of beer and go for another walk in the park? I so love it there in the evening, when the tourists have gone and it's quiet.' Juliet had even pre-planned this and brought her large patent orange tote bag with her to hold the beer. So, it was decided and they set off for the park after visiting the off-licence. Following the revelation of finding out more about her mother's past love-life than she really wanted to know, Juliet also had had the foresight to bring some condoms with her. She had decided that she wanted her relationship with Rick to progress to the next level and was sure he would too.

They strolled slowly in the vast park, hand in hand. The park was emptying of visitors and soon they saw no other people. After a while, they sat down beneath an ancient oak tree. Its branches spread out widely forming a canopy of bright green leaves. It was dusk and the sun was low, shining below the branches, warming their bodies and faces, and making them squint. Tall yellow and pink flowers mingled with the soft long grass beneath the tree. It was a romantic secluded setting. They sat quietly, enjoying the tranquillity of the moment, while the sun finished its descent behind the trees in the wood, enveloping the young lovers in half-darkness and shielding them from the sight of any curious passers-by. Rick wrapped his arm around her waist.

'Is that OK?' he asked anxiously. She replied with a smile and snuggled closer to him, feeling much more relaxed about their intimacy. Neither said a word, their bodies moulding perfectly into each other's gentle curves.

After a while, Rick tenderly enveloped her in his arms and kissed her lips, gently at first. She returned his kisses with increasing vigour and he reciprocated, cautiously at first. Her insistence gave him the courage to become more forceful and he tentatively manoeuvred his tongue between her lips. This time she responded with passion and they kissed till the urge to explore further became unbearable. Rick caressed her breasts beneath her T-shirt. He gasped as he realised she was braless and nearly came on the spot. He was delighted he would not have to struggle with any difficult clasps, but more importantly he appreciated that Juliet really did want to explore her sexuality with him. She groaned with pleasure, smiling to herself that she had got one thing right this evening.

Slowly, Rick pushed up her T-shirt, exposing the most beautiful breasts he had ever seen, more beautiful than he had imagined in his recent dreams. Juliet writhed with pleasure, enjoying the attention he gave her pride possessions. Her nipples hardened and their sensitivity became heightened as Rick caressed and kissed her. Juliet felt a sensation like an electric shock. It was a wonderful, exciting surge of electricity that welled up in her groin and shot through her torso, stimulating her lips as she returned his kisses, and circulating around her head firing her pleasure neurones. She felt faint, floating in a limpid sea of ecstasy. All she could think was, *Wow, please don't ever stop.* She felt her body take over from her mind. His penis was now so stiff that he desperately needed to release the pressure welling up inside him.

Rick had not touched a woman's clitoris, nor made love, for over a year, except in his dreams. But the urge to continue was so strong that all his fears and inexperience were forgotten. He found his hand had made its own way inside her knickers without his conscious intent and here he felt the moist soft furry region surrounding her vagina. He felt for the entrance of her vagina and gently inserted his fore finger, then his middle finger and carefully moved them up and down, stoking the walls of her vagina. His penis now knew what to expect when the moment of entry came. Juliet writhed and squealed with pleasure. She was floating in a spinning universe of stars; the World and reality no longer existed for her. Rick was still on planet Earth and quickly removed his trousers and pants, fumbling in his pocket for a condom. With enormous relief, he extracted the condom from its wrapper and placed it on his penis that was now so large it was hurting. He squeezed his penis into her damp vagina and came in a rush. Juliet lay breathless and defenceless, squashed beneath his sweat-covered body and the damp earth.

They lay exhausted in the long grass, sweat running from their pores in rivulets. The power that had taken them over now left them both completely immobilized. They lay without moving for what seemed an eternity, until reality finally began to reawaken their consciousness.

Wow, wow, wow, thought Juliet, though she quickly began to feel embarrassed by her nakedness in a public park, even though it was now quite dark. She moved her arms to free them from Rick's weight bearing down on her. He felt her discomfort and quickly transferred his weight to his elbows. Smiling down at her, he felt an enormous affection. He smiled at her disarranged hair and smeared mascara. She was even more beautiful when ravished he decided.

Juliet was floating on cloud nine, but desperate to replace her clothes. After all it was the first time she had made love with anyone and she was not completely at ease with her semi-naked body, or with Rick, her first lover.

Rick kissed her tenderly. 'Thank you, so much, you are truly beautiful', he said with a hint of embarrassment in his voice. She returned his shy smile. They cleaned their bodies with the long grass then replaced their crumpled clothes. Relief soon overtook them and when they next caught each other's eyes they couldn't help but laugh and laugh. It was a happy shared laughter of pure enjoyment and an acknowledgement of what they had achieved together. All the pent-up sexual tension of the new lovers was released into the ether and they were overpowered by a feeling of complete serenity.

Not knowing quite what to do next, they drank a beer each, to give them a quiet moment of reflection. They could be alone with their thoughts for a while. Both decided that what they had just experienced together was wonderful and each silently committed that they would try to nurture their mutual friendship and passion. Juliet did not feel traumatised by the loss of her virginity. On the contrary, she was delighted to have shared such a passionate first experience with Rick and he was relieved that she had enjoyed his love-making. He was also relieved that he had not ejaculated prematurely, though felt a bit guilty about rushing everything. He was an inexperienced lover too, but would improve with time and the perfect partner who he had in Juliet.

They strolled back through the park to the Queen's Oak pub, where they shared a few giggles and a bottle of cheap Languedoc Roussillon house wine, before Rick walked Juliet home. She was feeling nervous about seeing her mother, because she was sure her mother would guess what had happened by the stupid big smile on her face, that she seemed unable to erase. Rick left her at the front gate and quickly disappeared into the night, worried about having to speak to Juliet's parents after the events of the evening. Juliet was right to be nervous, as her mother welcomed her home with a hug, quick sniff and a knowing smile.

Shit, she knows, thought Juliet, who immediately said her "goodnights" and fled to her room to shower and dream of her lover.

She lay in bed reliving every second of the evening in which she had evolved from a serious schoolgirl to a sexually-awakened woman. She was in love for the first time.

9

Coralie was not her usual unruffled self today. It was 2nd September, the day before the fairies' annual fête, and she was far behind with the organisation and, unusually, very few fairies had volunteered to help, even though they were all chatting animatedly about the evening's entertainment. Coralie hadn't even decided what to wear! There were delegations of fairies coming from abroad this year, as word of the infamous fête had spread and attracted the interest of fairies around the world. Pablo was not helping, preferring to complain and criticise rather than getting his finger out. *Ggrrrrh*.

'Anyway,' he explained, 'I have to practise my guitar solos for the evening's entertainment and have no inclination to help with what I consider to be mundane practicalities.' As well as performing a short concert after the feast, he secretly planned to learn the first few bars of the visiting fairies' national anthems to introduce each nationality as they entered the arena for the grand parade. He wanted to surprise Coralie with his ingenuity.

Coralie consulted her checklist and made notes on the actions still outstanding:

1. **Fancy Dress Parade**
   I know that lots of the young fairies are working hard on their costumes and are very excited about the competition. I also know that many of the fairies visiting from abroad will be parading in their national costumes, which will be fun and educational for everyone.
   She wrote "ACTION – Get prizes" on her list.
2. **Blueberry Punch**
   This is being brewed by Calista and she has strict instructions to guard the punch and keep its location secret until the fête starts. I whole-heartedly trust her to be responsible about this. I well

remember the problem we had last year when an adolescent fairy found the punch hidden in the hollow trunk of a decaying tree in the afternoon before the fête started and spiked it by adding rather a lot of Partitim. It had a disastrous effect on those who were heavy imbibers. Two elderly fairies nearly died as a direct result of its powerful hallucinogenic effects. That was an experience definitely not to be repeated.

She wrote "SORTED."

3. Candyfloss

The local spiders' cooperative is busy eating sugar and strawberries and spinning their silken strands to make a sweet strawberry-flavoured candyfloss. It should be really delicious and this is one of my new innovations for the fête. It is the first time the spiders have been involved and they are determined to be successful as this will lead to further commissions and, anyway, they have found it fun eating lots of free sugar and strawberries provided by us fairies.

"SORTED."

4. Tombola

I haven't bought or commissioned any prizes yet.

"ACTION – Find a volunteer to make/find prizes – Try Zak and Benjie."

5. Face-painting

I haven't found a volunteer yet.

"ACTION – Find a volunteer; someone artistic."

6. Fawn Racing

The senior fawn, Shawn, is meant to be organising the contestants. He hasn't reported back to me yet, but that doesn't mean he has shirked his responsibilities. I'll search him out this morning. The Irish fairy, Padraig, is setting up a booth to take the bets. He should, in principle, be the right fairy for the job, with extensive experience gained at the Irish Grand National. As long as he doesn't drink too much, that should be OK. He has already told me that all is in order.

"ACTION – See Shawn."

7. Frog Baiting

This is a classic event, much enjoyed by most fairies, but no frogs have volunteered this year. I'll have to visit the pond and see if I can persuade some of the frogs that it would be fun to make fools of themselves. Perhaps I'll offer some form of inducement, or prizes for the frogs that perform best.

"ACTION – Go to the pond and offer frogs an inducement to participate."

8. **The Feast.**

This is well in-hand. The best fairy chefs in Sevenoaks have been devising the menu and perfecting the recipes for several months now.

"DEFINITELY SORTED!"

9. **Music, Dancing and Lighting.**

Pablo is busy practising his gypsy guitar solos and two of my favourite fairies, Zak and Benjie, gave me an Apple iPod that they found in the park two weeks ago. It contains lots of pop music. Naturally, I didn't ask too many questions about where it came from. I suspect the worse, but know it will make the party really rock, so I'm going to turn a blind eye to its provenance. The dance floor is currently being trodden flat and grazed by the deer. The fireflies are very keen to be involved and provide the disco lighting; I've seen them practising some artistic routines. The Pevi will also be there to provide more subtle lighting.

"SORTED."

All in all, she decided, perhaps things were not as bleak as they had looked when she had woken up that morning. She made herself a cup of dandelion tea and went to find Pablo. Pablo's guitar had been warped by the unusually hot and humid July weather and it was not giving him the perfection of sound he desired. He was not in the best of moods.

Best to leave him to it, thought Coralie. She went off to find Shawn.

Shawn was grazing near the visitors' car park, hoping to be fed by some children offering something more interesting than grass. Carrots were his favourite, or a nice crisp baguette from the baker's in town. He stopped eating when he saw Coralie approaching.

'Hi, Coralie, I know why you're here. I'm sorry I didn't get back to you with the list of entrants for the fawn races.

Don't worry, we have a full house. It's all sorted. We start with the mixed new fawns, under one year old. Then come the juveniles, one- to two-year-olds; males first, then females. Then we have an open event which will, of course, be the fastest; followed by the mixed-veterans' race. This year we've come up with a really special surprise race to end the competition. I'm loath to disclose the details of it to you, as it would be nice to keep it secret. What do you think? Do you want to know, or would you prefer a nice surprise on the night? You won't be disappointed I can assure you. Padraig knows all about it and is very excited.'

Coralie was delighted that Shawn had done such a thorough job. She decided to trust him and let him keep his grand finale secret. She gave him a big hug and a kiss and then went off to the pond to find some frogs.

The frog pond was warm and contained some pond weed, but the water level was good as it was fed by an underground spring. The mud at the edge of the pond was dry and cracked. The water lily petals were brown at the edges. It was not an ideal environment. It had been a hot summer and the frogs were not happy. They were not in a mood to be helpful. Coralie knew she'd need to really turn on the charm, but she was prepared for this. She was looking especially sweet and pretty today. She'd highlighted her hair with camomile, stained her toe and finger nails with berry juice, dyed her lips with pink rosebud juice, coloured her cheeks with bronze powdered bracken and was wearing a white damask dress which floated gracefully in the light breeze, revealing her elegant limbs. She knew she looked good and was sure she could charm some frogs into volunteering for the frog baiting event.

Not bad, she had thought when she admired her reflection in the mirror before she set off for her series of meetings to finalise the organisation of the fête.

'Croak, fucking croak,' said a large bullfrog when she approached.

Not a good start, thought Coralie. *He made no attempt to be civil and talk intelligibly to me.*

'Hi,' said Coralie. 'I'm sorry to see your plants around the pond looking so parched and sad. It must be hard to live here at the moment. I guess you are really hot. Perhaps the fairies can help you?'

'How's that?'

Well, at least he is trying to communicate now, she surmised.

'We have skilled fairy carpenters. Perhaps we could build you a pergola to shade you from the sun and a small boat for the children to play in on the pond. We would like to be your friends,' she proposed.

'So, what do you want in return?' he asked gruffly.

Coralie knew that he knew about the fête and the annual frog baiting competition.

She wondered, *How best to proceed?*

'We have some distinguished international visitors arriving tomorrow for our annual fête and we want this fête to be extra special. We would really like the frog community to continue to contribute to the success of the fête. What we are looking for are four frog volunteers to enter the exciting frog baiting competition. As you know, the frogs are only lightly struck by the fairies with a hazel twig, while tethered to a tree. It doesn't hurt and it has been our joint, if somewhat curious, custom for centuries. As I mentioned, an added incentive this year is that if you provide four volunteers, we will offer the frog community recompense for their contribution, in the form of a designer-built pergola and a small boat for the young frogs to play in. We will split the entry money with you as usual. What do you think? You just need to find four volunteers. You can't lose.'

A full ten minutes passed, before the bullfrog made his reply. Coralie waited patiently. Finally, the answer came.

'OK, affirmative. I will send four volunteers to the fête tomorrow night. You have my word. In the meantime, I will start designing the pergola and think about the best type of boat for the youngsters.'

'Thank you. You have great vision and are a true friend to the fairies.'

'No, I just look after my own,' he replied, then farted.

Coralie was happy to leave and escape the vile odour of methane and sulphur. Her next job was to find someone for the face-painting and some fairies to collect an array of prizes for the parade, races and tombola. Coralie already had two fairies in mind for the prizes; the same two who had found the iPod in the park. They seemed to have a knack of finding lost possessions and, if she didn't ask too many questions, she was sure they would do an excellent job. She headed back to the fairy grotto and soon found Zak and Benjie snoozing in the dappled shade under a chestnut tree.

'Hello, my gorgeous boys. How are you doing? Not too busy I observe.'

Zak opened one eye and saw a vision in a translucent white damask dress hovering just above him and Benjie.

'Hello your gorgeous self,' Zak replied. 'I suspect you are after our assistance for some urgent matter of state. What can we do to make you happy, darling? I think we've napped long enough for today. Time for a bit of mischief, Benjie!'

Coralie explained that she needed lots of prizes for the fête and had chosen Benjie and Zak to help procure them. She told them that she had great confidence in their ability and ingenuity and that she promised not to ask too many questions about the provenance of the prizes. Prizes for adults, children, fawns and visiting dignitary fairies were all needed. In return, they could join her at the top table for the feast and be waited on by the juvenile fairies.

Benjie and Zak did not need much persuasion to agree to help. After all, it would be fun and would test their ingenuity and it was a good few days since they had last played any tricks on the humans who frequented the park. Now they had their fairy queen's blessing to get up to some serious mischief.

So that only left the volunteer for the face-painting to be found. Coralie went to the nursery, but no one was there. She searched the glade behind and soon found a group of young fairies and their elderly minders.

'Hi kids, who's the most artistic fairy here?' she asked.

In unison, the juvenile fairies shouted, 'Chantal.'

Of course, thought Coralie. *How could I have overlooked her?*

A pretty dark-haired young fairy with enormous chestnut eyes, called Lulu, further expanded, 'Chantal's brilliant. She can make a tortoise out of a nutshell and some twigs, and a butterfly out of flower petals and stamens. She's painted murals on the walls of the nursery so it's like an exotic tropical island. She's brill!'

'That's her over there,' shrieked an overexcited Lulu.

Chantal, a modest middle-aged fairy was sitting quietly, weaving a basket from pond reeds. Not only was she a talented artist, but she also knew a lot about plants and was a formidable cook. She looked up and smiled meekly at Coralie. Chantal was a remarkably kind fairy and was pleased to volunteer when Coralie explained her dilemma and the need to find someone to do the face-painting for the fête. All the proceeds from the face-painting would go towards improving the community facilities.

Chantal suggested she spent the rest of the morning collecting dyes from the plants in the wood with the help of her young charges. Then, she would let her creativity run wild in the afternoon and sketch some striking designs to entice the fairy clients; young or old, male or female. She was secretly very pleased to have been selected and would throw all her artistic resources into the project. All the young fairies were jumping around, screaming and pleading to be allowed to help with the preparations and offering themselves as guinea pigs on which to try out the new designs.

Coralie thanked Chantal copiously and promised to reward her after the fête. Though she couldn't help wondering why she hadn't volunteered a few weeks ago, but had waited to be asked. She was undoubtedly the best fairy for the job. Still she had come though at the eleventh hour. Now Coralie could return to her palace and spend the afternoon creating her outfit and annoying or seducing Pablo... that would depend on his mood as much as hers.

10

Coralie awoke the morning of the fête with a splitting hangover. She and Pablo had imbibed a bit too enthusiastically the night before and had ended the evening with a wildly passionate encounter that had lasted well into the early hours of the morning; far too long considering the demands that would be placed on them today, but it had been fun and exhilarating at the time. Now she was rather regretting their wild abandon. Half a Nurofen should help. She still had almost a full pack left that she had found in the park. It worked much better than the fairy's traditional remedy of camomile and ground apple pips. Pablo half opened a sleepy eye and groaned in a gruff croaky voice.

'Great party last night, sweetheart. Got any Nurofen left?' He leant over and kissed her tenderly.

The problem had been that Coralie had had such a good day yesterday and her plans for her outfit had come together so well, that she had become overexcited last night and had rather forgotten to save her energy to handle her serious duties for today. Pablo had been highly responsive to her sexual advances and they had both drunk several glasses of fermented elderberry juice before and after their love-making. She knew that fermented elderberry always gave her a headache and that she should stick to fermented elderflower, but her gay abandon had overridden her logical brain. They took their Nurofen with a glass of dandelion tea in bed and held each other gently until the Nurofen became effective and their heads de-fuzzed. They finally rose at 10:00 am, feeling ready to face the world and enjoy the grand fête. The fête was not due to start till 7:30 pm that night, so there was plenty of time to check everything and even have a siesta before the first foreign guests arrived.

Coralie went off to see Zak and Benjie to confirm that

71

there were sufficient prizes. Not only did she find a vast pile of prizes, but each had been carefully wrapped and labelled with a cryptic description of the contents. She was overwhelmed with gratitude. Zak and Benjie grinned like two cats that had got the cream when she kissed and hugged them in gratitude. Goodness knows what the packages contained, but there were definitely sufficient of them. Coralie then dropped by Calista's place and was relieved to hear that the blueberry punch had survived the night intact, without being spiked.

On the way to see Shawn, she met the spiders who confirmed the candyfloss was delicious. Shawn was smiling broadly when she found him. He was happy with the arrangements for the fawn races; everything was organised. Finally, she went to inspect the dance floor, which was perfectly flat and well manicured. Goodness knows what the human gardeners would have made of it, if they found it during the day. They might suspect extra-terrestrials had been at work! However, a magical perimeter had been erected around the glade where the fête was to be held, so it was safely hidden from prying human eyes.

Coralie flew home and checked her list again; noting with pleasure how all her organisational efforts had come together today:

1. **Fancy Dress Parade** – "SORTED," she wrote.
2. **Blueberry Punch** – "SORTED"
3. **Candyfloss** – "SORTED"
4. **Tombola** – "SORTED"
5. **Face-painting** – "SORTED"
6. **Fawn Racing** – "SORTED"
7. **Frog Baiting** – "SORTED"
   Well, hopefully "sorted". I don't want to double-check and confirm that the aggressive bullfrog has found four volunteers, because that would only infuriate him.
8. **The Feast** – "SORTED"
9. **Music, Dancing and Lighting** – "SORTED"

Everything was organised, including her outfit which she had finalised yesterday afternoon, and now she could relax and enjoy a quiet relaxing afternoon to prepare herself mentally and physically for the festivities tonight.

Heaven knows what Pablo will wear, she thought, but that wasn't her problem.

The stands were all erected that afternoon in the glade adjacent to the dance floor and the trestle tables for the buffet and guests' feast were put up nearby and decorated with wild flowers and tethered butterflies. The magical fence, that had been set up around the entire area to protect the fairies from prying human eyes, was tested for the final time. Only the fawn races would take place outside the fairies' magic cordon and these would not start till the last visitors had left the park.

Around 6:30 pm, the distinguished visitors from foreign countries began arriving at Coralie's palace where cocktails were being served. Many of them were dressed in their traditional costume for the fancy dress parade, as they had promised. Coralie greeted them wearing her Dolce & Gabbana imitation gown that she had copied from a *Vogue* magazine, carelessly discarded in the park. She looked stunning in an asymmetric, off-the-shoulder dress in a fabric woven from cobwebs spun with daisy pollen and rosebay willow herb petals and decorated with downy baby sparrow feathers on the single shoulder. She wore a tiny funky hat of interlaced hazel twigs and her hair fell in cascades of chestnut curls. Not for her the fancy dress parade! Pablo, however, had decided that he should be dressed in keeping with his musical performance, so had opted for a gypsy prince outfit in gold and red with a bandeau and single golden earring. He could have entered the fancy dress parade (and won), but this was not his intention. He had dressed to please his artistic temperament, not to win prizes. They made a strikingly handsome couple.

Finally, the nightingale sang 7:30 pm and they all set off for the hidden glade, chatting happily about what the evening ahead may hold. Everyone was greeted by Calista who served them with a glass of blueberry punch decorated with a sprig of red currants and a paper cocktail umbrella. The blueberry punch was very well received, not too strong but definitely alcoholic. The young fairies were served with punch diluted with elderflower water, so they also felt part of the celebrations.

Coralie gave a short speech welcoming the local fairies and foreign visitors, thanking the helpers, and then declared the fête open. The Pevi and fireflies danced in the trees around the glade, creating a party ambience with their display of twinkling coloured lights. It was still light when the fête started, but soon the sun would set and the display would become more dramatic. Their display had been beautifully choreographed and they had practiced diligently to perfect their coordination. They would continue to dance until the last fairy collapsed exhausted and the fête was over. The Pevi always thoroughly enjoyed the fairies' fête and were proud to be part of it and contribute to the fun.

The first event of the evening was the fancy dress parade. At the head of the parade, came the visiting dignitaries in their national dress. To the delight of Coralie, Pablo introduced each national group by playing a couple of bars from their national anthem on his guitar. The visitors were followed by the young fairies in fancy dress, then various adult individuals who didn't mind making a spectacle of themselves, and finally the floats arrived colourfully decorated by various fairy associations. The parade was greeted with enthusiastic cheers and clapping. A small group of judges had been selected from the foreign visitors to choose the winning outfits and floats. When the parade was finished, the contestants grouped together in front of the judges and Coralie read out the results.

'We would like to thank our distinguished visitors for their spectacular display of national costumes, which was both a feast for the eyes and educationally instructive for our young fairies. We will not insult you by selecting a winner. Thank you again for your participation. Moving on to the fairies' fancy dress awards; first prize in the category "young fairies" goes to the pregnant mole; second prize goes to the squashed orange slug. Please forward come and select a prize.' The two winners tentatively approached the grandstand and looked at the bewildering array of packages with their cryptic descriptions. Zak and Benjie stepped in at this point so as not to disappoint the youngsters and guided them towards the presents they knew would be acceptable; a sweet lollipop and a packet of radish seeds. Respectively described as "Suck hard and enjoy" and "Radish your wife". Coralie wondered if asking Zak and Benjie to organise the prizes had been such a great idea.

'The winners in the adult section are... First, the zebra crossing and second place goes to the footprint. Please come forward to select a prize.' The adults took a little longer than the youngsters to select their prizes as they were determined to interpret as many of the clues as they could before deciding which to choose. Just as Coralie was beginning to lose her cool, they made their decisions. The zebra crossing chose "Breast-enhancer", which turned out to be a rather pretty and valuable brooch, and the footprint selected "Willy-wrapper" which was a packet of durex; not much use to a fairy, but they could always be used as balloons at a kiddies' party. Coralie hoped that things would get better and more family-oriented for the tombola prizes.

'Finally, the best float award goes to the Drama Society and second place is awarded to the Mushroom Appreciation Society. Will the chairperson from each society please come forward to choose a prize. Zak and Benjie, perhaps you can suggest an appropriate prize for our learned societies.' Sheepishly, Zak and Benjie came forward and gave a large box to the Drama Society, which turned out to be a children's lunchbox, decorated with a picture of a princess riding a white unicorn, that would hold enough food for a picnic for six fairies. They selected a smaller box for the Mushroom Appreciation Society, which contained a highly useful magnifying glass. The cryptic labels were swiftly removed and disposed of. Surprisingly, the prizes had turned out to be particularly appropriate for the winning societies and the chairmen both expressed their delight. Coralie had a quiet word in Zak's ear and suggested that he removed the labels for the tombola, as this was a family game of chance and needed to be appropriate for youngsters. She hoped that the presents would be suitable, but she need not have worried, as the two fairies had actually been relatively responsible for the most part and had tried hard to find interesting and useful objects left by visitors to the park, or in some cases, temptingly placed in an open handbag or back pocket. Their sense of humour had got the better of them during the wrapping, to relieve the tedium. It is a well-known fact that male fairies hate wrapping presents, but they had persevered for their queen.

Now the parade had finished, the tombola, candyfloss, blueberry punch, face-painting and frog-baiting stands opened for business. Background pop music was provided by Juliet's iPod and speakers. The bullfrog had been true to his word and had sent four reluctant young frogs to be the victims for the frog baiting. Frog baiting is a highly popular sport with fairies, who are generally gentle creatures, but once a year release some of their pent-up frustration by hitting frogs with hazel twigs. They are not allowed to hit very hard, so it doesn't hurt too much, but is highly irritating for the frogs who are tethered to a tree on a long leash in the centre of a small arena and do their best to dodge the blows. The fairies pay ten pence for the twig and five minutes in the arena, then another two pence for every direct hit they make. This money is split fifty-fifty between the frogs and the fairy community projects. The fairies who score the most direct hits in a five-minute session are declared the winners. There would be a prize for the best male, female and juvenile fairy of the evening and the stand would only be open for one hour; one very long and annoying hour for the "volunteer" frogs. Coralie was not completely convinced that this practice was politically acceptable, but it was such a firm favourite with the fairies that she had decided to allow the practice to continue for the time being, or at any rate, as long as frog volunteers could be found.

Coralie and Pablo both distanced themselves from the frog baiting stand, preferring to frequent Calista's blueberry punch stand.

The juvenile fairies were all overexcited; decorated with face-paint and with remnants of pink candyfloss stuck to their hair and clothes. The strawberry candyfloss was a real hit this year, though some of the young fairies were nervous of the spiders who sold it.

Two hours after the fête opened, everyone sat down at trestle tables to enjoy the feast. The chefs had created a work of art for each dish. As fairies do not eat very much, good presentation is deemed more important than the actual food. The chefs had undoubtedly excelled themselves in this respect this year. Each course was devised to represent a different colour of the rainbow. The first course had a red theme, preserved berries and rose hips. The second course was orange segments decorated with marigolds. The third was a beautiful creation of buttercup flowers and dandelion stamens, with a royal jelly compote. And so it continued, each course being more impressive than the last.

During the final course, of purple flowering broccoli and plum jam decorated with a confetti of violet petals, Pablo entertained the congregation with his gypsy guitar compositions. He had devised a programme containing a mixture of his own compositions and well-known favourites. He looked dramatic and sexy in his colourful gypsy outfit. His fingers moved with lightning speed over the frets, enthralling the fairies and the hypnotic rhythms floated in the breeze over the park. The Pevi and fireflies swirled around him like wild dervishes, enhancing the thrill of the spectacle. Pablo played to enthusiastic cheers and applause until his fingers bled from strumming the strings so persistently. He ended his performance with a romantic number dedicated to his beloved fairy queen. His display had been professional and exhilarating and Coralie was so very proud of him.

When the applause had finally died down, Shawn the fawn stood up and announced the start of the fawn races and the programme of events: mixed new fawns, juvenile males then females, the open event, mixed veterans and, finally, a surprise speciality event. Coralie still had no idea what this would be and was highly intrigued. The new fawns participating in the first event paraded nervously around the glade closely scrutinised by the fairies. The fairies were trying to analyse all the variables as there was no known past form in this first race. Who had the longest legs? Who had the strongest legs? Who had the strongest character? Who looked fittest? Then the young entrants all set off for the start line and, hopefully, victory. They would run twice round the circuit that had been mapped out using pebbles and string.

Padraig opened his betting booth and a queue of excited fairies immediately formed at the window. A pretty young fawn called Beige was soon declared favourite at 2:1 and indeed this proved a good bet as she passed the winning line three lengths ahead of the closest opposition. She was unable to contain her emotions and cried copiously when presented with her rosette and prize. The rest of the races followed one after the other and many of the fairies had lost a lot of money by the time it came to the final event. Padraig, however, had had a profitable evening as no other favourites had come home in first place after the first race. There would be no betting on the final race. It was strictly just for fun.

Shawn stood up again and announced the final race. This would be a relay race consisting of three legs: a wheelbarrow race, a six-legged race and a two-legged race. Each team contained five members and they had not been allowed to practice, for fear of giving the game away if spotted, so it should, indeed, be a highly amusing and uncoordinated display. The four participating teams lined up at the start line. Two fawns would participate in the first and second legs and one in the final leg. The rules for the first leg were that the fawn in front could only use his forelegs, his rear legs were placed around the neck of the fawn behind, who was allowed to run normally.

The starting pistol sounded and the four teams set off to

much hilarity. Even the entrants were laughing so much that they could hardly coordinate their movements. There were several collisions and bruised fetlocks, but they all made it round the course eventually and passed over to their two team-mates who comprised the second leg, the six-legged race. These two fawns run side by side, with the inside hooves of one member tied to the inside hooves of the other fawn. This needed exceptionally close coordination and timing. The lack of practice had definitely not helped and the teams struggled to keep up a good speed. Whether the fawns or fairies were laughing loudest, was hard to tell. The final leg consisted of a single fawn running on his hind legs. It was a wonderful sight to see and the spectators were surprised by the speed and agility showed by the final participants. Who won was irrelevant, it was the frivolity that was important. Several fairies laughed so much that they were physically sick. All the contestants were presented with a rosette and prize to commemorate the event.

Shawn's relay had been a magnificent inspiration. He wondered how he would be able to top it next year.

Now all the formal events were over, the fairies could enjoy the disco and dancing. Benjie and Zak had mastered the technology of the iPod and were selecting individual dance tracks and taking requests at ten pence a time. The fairies pirouetted and circled the dance floor well into the early hours of the morning, touching each other fleetingly and immodestly, as was their custom; their antics lit by the resilient Pevi and fireflies who never shirked in their duty to provide funky disco lighting for the dance floor. The final fairy dropped, exhausted, to the earth at five in the morning. The 205th Grand Fairy Fête was over and no one had been seriously injured or died this year. It had been a resounding success for the fairy community.

However, nearby, two young humans who were engrossed in each other's company and experimenting with their new-found sexual desires, would not end the evening on such a high note.

11

Juliet and her two girl friends had arranged to meet up with Rick and the boys on Saturday evening in the Queen's Oak pub. Juliet had not told her friends about the secret meetings she had had with Rick and how events had unfolded. Rick had also failed to mention his recent two dates with Juliet to his friends. However, they had been spotted leaving the pub together on Monday by Andy, who happened to be driving past at the time, and he had phoned Niall and Stan with the news. They had been unsurprised and were pleased for Rick.

When Juliet walked into the pub, Rick thought how stunning she looked in her short straight denim skirt, figure-hugging simple T-shirt, and flat silver sandals. She had her hair tied back in a pony tail to let the breeze cool her neck and her bronzed legs were elegant and endless. He was so lucky to have found her. Rick was looking casual in navy Cargo shorts and a pale yellow polo shirt. They had both brought a sweatshirt to put on later when the sun sunk below the horizon. They complemented each other perfectly. She smiled coyly at him and he shot her a sly wink in response, causing her to blush.

Rick opened the conversation by telling everyone that he was excited because he had just been offered an invitation for an interview at the science park nearby, at Sittingbourne. The interview was next Friday with a company, called BioEnerFuels, that was researching new sustainable methods to produce energy. This was exactly the type of research that appealed to him. He had spoken on the phone with their Chief Scientific Officer and had come away with a strong impression that she was an enthusiastic scientist, with an in-depth expertise in innovative ways to create renewable energy. It certainly sounded like a fascinating company; small and focussed, yet dynamic; somewhere he could develop valuable experience and directly see the impact of his contribution to the company's research portfolio and perhaps even help in a small way to improving the environment of the world. Everyone was pleased for him and wished him luck.

The friends chatted away for a couple of hours, talking about their opinions on newly-released CDs and DVDs. The fourth Harry Potter film, *Harry Potter and the Goblet of Fire*, was due out at the end of the year and it transpired that Andy was excited about this because he had a crush on Emma Watson who played Hermione Granger.

Juliet and Rick made their excuses at around 8:30 pm and left the rest of the group to conjecture on where they were going and what they were up to. You didn't need a university education to know the answer to that question. They strolled hand in hand until they arrived at the hidden gate that gave them access to Knole Park. They entered the park and slowly made their way to the same spot where they had made love earlier in the week. It was dark tonight as there was a new moon that cast little light, but the town lights in the distance provided sufficient light for them to make out the paths and trees in the park. The atmosphere seemed strangely energised and Juliet wondered whether there would be a thunderstorm later that night. The cool night breeze gently stroked the downy hair on their limbs, causing little tingles of merriment to run up and down their exposed skin.

Juliet and Rick sat beneath "their tree" talking about the future and wondering where and when they would be able to meet now their lives had taken such different courses. They had brought a bottle of rosé wine, two plastic glasses and a corkscrew with them. Somehow chatting and bonding seemed to both of them more necessary than passion for the moment. Both needed support that they were making the correct decision about their future, and Juliet's decision obviously meant that they would not be seeing as much of each other as they would like. It was hard for her to tear herself away from Rick, but Switzerland was such a great opportunity and her mother had been so generous with this offer and had promised to give Juliet a good allowance so she could benefit fully from the experience. She knew that she would miss Rick terribly, even though they had only been lovers for a very short time, they had quickly become soulmates and were surprised at how similar their views on life were. Life was both easy and exciting with Rick and their sexual chemistry had been supersonic when they had made love in the park earlier that week.

After a while, Juliet became distracted by a faint glow in the distance that seemed to vibrate and she clearly saw pinpoints of coloured light that appeared to move in unison, almost like a disco. She thought it must be some surreal effect of the town lights and the electrically charged atmosphere (or was it the rosé?). Strangely, Rick could not see anything despite her protestations and wild gestures in the direction of the lights. Confused, she dismissed the phenomenon and refocused her attention on her lover. She hoped that she would find an article in the local paper next week that would explain the marvel she had seen. She recalled the night of the party when everyone had got unexpectedly drunk. It seemed that unusual things happened when they were in Knole Park together.

Next it was Rick's turn to see an apparition.

'I just thought I saw a deer with six legs and two heads. Just over there, by the small hillock,' he exclaimed, laughing loudly.

'Don't be ridiculous,' replied Juliet, but before she had finished speaking, she also saw the same weird creature, crashing ungainly through the bracken. 'It must be a freak of nature, but why haven't the owners done something about it? No wait, there are four of these strange creatures. Surely not! Hey, where did you buy this wine? It must be spiked.' Juliet was beginning to feel nervous and wondered if Rick had, indeed, intentionally laced her drink with some narcotic. Perhaps she had misread him and he wasn't as kind as she had thought. After all, she would be leaving him for Switzerland soon, so perhaps he was taking his revenge.

Rick took Juliet's face in his hands and stared imploringly into her panicked eyes.

'Do you really think I'd spike your drink? What a cruel accusation. Let's go and investigate what we *both* just saw.' But Juliet was strangely reluctant and preferred to remain still, hidden under the branches of their tree.

'Sorry, that was unfounded,' she whispered apologetically.

Rick took her in his arms and kissed her. 'Don't worry, I'm sure there's a logical explanation for all this,' he reassured her, but he was also very concerned about what they had apparently seen. 'Do you want to go home?' he enquired. Juliet was not one to be frightened easily; she was resolute that she would stay and that tomorrow they would laugh about their stupidity. She returned his affection and soon they were lying together in the long soft grass, exploring each other's body, oblivious to the second and third legs of the fawn's relay race.

It was at this time that Coralie and Pablo came flying by. They had escaped the noise of the fête after the fawn's relay race had finished, to enjoy a brief period of peace and solitude, when they came upon the young lovers. They hovered close to the entwined teenagers, feeling their passion.

'Perhaps we can learn some new techniques from these humans,' ventured Pablo with a wicked glint in his eye. But Coralie was not interested in voyeurism and insisted they should leave immediately to find the solitude they had set out to discover. Just at that moment, Juliet cried out in pain. 'We won't learn anything useful from these amateurs,' Pablo remarked cynically. 'Let's go.'

Juliet screamed again. An agonizing sharp pain had enveloped her right thigh. She felt it spreading through the veins in her leg. Rick jumped up, shocked by Juliet's cries and frightened that he had hurt her. Then he saw something wriggle away into the long grass. He realised that Juliet must have been bitten by a snake. She must have disturbed an adder during their love-making. He knew adders were generally timid creatures that avoided human contact, so she had been incredibly unlucky.

'Juliet, are you alright? I think you have been bitten by a

snake. Oh, Juliet, does it hurt terribly? What can I do?' But Juliet was in too much pain to reply. She just cried out again and again and clung to him tightly, looking imploring into his eyes for help.

Rick tried to keep calm. He wondered whether he should apply a tourniquet or suck the venom from the wound. He had seen both these attempted cures played out in cowboy movies, but he was unsure of their utility. Definitely, he should call an ambulance, even though he realised they would be hard to find in the dark in the middle of the park and he would have some explaining to do. He didn't think he should move her and perhaps the 999 service could advise him what to do. Juliet was becoming delirious with pain and her whole body was shaking. He knew he had to act quickly. He phoned 999 on his mobile and got through to the ambulance service. As he had surmised, they were concerned that they would have trouble locating the couple in the dark, but assured Rick that an ambulance would be sent immediately. Coralie and Pablo watched the drama unfolding, highly distraught, but unable to help. Fairy magic and healing were not effective on humans. They could do nothing but observe and sympathise.

The ambulance service advised Rick that the best course of action was to keep Juliet warm and as still as possible, and definitely not to try to suck out the venom or apply a tourniquet. They reassured him that by seeking medical attention immediately, he had done exactly the right thing and there should be no reason to be unduly concerned. It had been a shock, but she would be fine. Snakebites were rarely serious and very rarely fatal in the UK. They asked him to describe the snake, though, unfortunately, he could not do this accurately because it was too dark to perceive the snake's colour and markings.

Rick took off his sweatshirt, wrapped it around Juliet's shoulders, then held her gently, hoping his body heat would provide some comfort and warmth. After a few minutes, Juliet began to experience breathing difficulties and was wheezing slightly. Rick was concerned to see the shape of her face changing as the region around her lips and eyes started slowly swelling. She was very pale and looked grey. Worse still, she had now gone very quiet and he could barely detect a pulse. He began to panic, asking himself why her facial features were changing so radically; she hardly looked like his sweet Juliet any more.

Where was the ambulance? Rick wondered.

Unbeknown to Rick, Juliet had suffered a severe allergic reaction to the snake venom and had gone into anaphylactic shock. Anaphylactic shock can be treated very effectively by giving a shot of adrenalin, but it must be administered quickly, especially if the reaction is severe. It was essential that the ambulance arrived in the next few minutes to administer adrenaline, before Juliet's blood pressure dropped too far and her bronchial tissues swelled too much, causing choking and then collapse. Her condition was deteriorating steadily and that was a serious sign.

The ambulance crew were delayed because they had had trouble gaining vehicular access to the park so late at night, and had needed to wake the gamekeeper who lived in the gatehouse and get him to unlock the gates, so loosing precious time. Rick saw their headlights as they entered the park and he gently laid Juliet on the grass then he ran as fast as he could towards the ambulance, shouting and waving his arms. But the ambulance driver failed to see him in the dark and set off in the opposite direction, driving further away from Juliet. Rick rushed back to check on Juliet. He was really worried about how still she had become.

He repeated the words of the woman on the phone in his head, *Snakebites are rarely serious and very rarely fatal in the UK,* but this was not what he was seeing. Juliet's condition looked very serious to him.

The ambulance circled the park for fifteen minutes trying to locate the teenagers. Finally, they saw a figure frantically waving and drove over in Rick's direction. They were joking together about what the teenagers had been up to so late in the park, unaware of the seriousness of Juliet's condition.

When they finally found the teenagers, it was too late; Juliet had gone into a coma, caused by her anaphylaxis. She died a few moments after they arrived, before their administrations and injections could work. It was a tragic and extremely rare event.

Rick could not tear himself away from Juliet's lifeless body. He kept cradling her in his arms, rocking her gently, beside himself with grief and crying into her hair.

He asked himself, *How could this have happened? The evening had started out as such fun with their friends in the pub and the future was so bright for Juliet. She did not deserve to die.*

The ambulance men stood silently by, not wanting to disturb Rick, and feeling guilty about their banter in the ambulance. Neither of them had ever seen someone in an anaphylactic shock, but they recognised her textbook symptoms; the grey pallor, the swollen face and limbs. This was a highly rare reaction to adder venom, essentially because people are not frequently bitten by adders in the UK, but it was a relatively common and serious problem for people with severe allergies to bee or wasp stings, for example, or those with allergies to certain foods, such as peanuts or shellfish. They knew they could have saved her if they had arrived ten minutes earlier and administered the shot of adrenalin. It was such a pointless waste of a young life.

Rick was now in a state of advanced shock, hardly aware of anything around him. He was taken to hospital in the ambulance, lying on a stretcher next to his lover's still body.

Coralie and Pablo were also shocked and vowed to do whatever they could to help the young male human come to terms with his loss. So often when life was going wonderfully, tragedy lay just around the corner, looking for an unsuspecting victim on which to pounce and turn their world through one hundred and eighty degrees.

12

After a troubled sleep, during which he was haunted by visions of Juliet's grey and swollen face, Rick woke late the next morning to find himself in a strange bed in a strange room. His initial panic quickly turned to deep remorse as he recalled the events of the previous night. Juliet was dead.

He looked around the neat and tidy bedroom. Chintz curtains, Laura Ashley wallpaper, ironed sheets. This was definitely not home. The view from the window confirmed his suspicions. He was in Juliet's house. He tried to remember what had happened after the ambulance had arrived, but he could not remember anything after realising that Juliet was dead and holding her lifeless body in the park. He pulled on his clothes, still smelling of grass and Juliet's scent, splashed his face with cold water and went downstairs to face the music. He found Juliet's parents sitting over cold cups of coffee in the kitchen. They turned and looked at him, their eyes red and tired from shedding too many tears and passing a sleepless night.

'Would you like a coffee?' offered Kathleen, clasping a tissue to dry her cheeks.

'Thanks,' replied Rick, relieved that the conversation had started with a simple question. The difficult questions would no doubt come later. He sat down at the kitchen table and waited for the next question. When his coffee arrived, he took a sip and waited for the interrogation to start. But Kathleen and Robert were both lost in their own thoughts and left him to drink his coffee in silence.

After ten awkward minutes, he asked Kathleen what he was doing here as he had little recollection of the events of last night after the ambulance had arrived. Kathleen explained tearfully that Rick and Juliet had been taken directly to the hospital, where Juliet had been pronounced dead: the cause of death being a severe anaphylactic shock caused by an adder bite. The police had arrived at their house in the early hours of the morning and had delivered the tragic news. The policewoman had been professional, but also very kind and sympathetic, not an easy job for her, and had driven Kathleen and Robert to the hospital, where they had said their goodbyes to Juliet. They were taken to a small private ward with two beds. One contained Juliet's lifeless body, the other was occupied by Rick, lying in shock, delirious in his sleep. A nurse was sitting beside him and watching a monitor, connected to his wrist. She had quietly left the room when Kathleen and Robert arrived to leave them in private with their grief. She had returned ten minutes later accompanied by a doctor.

'The doctor told us that you were no longer in any danger physically, but you should not be left alone all night. The hospital urgently needed the beds for two youths who had been injured in a car crash. He explained that the police had been unable to contact your parents. He then asked us if we could take you home for the night and keep an eye on you. Although we had never met you, Juliet had told us all about you, and so we agreed to look after you and here you are,' Kathleen explained.

'Thanks,' said Rick. 'It was very kind of you.' He didn't know what else to say to these people he barely knew, but who were suffering the same loss. He remembered that his parents had gone away to Eastbourne for the weekend to celebrate their wedding anniversary. Although they were rarely overtly loving to each other, their relationship had endured twenty years and basically, they were happy living together and sharing their life, their limited aspirations and their problems. He wondered if he would ever find another soulmate with whom to share the rest of his life. Then he became overwhelmed by sadness, lost his composure and broke down in tears. Kathleen pulled her chair over to be beside him and held him tenderly while he shook with grief as all the events of the evening came flooding back. Kathleen had exhausted her reservoir of tears, but felt some comfort from the close contact with her daughter's lover's warm body. Giving sympathy and caring for someone else was therapeutic for her at this time and helped her momentarily forget her personal grief. Robert was lost to the world, deep in his own memories of his treasured daughter.

Slowly, Rick recovered his composure and felt a strong desire to talk to Kathleen about his love for her daughter and the tragic events of last night that had taken her away from him after such a brief period of happiness. He had not met Juliet's parents before this morning, but he already felt a close bond forming between Kathleen and himself. Maybe they could gain some comfort from talking together about their different Juliets, the daughter and the lover.

Kathleen also felt a strong attraction to this sad boy who had won the heart of her Juliet. He was handsome, not strikingly so, but definitely good-looking, with a kind face and demeanour. He was also tall and intelligent, both attributes were essential for an ideal boyfriend in Kathleen's view. Juliet had chosen her first serious boyfriend well, but there would be no wedding to look forward to; no heated mother-daughter debates about the best couturier to design the dress, the optimal complementary colour for the bridesmaids' dresses, the ideal location for the marriage and the wedding breakfast and the ever-contentious guest list; friends and family members who should and should not be invited.

Kathleen and Rick spent the rest of the morning listening to each other's stories and memories of Juliet. Talking about Juliet gave them both strength. Robert remained silent, too upset to speak. After a light lunch of bread and cheese, washed down with a bottle of good Bordeaux, Rick decided he should go home and leave Juliet's parents to their own grief. He bade his farewells and asked if he could come back to see them in a few days' time. Kathleen was delighted and thanked him for his company this morning. The house felt horribly empty after he had left.

Rick walked the long way home with tears in his eyes,

following some of the backstreets he and Juliet had walked down a week and a half ago, and remembering her laughter. He didn't want to meet anyone he knew; he felt a great hole in his heart and in his life. Juliet had been such a wonderful companion and he had hoped they would stay together. He would have waited for her to return home from her Swiss finishing school; he would have remained faithful. How could he tell his parents and friends what had happened? His parents would still be away on their weekend trip to Eastbourne. He was walking towards an empty house with no one to comfort him. He fought back his tears. The few people he saw were all smiling and enjoying their Sunday afternoon. He doubted he would ever smile again.

He finally arrived home to a silent house. He climbed the narrow stairs and fell exhausted into bed. He cried himself asleep and slept fitfully for the rest of the afternoon. His parents arrived home at 7:00 pm and found him still asleep in his room, his pillow soaked with salty tears. They had had a lovely weekend away by the sea and felt refreshed and in love again. They sat down on the edge of his bed and listened to his story, hearing the tragic events of his weekend and sharing his sorrow.

13

Juliet's funeral took place on Thursday 8th September and five days later, Rick phoned Kathleen and they arranged to meet for coffee in Caffè Nero in Sevenoaks. Rick was feeling uncomfortable with his emotions. On the one hand, he was excited because his interview at BioEnerFuels, on the day after the funeral, had gone exceedingly well and he was convinced that he would soon be offered a job as a technician in their research team. However, his excitement and enthusiasm for the job were making him feel guilty, because he knew that, unlike himself, Juliet would never be able to realise her dreams for the future. He had found it so hard to be dynamic and positive at the interview, following so close after the funeral, but somehow he had managed to impress them. He felt a strong need to talk to Kathleen and ask for her understanding of his mixed emotions. Although his underlying emotion was one of extreme sadness and loss, he felt that he needed to be forgiven for feeling excited on occasion.

Kathleen was already seated at a discrete table in the corner of the coffee shop when Rick arrived. She looked elegant, yet understated, in jeans, a white blouse and beige linen jacket. Despite her make-up, he could see that her eyes were slightly bloodshot and it was clear that she still carried her grief heavily. She smiled and stood up when she saw him and beckoned him over. She took his shoulders in both hands and greeted him with a kiss on both cheeks. Rick decided that she seemed genuinely pleased to see him, despite her sorrow and his involvement in her daughter's untimely death.

'Hello, Rick, what can I order for you; a cappuccino, a latte, or would you prefer a double espresso? I'm going to enjoy a cappuccino and a blueberry muffin. I'm slowly regaining my appetite now, after not having eaten for days.' Rick asked politely for a double espresso and a croissant; he wasn't hungry but it would be rude not to join her in something to eat.

Kathleen went up to the counter to order and returned with their coffees and side orders. She sensed his discomfort and immediately put him at ease, by expressing her delight at seeing him again and thanking him for attending the funeral and for the wreath of lilies and purple irises he had sent. She explained that purple irises were her favourite flower; she adored their bold shape and strong colour. They drank their coffees and discussed the funeral. It had been a relatively small affair, attended by close family, Juliet's closest girl friends and Rick. Kathleen had not wanted to invite too many people from the school, but had preferred to restrict the congregation to people who really knew and cared for Juliet.

The local vicar knew Juliet well and had composed a glowing tribute to her, highlighting her caring character and the sporting achievements that she had made in her short life. Robert had plucked up his courage to also pay tribute to his daughter with a short speech about his memories of her growing up and Juliet's friend, Claire, had bravely read an uplifting poem by Wordsworth. The service had been moving and the professional choir had sung beautifully, so the sad tuneless voices of the congregation had been drowned by the melodic harmonies of the professionals. Luckily, the weather had been sunny, which they agreed had been a relief, as no one wanted a cloudy rainy day to further depress the congregation.

At the end of the tributes and prayers, Rick had felt his eyes boring into the coffin, trying to visualise the body inside for the last time. Then, the curtains had closed around the coffin and Juliet's body had been given to the furnace below. There was no turning back now, no miraculous reincarnation was possible. He felt a solitude unlike any emptiness he had felt before. This tragic event was so unfair, so cruel to Juliet and him.

Rick had found the whole event so very stressful. He had

wanted to cry out loud, a long, bitter cry from the heart, damming God, but he had felt too inhibited and had had to contend himself with quietly sobbing into his handkerchief. It was the first funeral he had ever attended and of the congregation, he only knew Claire and Susie, and he did not know them that well as they had only been friends for three weeks.

He had not stayed long at Juliet's parents' house for the wake. Although Juliet's parents were kind to him and did not seem to blame him unduly for their daughter's untimely death, several of the relatives who knew the details were giving him rather unpleasant looks and he felt awkward and responsible. He had walked home slowly, taking the long route through the park but avoiding the fateful spot where Juliet had been bitten. When he was sure no one was around, he had let all his pent-up emotions escape into the ether with a series of long sorrowful cries and an abundance of salty tears, which Coralie and Pablo had heard from a distance and recognised as Rick's mourning for Juliet's lost life.

After Rick and Kathleen had exhausted discussing the events of the day of the funeral, Rick turned his mind to the future and told Kathleen about his interview at BioEnerFuels and how excited he was about the research that the scientists were undertaking there into new cleaner energy sources for the future. He felt it was a great opportunity for him to make a real mark on the world and improve the environment in the future. He also explained his dilemma about his tangled emotions. He found it so much easier to talk to her than to his own parents, who were kind and tried to be sympathetic, but found it hard to empathise with him having never met Juliet. Kathleen listened attentively and provided support for his ideals. But she could offer little advice for his and, indeed, her own sorrow other than "time", which would ultimately heal everyone's wounds (a rather hackneyed yet accurate piece of advice), and that Juliet undoubtedly would want him to live his life to the full, yet to sometimes find time to remember her with happiness for the short time they had spent together. The eyes of both Kathleen and Rick began to fill with water as they again started thinking about their loss. They sat in silence for a while, till Kathleen broke the impasse by suggesting that they meet again in a couple of day's time and Rick could tell her whether or not he had got the job he so badly wanted. She also promised to bring him a recent photo of Juliet.

As Kathleen walked home through Knole Park, reminiscing about the happy times they had spent there as a family, she realised that she did not know the exact location where her daughter had tragically been bitten by the snake. She resolved to ask Rick next time they met to walk with her in the park after coffee. It was important to her to know as much as possible about Juliet's last few hours alive.

Rick walked slowly home through the town, desperately hoping that the postman would have delivered him good news about the BioEnerFuels' job. He had enjoyed meeting Kathleen again and felt relieved that she had seemed genuinely happy to meet him again. A friendship was forming between them that he valued.

When he got home, his mother was clearly agitated; she was clasping a letter addressed to him from the research company. She handed him the letter and he retired to the privacy of his room to read the contents, just in case it was a rejection. Yes, it was the news he had dearly waited for, he had been offered a job working as a technician reporting directly to Doctor Macferson, the company's Chief Scientific Officer. The salary offered was pretty good for a school-leaver and his employment could begin in one week's time, on Monday 19th September, if he chose to accept their offer. He would be on a three months' probationary period and, if he worked diligently and showed promise, they would consider allowing him to study at college one day a week the following year, so he could obtain a higher qualification. Everything he wanted had just been offered, but there was no one extra-special to celebrate with, no Juliet. He decided to email his friends, Andy, Stan and Niall, with the news and arrange to meet up for a beer that evening. He then phoned his Aunt Sarah who was overjoyed that he would be following in her footsteps and pursuing a career in research science. She reassured him that it was the most rewarding career path and that he would never know boredom at work if he kept true to his ideals and desire to help the human race and to advance scientific knowledge. Finally, he went downstairs to give the good news to his anxious mother, who was delighted, and opened a bottle of Spanish Cava at lunchtime to toast his success, with strict instructions not to tell his father about their little indulgence.

Two days later, Rick met up with Kathleen again for coffee. This time he ensured he arrived first and paid for their refreshments. He wanted their relationship to be one of equals, not parent child. His mother had given him some money that morning and he had been shopping in Sevenoaks for new clothes suitable for work. He still had just under a week of freedom before he started his first proper job and he was looking forward to spending some time researching novel methods of energy production on the web. Kathleen had brought him a recent photo of Juliet, as she had promised. It had been taken on a beach that spring during a family holiday to Alghero in Sardinia. Juliet was slightly tanned and wearing a sexy short tangerine summer dress. She looked exceptionally pretty and had a lovely genuine smile in the photo.

Kathleen complained, 'Why is it so difficult to find that perfect picture of someone you love, or even just a good picture? Most of the recent photos of Juliet were either slightly out-of-focus, or she didn't have a good expression, or the location wasn't suitable, or there was a fly on her nose. It took a while to find a photo that really captured her true personality and beauty. I hope you like it. I can email you a jpeg if you like?'

Rick accepted her offer and admired the photo of his lost lover. It was the only photo he had of her, but it was perfect, he would treasure it. They both sat and reflected quietly on their respective Juliets for a moment; sadness welling up in their hearts, eyes gently watering. There had not been sufficient time for them to move on and feel happy about what Juliet had achieved in her short life. Seeing the photo had brought back a flood of memories and suppressed emotions. They were crying for their own personal loss, as much as for the young life that was cut so short; an almost selfish, yet highly understandable feeling. Rick handed Kathleen a tissue, which she gratefully accepted, and gently wiped the smudged mascara from around her eyes. He blew his nose, hoping nobody in the cafe had noticed his tears.

After a few minutes of complete silence, the conversation became more animated as Rick tried to lighten the atmosphere. He told his news about the job offer and they chatted away about his future and the potential value the new energy technology could bring to future generations. Kathleen was genuinely interested in his career. She could no longer plan for Juliet's future, but she took some solace in supporting Juliet's boyfriend and hearing about his ideals. She found he had an engaging personality and she appreciated his company.

After they had finished their coffees, Kathleen and Rick strolled in Knole Park. The park was always busy at the weekends, but it was peaceful during the week and they saw very few people as they slowly made their way towards the location where Juliet had met her death. They both felt an enormous dark cloud descend as they neared the tree, but Kathleen was trying hard to keep the atmosphere light and was hiding her fear by asking Rick lots of questions about BioEnerFuel's technology. She had a reasonable grasp of biochemistry as she had studied for a degree in chemistry and had worked as a research scientist for a pharmaceutical company for five years when she was first married, looking for new treatments for breast and testicular cancers. Rick was not yet informed enough to be able to answer many of her questions as they were quite technical in nature. He knew the company worked on developing microbial fuel cells to generate electricity, but the scientific details were still rather hazy. However, he would make sure that he could answer her questions next time they met. He would take another look at BioEnerFuel's website and educate himself better to impress her. It was nice to talk about Juliet, but he also enjoyed the opportunity to have a quite scientific discussion too.

Someone else was also out and about in the park at the same time. Edmund, the chief Pevi, was circulating the park with Coralie, the fairy queen. Edmund was telling Coralie about the Pevi meeting that was planned to occur in a few days' time, where they would endeavour to find a solution to the problem of the depressed young Pevi and the weakening Pevi immune system due to the reduction of positive ions in the atmosphere. The Pevi's best scientist, geographer and historian would present their ideas and debate the problem with the Pevi community as a whole. He hoped there would be some interesting and novel suggestions, but Edmund was not convinced that any of the proposals that they could come up with would work in practice and anyway, they did not yet know what caused the problem.

Coralie listened with genuine concern, but felt helpless to make any intelligent suggestions. She offered to contact Professor Theodore, the fairies' most accomplished physicist and mathematician, to see if he had any inspirations. He was Spanish, but lived in the south of Holland. She was sure he would be happy to visit Sevenoaks for a few days to meet the Pevi and talk about their concerns. He was an old friend of Pablo's and would enjoy speaking Spanish with him and listening to him playing traditional folk guitar music.

They then began chatting about the sad death of the teenage girl the other week. Coralie had been badly traumatised by witnessing the event and they were discussing if they could do anything to help the teenage boy who was with the girl at the time. Coralie immediately recognised Rick when she saw him in the park with Kathleen and pointed him out to Edmund. They hovered behind the couple strolling in the park, listening in to their conversation. It became apparent that the woman was the teenage girl's mother, because they were talking about the tragedy and

Rick was pointing to the site beneath the tree where they had been sitting when tragedy struck. Edmund, however, was more interested in the parallel conversation the humans were having about renewable energy and creating electrons and protons in an environmentally-friendly and sustainable way. It was a shame that the boy was still rather unsure of any details, but he had promised the woman that he would do some more research into the technology before starting his job, so he could tell her more about it next time they met.

Kathleen and Rick sat on the dry grass beneath the lover's tree for some time, while Kathleen reminisced about Juliet. She clutched a paper tissue and frequently dabbed at her eyes to remove a tear while she spoke, stopping from time to time to compose herself. Being an only child, Juliet had often spent quality time with her mother and they had enjoyed shopping, walking and swimming in the pool together. Kathleen explained that Juliet had been quite reserved by nature and had not confided her deepest thoughts to her parents, but she had always been loving and respectful to them.

Rick listened with interest to some of her tales about the young Juliet growing up and her battles with her parents as she fought for freedom to express her own personality. How her father didn't want her to have her ears pierced or wear short skirts. But, essentially, she was a devoted daughter who really didn't cause much trouble at all for her parents. She was not a wild child like some of her contemporaries at school and always respected her parents' viewpoint, even if she didn't agree with them. Kathleen told Rick that he was Juliet's first serious boyfriend and that her sexuality had only blossomed in the last few weeks (which he already knew). Kathleen explained that Juliet was not very like her mother in that respect, which made Rick chuckle.

After a while, Kathleen asked to be left alone beneath the tree to reflect about her daughter and try to understand her own feelings and how she could come to terms with her immense loss and sadness. Rick thanked her sincerely for sharing her precious memories of Juliet with him at such an emotional time and kissed her on the cheek as he said farewell. He also needed some time alone with his grief.

Coralie and Edmund watched them silently, sympathising with their sorrow but intrigued by their earlier scientific conversation and feeling the strong mutual attraction radiating between the two humans.

Coralie wondered, *Where will they end up; friends or lovers?*

Edmund was looking forward to hearing more about the technology when they next met. A machine that could generate "protons", which were small positive ions, was just what the Pevi needed right now.

14

The following morning, Rick logged onto his laptop computer and went to look at BioEnerFuels' website to see if he could better educate himself on their technology. He found their website was full of interesting information about environmentally-friendly ways of producing electricity. For the moment, he would concentrate on microbial fuel cells as this would be the project he was going to be working on when he started work at the company in a few days' time. He had done some preliminary studying prior to the interview, but now he needed to undertake a more detailed investigation and make an accurate crib sheet for himself. He was determined to impress the Chief Scientific Officer, Doctor Josephine Macferson, his new boss, on his first day in the labs. He also badly wanted to impress Kathleen with his technical knowledge.

Rick took out his favourite fountain pen, the Parker pen given to him on his first day at secondary school by his Aunt Sarah, and started to make some notes.

Microbial fuel cells, also known as biological fuel cells, are a bioelectrical system that generates an electrical current using bacteria. The cells usually work by mimicking biochemical interactions already found in nature.

The cell converts chemical energy into electrical energy (electrons) and protons (the positive ionic form of hydrogen) using bacteria to oxidise fuel using catalytic reactions. A catalytic reaction is one that is helped to go faster by utilizing an intermediary compound or protein to facilitate the reaction. The catalyst is commonly an enzyme found in nature.

The electrons are transferred to the "cathode" compartment via an external circuit, producing electricity which can be used to run machinery or provide lighting etc. The positive ions, generated in the "anode" compartment, are not used; they are just a by-product from the production of the valuable electricity.

There are two main types of microbial fuel cells:
"Mediator" microbial fuel cells
"Mediator-less" or "Non-mediator" microbial fuel cells

Early mediator fuel cells needed chemical mediators to assist in the electron transfer, and these were both expensive and toxic. The mediator fuel cell technology was therefore not ideal to pursue much farther.

More recently, non-mediator fuel cells were being developed by a very few small biotechnology companies, such as BioEnerFuels, and university research departments, including an Institute of Science and Technology in South Korea. These non-mediator fuel cells, as the name implies, do not require a chemical mediator, but instead use bacteria themselves directly to transfer the electrons. Some bacteria have small hairs on their surface which they use to transfer the electrons. These types of fuel cells can generate electricity using wastewater or aquatic plants as the fuel source.

BioEnerFuels is developing this technology based on living algae and/or pond water, which has major long-term ecological advantages for the planet and obvious practical applications for people living in poor remote areas who can only dream of a local supply of clean water and a cheap reliable source of electricity.

Microbial fuel cells have several potential uses, including:

- *Generating electricity and clean water from wastewater*
- *Generating electricity from crops or algae*
- *Creating batteries that do not need recharging.*

Even that very basic level of research made the technology more understandable to Rick. There was a lot more information on the company's website and other academic websites bookmarked there, but much of it was technically too complex for him at the moment, though he had no doubt that he would fully understand the principles once he started working on a real project. He was surprised that so little research had been undertaken on creating efficient fuel cells, since the idea had first been postulated in 1911 by M. C. Potter, who used the bacteria, *E. Coli,* to generate electricity. It seemed such a sensible and logical way to generate power, without the horrible environmental problems posed by nuclear fuel or coal- or oil-fired power stations. He was now even more excited about starting his new job and working towards a better future for mankind.

He phoned Kathleen, keen to share his new knowledge, and arranged to meet her that afternoon in the tearooms in Knole Park at 3:00 pm. Kathleen was a little surprised at his enthusiasm to meet again so quickly after their last encounter, but she was feeling a closer and closer bond with Rick every time they met and enjoyed his company. He kept Juliet alive for her. Robert was still deep in depression and had not yet gone back to work. She hated hanging around the house which was so full of memories and sadness. She hoped she was not making an idiot of herself. Did Rick view her as a friend, a mother figure or something more sexual? She certainly felt a certain attraction towards him that she hadn't experienced for almost two decades and while this deeply troubled her, it also gave her a focus in life which she needed at the moment and stimulated her to take a renewed interest in her appearance. She put down the phone after talking to Rick, then dialled her hairdresser and made an appointment to have her highlights redone the following morning.

Kathleen and Rick met later that day in the small courtyard of the tearooms and shared a chilled bottle of Sauvignon Blanc in the sunshine. Rick immediately started to tell her all he had learned about microbial fuel cells. Kathleen was genuinely interested and listened intently, keen to fully understand as many of the technical details as she could. Edmund had spotted them arrive and was sitting on Rick's shoulder listening with great interest. He had contacted Coralie and she was on her way with the fairies' top mathematician and physicist, the Spanish Professor, Theodore, who had arrived from his home in southern Holland the previous evening, keen to help the Pevi resolve their life-threatening positive ion problem.

Edmund reflected, *Could this young human teenager actually be the source of salvation of the Pevi race? Could he find a way to generate positive ions for them from an ecologically renewable source such as pond water? The frog pond in the park nearly always contains water, it rarely runs dry, so could potentially be used as the input source for the fuel cell. It seems that the humans aren't even interested in the positive ions, just the negative electrons to generate electricity. The positive ions are merely a waste product from the reaction. How can I communicate our problems to him? Maybe Coralie can help because Rick doesn't seem to sense my presence on his shoulder at all.*

To Rick's surprise, Kathleen seemed to have stopped listening intensely to him after a while and, instead, was looking at him with a bemused expression.

'You know this is really strange, but I seem to be able to see your aura, or part of your aura anyway. There is a strange purple glow emanating from your right shoulder. What on Earth can this mean?'

Coralie and Professor Theodore arrived at that moment. Coralie implanted a temporary rewind button into Rick and Kathleen's minds, prompting them to repeat their discussion on microbial fuel cells in its entirety for the benefit of the two newly arrived fairies. Kathleen had a strong sense of déjà vu and feeling that she was being watched, but her senses were not developed enough to detect the fairies. Coralie and Theodore listened to Rick re-explain the technology with great interest. The teenager was obviously relatively technically naïve at the moment, but it certainly sounded as if he would soon improve his understanding of this fascinating technology. He was undoubtedly intelligent and seemed determined to impress his new employers and his companion, Kathleen, with his knowledge and enthusiasm.

When Rick had finished talking, Coralie summarised her observations to Edmund and Theodore.

'Well, not being a scientist, I didn't follow everything that was discussed just now, but I grasped a few important concepts about what the technology is about. The boy is young but intelligent and so is Kathleen. She was asking some relevant questions, so she clearly understands what he was talking about. The technology is very new, but apparently proven on a small scale. I believe we should follow up this technology and try to communicate the Pevi's problems with these humans. Unfortunately, Rick appears to be impervious to the forces at work here in Knole Park, to the fairies and Pevi's presence, but I detect a sensitivity to both our races from Kathleen. Professor Theodore, what is your view?'

Professor Theodore was deep in thought, internally speculating on what this technology might be able to achieve. He was a brilliant scientist and, like all scientists, was prone to cutting himself off from the world when analysing data and weighing up the relevance and importance of new information. Edmund and Coralie waited patiently for a while, then Coralie repeated her question a little louder.

'Professor, what is your view?'

'I'm afraid that this is all new to me, Coralie. I haven't specifically been keeping myself up to date on new sustainable energy ideas. However, what I can say, from my extensive experience of working on fundamental biochemistry and physics principles, is that I certainly believe there could be a possible solution here to the Pevi's problems, though whether field trials have been undertaken already or whether this is merely a laboratory exercise we don't know at the moment. I agree with you that we need to open channels of communication with these humans, but without alarming them too much. Do we know if they live nearby, or come to the park frequently?'

Edmund replied that Kathleen had been visiting the park regularly for many years with her family, but he had only noticed Rick relatively recently, when he had started visiting in the evenings with Kathleen's daughter, the girl who died.

Coralie was keen to immediately open up communications with Kathleen and Rick, but Edmund and Theodore preferred to wait until they had more concrete evidence about the effectiveness of the technology and, furthermore, better understood the characters of the two humans. They also wanted to involve the Pevi scientist, Dr

Cedric, in any further discussions which might take place with the humans.

Kathleen and Rick finished their bottle of Sauvignon and went for a stroll in the park, followed closely by Coralie, Professor Theodore and Edmund. Both humans were lost in their own thoughts. Kathleen was still pondering the significance of the purple aura she had seen around Rick, while Rick was remembering the strange sights he and Juliet had seen on that tragic night in the park; the vibrating lights Juliet had seen and the six-legged, two-headed deer they had both seen; strange forces seemed to be materialising in the park. He started trying to recount this information to Kathleen, but it sounded juvenile and he stopped. He realised that he would never understand what they had or had not seen that fatal night.

Rick and Kathleen agreed to meet the following Saturday, by then, Rick would have started work and he would have lots to talk about.

The fairies and Edmund agreed to meet up again in the evening to discuss how best to approach the humans and find out more about BioEnerFuels. They then went their separate ways to ponder their tactics and benefit from a short siesta.

15

Two weeks after the fairies' fête, the Pevi had recovered their fitness sufficiently to hold their debate on the positive ion crisis. Hangovers had long been erased, heads had been cleared and Edmund was pleased that the time had come for the first (no doubt of many) meeting to discuss the future of their community in Sevenoaks. He had had preliminary discussions with his chief advisors, who had begun their research over two weeks ago, and were in full agreement that a meeting of the entire community should now take place.

A formal agenda had been circulated:

The problems – Chief Pevi, Edmund
Is it a global or local phenomenon?
 – Chief Pevi Geographer, Eve
Can we learn anything from our history?
 – Chief Pevi Historian, Harry
Scientific explanation and ideas
 – Chief Pevi Scientist, Doctor Cedric
Open discussion – All Pevi
Action plan

The Pevi gathered together in the Twisted Oak in the centre of Knole Park, just next to the glade that had been the fairies' dance floor two weeks previously. It had rained during the day and the temperature had dropped, so everyone was feeling chilly and hoping this evening's meeting would not last too long. After a hot sunny August, September had got off to a wet start. Rainwater was still dripping from the oak leaves and making the Pevi's fur cold and damp. Spirits were low. Edmund welcomed everyone to the meeting and gave the opening address which succinctly summarised the problems. This was a time for action, not extended speeches.

'Beloved Pevi, welcome to the first general meeting called to discuss our future and better understand the threat we currently find ourselves under. As you know, a few weeks ago *The Pevi Weekly* reported on a series of related problems that are threatening the existence of our race here in Sevenoaks. I'm sure you have all read these reports, but I will summarise them anyway. The first problem is that there has been a decrease in the concentration of positive ions in the Sevenoaks region, which, if it continues, will significantly decrease our strength and weaken our immune systems, leaving us vulnerable to disease. The second problem is that there is also an increasing occurrence of depression which has recently been noted, especially among the younger Pevi, and it is thought that this could also be directly related to the decrease in positive ions. With that depressing news, I hand the platform over to Eve, our esteemed and highly knowledgeable geographer, who will tell you about the early results from her global enquiries.'

Eve was a mature female Pevi with voluptuous curves and thick soft fur. She had spent many years teaching young Pevi in school; training them in the art of reading, writing, arithmetic and the French language and so she was well known and respected in the community. She was a spinster, having never found love among the male Sevenoaks community. She had stopped looking for a mate now and had concentrated her energies on finding out more about the world and its various cultures outside of Sevenoaks. She had read extensively about other countries and Pevi communities and had a strong urge to go exploring and see new sights before she got too old. She believed that this impending catastrophe might well give her the impetus she needed to begin her travels. She certainly intended to make sure she was included in any travel plans.

'Thank you, Edmund,' began Eve. 'I only have preliminary results from the enquiries that I have sent out, but it appears the situation may be relatively localised to Kent and possibly the centre of England at the moment. I have requested information from all our communities in the UK which includes those in the London and Market Harborough. I have also contacted some of our communities in Europe, specifically, France, Holland, Poland and Sweden. The anecdotal information is that they have not noticed any severe problems, but, having said that, they all mentioned that we are near the end of summer and, in general, most Pevi are busy enjoying the last of the summer's sunshine and not taking life too seriously at the moment. Everyone has been involved in summer fêtes and music festivals, so I cannot treat their rather flippant responses with one-hundred-percent confidence.

Unlike in Sevenoaks, no formal monitoring of positive ions is made on a regular basis by our other communities and, as far as I am aware, our measurement equipment is far more sophisticated than that in any of the other communities. We are lucky to have such a diligent technical team, who look after our environment here. I have of course requested urgent measurements of the positive-ion levels around Europe, but this will take a while as it is the holiday season and the results may not be of the accuracy I would like. I expect that it will be best for us to travel to some other communities to undertake the measurements ourselves and then we can have complete confidence in the results. So in summary, I'm afraid we will have to wait a bit longer before we can categorically state whether it is a local or more widespread problem. I apologise that I cannot be clearer on the subject at this stage in my investigations. I now hand the platform over to our esteemed historian and my good friend, Harry.'

'Well I've had such great fun searching our historical archives recently for any similar phenomena that happened in our past. I've even learnt a thing or two about the origins of the Sevenoaks Pevi,' pronounced Harry with great enthusiasm.

Harry was a devoted historian who spent so long in the archives that you could always tell when he was near, by an overpowering smell of dusty old parchment. He was the oldest Pevi in the community and was the subject of much teasing by several naughty young Pevi who frequently stole his spectacles or hid his historical books and ran away before he could chastise them. But he was popular as he never lost his temper and always had a kind word for everyone; young or old. His fur was mottled, turning from grey to pure white in places, which made him look highly distinguished, and his rich voice served to increase his air of authority. The Pevi audience waited with bated breath to hear about Harry's findings.

'I can advise you,' he continued, 'that this is not the first occurrence of such a phenomenon. Back in 1666, there was a great fire in London and I would surmise that this would have had a significant impact on the environment in the South of England and would have certainly caused a change in the ionic balance of the atmosphere, though in quite what manner I do not know. The South of England Pevi, who at that time mostly lived in the parks and woods in and around central London, fell seriously ill about this time. It is reported in the archives that they were rescued by the fairies who flew them further south, into Kent, where the atmosphere was cleaner and much healthier for them. In fact, the Sevenoaks community is first mentioned in the archives in 1670, relatively soon after this evacuation from London. Had the fairies not organised the evacuation, the London-based Pevi would certainly have died because they were too weak to fly themselves. So I believe that this relocation in 1666 was most probably a result of atmospheric change, but of course we have no hard measurements of ionic concentrations from this far back. It also explains why we feel so attached to our fairy friends; they were our saviours. Therefore, it is vital we continue to monitor the environment and carefully watch out for signs of weakness among the general population here in Sevenoaks. We may well need to relocate if the health of the community deteriorates significantly, before it becomes too late. It is important that we keep the fairies well informed because, if the worst comes to the worst, they may need to save us again.'

Edmund then introduced Doctor Cedric, their scientific expert, who few recognised.

Cedric was middle-aged and rather serious. He had shaggy fur, which he rarely brushed, and always appeared a bit dishevelled because he was uninterested in his personal appearance and hygiene. Cedric was much happier reading about science than standing on a podium to address his fellow Pevi. He had spent so much of his life pouring through scientific texts and developing his own theories about the nature of matter and the universe that, on taking the stage, he discovered himself in front of an audience of virtual strangers. He felt slightly overawed by the sea of eager faces smiling up at him, hoping for a solution to their problem. He made a commitment to himself there and then, that he really should get out and about a bit more and meet the members of his community; perhaps even spend some time with the young Pevi who were apparently feeling very depressed at the moment. He had completely engrossed himself in the positive ion problem over the last week and had developed several plausible theories concerning the possible reasons for the shift in ionic matter, but, they remained theories at the moment, not proven facts, and he had no magical solutions.

'Hello, Pevi; young, middle-aged and old alike,' he began, peering over the top of his reading glasses and surveying his audience. 'First, let me apologise for knowing so few of you on first-name terms. This is my shortfall because of my unerring dedication to science and extending my knowledge. Seeing you all gathered here today has been a bit of an eye-opener for me and I have already made a personal commitment to get to know more of my fellow Pevi over the next few weeks. Maybe I could even take on a couple of young apprentices to train in the scientific wonders of this world. I'll ask for volunteers later.'

'Anyway, to get down to business, I believe there could be many reasons for a decrease in the concentration of positive ions in the air. I will tell you about five of my strongest theories.'

'My first theory is that it may be an effect due to changes in our universe, such as a change in the activity of sunspots or a slight shift in the axis of the moon. There is obviously nothing we can do to reverse these changes, if this is the case. The Pevi cannot battle against the wonders of our ever-changing universe.'

'An obvious culprit is global pollution. A worldwide problem caused by man's activities and his farm animals and, again, one we can have little influence on.'

'A third possibility is that there has been a volcanic eruption in a distant country, which has brought increased levels of dust into our atmosphere here in Sevenoaks. Again, there is probably nothing we can do about this, but its effects should not be permanent and the environment will recover, but the timing is unknown. Information from our other communities on their environment and information on any global eruption they are aware of and an analysis of wind directions will allow us to determine the probability that this is the cause.'

By now, Cedric had got into his stride and was beginning to enjoy holding centre stage.

He continued, 'On the other hand, there may be a purely local change in the environment caused by the construction of a new factory or mine in the region which emits pollution, or a significance change in agricultural land use in the fields around Sevenoaks. This can be investigated by sending out teams of Pevi to reconnoitre the local region in a systematic way. Our course of action will probably be limited and will depend on the change observed, but at least we can do something about this theory and investigate it now.'

'Finally,' he wisely brought up a practical, technical detail. 'We must of course be one hundred percent sure that our measurement equipment is not malfunctioning in any way, so we should send a small team to measure positive ions in other Pevi communities and compare results with their local, if less accurate, measurements.'

He concluded, 'So, I suggest we start by tackling the last

two of these issues because we may be able to take some action to limit the problem if it is due to local land use, and we must, of course, have complete confidence in our measurement equipment.'

Edmund thanked Cedric for his theories and opened the floor for general debate.

After a few hours a plan of action had been agreed.

Cedric would talk with the technicians about better ways they could invent to standardise the positive-ion measurement equipment across Pevi communities worldwide and ensure its accuracy and consistency. This would be a longer-term project as it would be necessary to build and validate new equipment, which would take time.

Eve would lead a small team of technical Pevi to visit two chosen destinations in the UK and one on the European mainland, to test their equipment and determine how local the problem was to Sevenoaks. She would also have the opportunity to discuss the problem with these other communities and seek their help. It would be advisable to have good relationships with other communities who may be able to accommodate them should they need to relocate quickly.

Cedric would put together four groups to research land use to the north, south, east and west of Sevenoaks respectively.

In the meantime, Harry would research the archives for old maps that would show land use in the past, so major changes could be identified.

It was hoped that this could all be achieved within a month's time.

With that, the meeting was terminated and Edmund's partner, Laura, opened up the cocktail bar in the hidden hollow of the Twisted Oak, so the Pevi could drown their sorrows and pontificate on how serious the problem actually was and what changes they might see in the near future. The Pevi were all damp and chilly after remaining seated for so long and welcomed the chance to warm themselves with a few glasses of alcohol. Cedric immediately set about finding volunteers to reconnoitre the local region, while Eve opened discussions with the technical team to choose a small experienced group to travel with her. There was no shortage of volunteers willing to be part of the research teams. They planned to spend the next fortnight making all the arrangements and would then set off on their travels.

Laura got out her guitar and sang some of the jollier ancient songs about life in the jungles of Venezuela and generally tried to cheer up the damp and despondent community with her lovely voice and good humour. Several Pevi danced together to warm themselves. Gwyn, Laura's friend and admirer, provided the backing vocals. They had become friendly last year when Gwyn had suffered from agoraphobia and was too frightened to leave her home. Laura had provided her with counselling and helped her analyse and overcome the roots of her fears. With Laura's support, Gwyn had been able to resolutely fight her fears and had recovered sufficiently to lead a normal life again. Laura was now her mentor in life.

Edmund looked on, feeling so proud to have such an inspirational wife, who refused to allow herself to be downtrodden by recent events. She always had a good word for everyone and could raise the spirits of the young and old alike, allaying their fears about the future. He secretly acknowledged that she would have made a more motivational leader than him, but he would never tell her that. She was his highly-prized asset. He was relieved that a firm course of action had been decided upon and had confidence in the intelligence of his senior advisors, Cedric, Eve and Harry.

16

Rick felt nervous when he arrived for his first day at BioEnerFuels on 19th September. He had underestimated what a big step leaving the security of school and actually applying all his learning in the real world would be. He was looking relatively smart in his classic "uniform" of chinos and polo shirt which helped his self-confidence. He had noticed at his interview that the scientists wore chinos or jeans rather than suits, even the senior managers, and he wanted to fit in.

He had been told to arrive at about 10:00 am and was welcomed by the security man on the gate at the entrance to the science park who had been informed about the new employee starting today. He was directed to park his motorbike in the BioEnerFuels' staff car park, just around the corner. For the moment, he had no entry pass for the laboratory building, so had to ring on the front door of the laboratory and wait for someone to answer. A buzzer sounded and he pushed the door open and walked into the reception area where he was greeted by the receptionist, Janet. She called the Chief Scientific Officer, Dr Josephine Macferson, who arrived bearing a pile of letters which needed posting to the company's investors, informing them of the up-coming shareholders' meeting. She gave the letters to Janet with instructions to take them immediately to the Post Office, then shook Rick warmly by the hand and led him down the corridor to her lab, talking enthusiastically all the way about how well the research was going at the moment.

Josephine Macferson was in her early forties. She had short straight hair, cut in a bob, and lively hazel eyes. She usually wore dark trousers, a white shirt and a cotton or linen jacket to work. Her rimless glasses contributed to her intellectual appearance. She was an inspired, dedicated and enthusiastic scientist, with an optimistic outlook. She found it easy to encourage and motivate her employees and naturally commanded their respect.

Rick was given a desk next to another young scientist, a Chinese girl called Wei, who had started three months previously at BioEnerFuels, after completing a BSc then an MSc in molecular biology at the University of Kent. Wei had achieved a first for her BSc degree and had then undertaken a one year practical thesis to obtain an MSc. Her project had been on microbial fuel cells, so she had excellent grounding prior to starting with BioEnerFuels. Wei's appearance conformed in part to the western stereotype of Eastern Asian women; she was small and slim, with dark almond-shaped eyes; but her hair was contemporary, dyed deep-mahogany with pink streaks and cut in a short asymmetric style.

Josephine Macferson left Rick in Wei's capable hands, with directions to get him a security pass, lab coat, stationary and generally show him around and introduce him to the other employees. Dr Macferson apologised that she was busy this morning, meeting with potential new investors, but she hoped to have some time to talk to him that afternoon. With that, she retired to her office next to the lab and firmly closed the door. Rick could still see her through the glass pane located between the lab and her office. She saw him looking at her through the window and gave him a warm smile. He realised that she wanted to keep in close contact with her technicians.

Rick quickly found out that Wei was a complete sweetheart. She was a very lively, but kind and gentle person, who appeared to be highly effective at her job and was obviously well liked at the company. She arranged for him to be photographed for his security pass and got together a starting set of stationary and a lab coat that was a little on the big side, but that was better than being too small. When these tasks were completed, she suggested coffee and took him over to the communal restaurant shared by all the companies on the science park. Rick bought them both a cappuccino and blueberry muffin. Wei chatted away about her role in the company. Like Rick, she reported directly to Dr Macferson, and this was in her opinion the ideal job, because they had more freedom to experiment with new ideas than the scientists in the other labs, who were more focussed on improving known technology than undertaking ground-breaking research into the science of biological fuel cells. Wei loved her work and frequently stayed in the labs till after 8:00 pm to complete her experiments. She explained that everyone was quite relaxed about time, so if she worked exceptionally hard one week, Dr Macferson often gave her an afternoon off the following week. The atmosphere was more like a university than a factory. Working with people who were dedicated to their research was a real joy for her and this promoted a spirit of motivation throughout the company and a wonderful feeling of community. Everyone was working on an interesting project and the success of the company depended directly on everyone's efforts. There were no freeloaders at BioEnerFuels.

After they had finished their cappuccinos, Wei took Rick on a tour of the Science Park, pointing out the different companies and the location of the various support functions that were accessible to everyone. Apart from the restaurant where they had just had coffee, there was a lecture theatre, a library, a small gym with a few exercise bikes and a rowing machine, and there was even a hole in the wall to withdraw cash. Wei explained that the nearest shopping centre was ten minutes away by car and, although it was not anything exceptional, you could find shops to purchase the main necessities for life, including a supermarket, chemist and post office. After twenty minutes, they had completed their tour and returned to the BioEnerFuels laboratory building.

Wei was keen to discuss her project with Rick and get him started in the lab. He would initially be working under her guidance and learning techniques from her, until he became more experienced and was able to work independently. Wei was working on mediator-less fuel cells that exploit pond water or living algae as the power house to generate electricity and clean water from, essentially, polluted pond or sea water. She had an impressive collection of samples of pond and sea water collected from all over the UK, which contained different species and mixtures of fresh and seawater algae. Her vision was to find the optimal biomolecular conditions to enable her to construct a battery the size of a suitcase, which could be used to purify drinking water and create small amounts of electricity in remote villages in the Third World, without needing recharging. Ideally, a system that would be reliable and could work for many years without intervention, and one that would be relatively cheap to build and distribute. She was passionate about the impact she hoped her research would have on improving the lives of people living in extreme poverty away from industrial centres. She also acknowledged that the real driver behind the science was Dr Macferson and that she herself was still a pawn, albeit a quite valuable pawn, in the company's hierarchy.

Later that afternoon, Dr Macferson found time to visit the young scientists in her lab. She told them she had had a very positive meeting with two potential new investors that morning; a rich industrialist who was now searching for a good cause to support in his retirement and the chairman of a charity that builds wells in rural villages in Africa and was looking to diversify into other projects to improve the livelihood of villagers in remote areas. Both these were significant potential new sources of income for the company which would necessitate the issue of new shares in BioEnerFuels to the new investors. Although the company was in good financial shape, due to the strict control that the Chief Finance Officer put on their budget, more money for research would enable them to move forward more rapidly and move successful projects on from the research stage to actual production.

BioEnerFuels was a public company listed on the AIM stockmarket in the UK, but a large proportion of the shares were owned by the senior directors and the venture capitalists who had invested in the company when it launched. The directors were heavily incentivised to be successful. If they produced a commercially viable product and made a profit within five years, then they would receive additional shares in the company, amounting to approximately thirty percent of its current listed value. In effect, they would all be well-off, not rich in the Silicon Valley sense of the word, but certainly exceedingly comfortable.

17

It was nearly three weeks since the fête and Coralie decided it really was time she paid a visit to the bullfrog, to discuss the payment they had agreed on for providing four frogs to participate in the frog-baiting competition. She also wanted to take another closer look at the pond to see how much water and algae there were, and whether she thought the technology that Rick had talked about to Kathleen may be able to help the Pevi. Not that she had sufficient information to make any scientific evaluations, but she just wanted to see the pond again and look at it in a new light. She was not looking forward to meeting the aggressive bullfrog again, but she could no longer procrastinate. She decided to take Benjie with her as he was the most accomplished carpenter in the fairy clan and could advise on the structural requirements and the design of the pergola she had promised the frog community. He would also provide useful support and a no doubt much-needed sense of humour. There was also the question of what to do about finding or building the boat for the young frogs.

She found Benjie resting under his favourite chestnut tree, chewing absent-mindedly on a stem of grass and humming his favourite song, *If I ruled the world*.

Luckily, he doesn't, thought Coralie.

'Hello, Tony. Oh it's you, Benjie! I could have sworn I heard Tony Bennett singing. Oh well, I guess you will have to do for now. Please will you come with me to see the bullfrog and discuss his pergola and the boat for the young frogs? I've already left it far too long since the fête.'

Benjie opened one eye slowly and the face of his queen slowly came into focus. He never failed to be amazed by her beauty, especially when she was in soft focus with the sun shining through her chestnut hair. 'OK, no problem. Let's go. You can treat me to a beer when we get back. I expect we will both need it. Let's hope he's in a good mood. Though I'm not sure that personality trait exists in him; grumpy bastard that he is.'

They set off together, glad to have each other's support for the meeting ahead. As they neared the pond, they could hear someone singing *If I ruled the world* in a discordant, gruff voice. Benjie recognised the tune immediately and vowed to find himself a new favourite song as his current one had obviously been hijacked by the unpleasant bullfrog.

' 'Bout time you fairies turned up to honour your debts. What kept you so long?'

'And greetings to you too, sir. We trust you and your family are keeping well. As you accurately surmised, we are here to discuss the construction of your pergola and the children's boat. Do you have a plan for what type of pergola you would like? I'd like to introduce you to our artisan carpenter, Benjie, who will be in charge of the construction project and, if it's convenient with you, we would like to start soon while the weather is still fine.'

The bullfrog was slightly taken aback by Coralie's politeness, so immediately muted his aggressive tone. He had indeed spent many hours planning the design of the pergola and thinking about the associated planting scheme. He was very excited by the project, both aesthetically and practically. It had been an unusually hot summer and he needed more shade around the pool to hide from the sun's rays and hopefully to reduce the water temperature by a degree or two. The pergola would also be useful in winter to shelter from the snow. He described his ideas to Benjie, who took copious notes. The pergola should be twenty-five centimetres high, forty centimetres deep and sixty centimetres long; just big enough to shelter all the frog community. He wanted it built in oak, with a contemporary feel, definitely not rustic with knots and twigs showing, but something highly polished with straight clean lines. He wanted one end to be semi-enclosed to hide the baby frogs from predators.

This should represent about one-third of the total length. Benjie was concerned that it would be difficult to camouflage a pergola with such a modern design. He tried to persuade the frog to go for something more natural looking that would blend into the rushes and bushes around the pond, but the bullfrog was adamant, he wanted something modern and it was up to Benjie and Coralie to find a way to camouflage it from prying human eyes, maybe by using fairy magic.

The bullfrog also discussed the planting scheme with Coralie, asking for her advice as he was not much of a gardener himself and wasn't sure what plants would provide year-round cover and a splash of colour. They finally agreed on a scheme with pink dog roses at the four corners of the pagoda and with alternating passion flowers and variegated ivy climbing up the vertical supports. The ivy would ensure there was some foliage in winter to protect against the cold. Coralie reassured him that the fairies had long held knowledge of how to grow miniature versions of all these plants which would ensure the design looked in-keeping with the overall scale of the pergola project. And yes, they would use fairy magic to hide it from humans' eyes and protect the frog community.

With the design of the pergola agreed, they went on to discuss the boat project. The bullfrog had also taken this project very seriously and was obviously not going to let the fairies off lightly.

He told Coralie 'I have big plans for the boat.' At which comment, her heart dropped. 'I want a miniature tea clipper, fully rigged,' not the simple coracle that Coralie had been thinking about.

He continued in his gruff voice, 'We have had a meeting to discuss the boat and one of my young frogs showed us a page from a yachting magazine he had found in the park, which showed a photo of the Cutty Sark tea clipper at Greenwich. All the frogs gathered round the dew-sodden image and unanimously agreed that this was exactly what we wanted as it would be great fun rigging the sails and learning how to control the boat when it was windy; very educational for the young and old alike. A simple coracle or rowing boat did not appeal to anyone, far too slow and boring for our adventurous young explorers.' Coralie was rather taken aback and explained that this would have to be further discussed as the fairies did not have the expertise for such a complex project.

Coralie was beginning to wonder if she hadn't been a bit too generous with her offer of payment to the frog community for providing volunteers for the frog-baiting competition. But at least the pergola design had been agreed and was very achievable. It would provide a useful amenity for the frog community, young and old alike, and would endear the fairies to the frogs, if not to the big bullfrog. She was also pleased to observe that the pond still contained a reasonable level of water despite the dry summer. The bullfrog explained that it was fed by an underground spring and the water level remained quite constant throughout the year. She also noted that there were some miniature algae in the water, possibly useful raw material for the BioEnerFuels' project she surmised, and overall the pond was not too green and dirty.

The bullfrog politely thanked them for coming and said they could start the pergola construction as soon as they liked. He even offered to help them himself with the construction, that way he could keep an eye on them and make sure they did a good job. He held out his front leg to shake their hands and seal the deal. Neither Coralie nor Benjie were too enthusiastic about touching his slimy, wart-covered skin, but the gesture left them with no way of escape, so they genteelly proffered their hands in return and tried not to grimace too much.

Everyone went away happy. Coralie and Benjie were pleased that the pergola was not too onerous a task and that the bullfrog had been relatively polite and friendly at last. The bullfrog was delighted that the pergola was agreed and that they had not immediately dismissed his tea clipper project. He had expected Coralie just to say "No, that's a preposterous request". He knew it was way beyond their capability, but he also knew that fairies were far more resourceful and intelligent than bullfrogs and just maybe they would come up with a halfway house solution which would delight the young frogs and be delivered in time for Christmas.

Strolling back to Coralie's palace, Coralie and Benjie discussed which fairies could help with the pergola construction. A team of six was quickly agreed on. Benjie would be project manager and senior carpenter. He was already training two young fairies in carpentry skills, Freddy and Rosie, so they were the obvious candidates to assist him with the construction. Coralie herself would oversee the planting alongside the artistic fairy, Chantal, who had done the face-painting at the fête and a fairy that neither of them liked, secretly nicknamed "Nasty George", could help with the on-site erection. George's character was a nasty mix of arrogance and ignorance, but he was big and strong, and would do what he was told, providing it was not a woman giving the orders. They both secretly hoped that Nasty George's time on this earth would soon come to an end. He was the result of a rather unsuccessful randomised rebirth and everyone in the community hoped that the next chance they got to scramble his genes would give rise to a more caring embryo fairy.

Benjie suggested, 'Perhaps there could be an industrial accident during the erection of the pergola?' But his fleeting vision of George falling from the pergola into the pond, quickly followed by the heavy weight of the oak structure pinning him to the soft muddy floor of the pond, was dismissed immediately. He knew that the reality was that he took personal security seriously on a building site and would never allow his team to be dismissive of safety procedures.

The bullfrog's request for a high-quality reproduction tea clipper became the topic of their next discussion. What to do? Would the bullfrog accept a simple sailing boat with two sails, something more like a Mirror dingy? That would definitely be achievable and far more reasonable. Unfortunately, the entire frog community was now in favour of this ridiculous, over-engineered project, which was far beyond the fairies' capabilities. They could just imagine how the discussion had got completely out of hand and that the young frogs were now overexcited about their desired Christmas present and were spending their nights dreaming of being the captain of a tea clipper sailing around the oceans of the World.

'Don't forget you promised me a beer,' Benjie reminded Coralie.

'Come back to my place and we can share a six-pack of chestnut beer on the veranda. Perhaps the alcohol will stimulate our neurons and ignite our creativity regarding this ridiculous boat project.'

Benjie and Coralie sat on her veranda watching the sunset over Knole Park and lamenting the fact that autumn was here and they would not have many more days to enjoy the delights of a warm evening, watching the fawns and rabbits playing in the lengthening shadows. Pablo was playing a Spanish folk song to entertain them. It was a perfect evening.

18

The Saturday after Rick started work, Kathleen and Rick met again in the courtyard of the tea rooms in Knole Park and there was a hidden welcoming committee already waiting for them. They ordered a large glass of Sauvignon Blanc each. Rick was incredibly excited about his work at BioEnerFuels; he felt like a real research scientist after only one week with the company and he was already contributing sensible ideas during their scientific discussions. He believed that he had really found his niche in the working world.

In fact, he was so excited that he failed to realise how especially beautiful Kathleen was looking that afternoon. She was dressed, as always, in a sophisticated but casual style, wearing tight denim jeans and a white cotton blouse, with a new purple leather handbag and matching belt. She had applied her make-up with great care and dexterity and her nail varnish coordinated perfectly with her leather accessories. She had visited the hairdressers that morning for a deep-conditioning hair treatment and scalp massage. She felt relaxed and beautiful, but wondered when, or if, Rick would notice her and stop talking about himself. She wanted his approval. Robert didn't notice what she wore anymore and had long ago stopped giving her compliments on her looks. Coralie also noticed with interest how stunning and vibrant Kathleen was looking that afternoon.

Rick was still talking about his research plans when they finished their drinks. Kathleen had again noticed a distinct purple aura on one side of his head (where, unbeknown to her, Edmund was sitting on his shoulder), but this time there was a yellow aura on the other side (where Dr Cedric was sitting). This was different to the aura she had seen last time in the park, which had only appeared on his right side, and she was quietly pondering the significance of the pale-yellow light emanating from his other shoulder. She suggested that they took a walk in the park. They left the tea rooms and strolled along the wide tree-lined boulevard by the side of the manor house, enjoying the warmth of the low autumn sunlight on their faces. No one was around and it was at this point that Coralie interrupted their conversation.

'Hello,' she said adopting a straightforward initial approach. Rick and Kathleen both stopped and turned round, but saw nobody, so continued on their trajectory.

'Hello, Rick and Kathleen.' The voice came from close by for a second time. This time it was more insistent. Again, they stopped and looked around. Again, they saw no one, but this time they were curious and waited to see what would happen next.

'Kathleen, I am sure you will see me if you just relax and open your eyes to the beauty of the trees and flora that surround you. I am here, just in front of you. I am a creature of this park, a fairy queen to be more accurate.' Kathleen looked incredulously at Rick, who returned her look of dismay. They had both heard the voice, but fairies were found in fairy tales, not in Knole Park. This must be a curious joke of some sort.

Coralie insisted, 'Kathleen, I know you are a sensitive human being and you do have the ability to see me if you can just feel at one with nature in this magical park. Close your eyes and breathe deeply, inhale the essence of the nature all around you and feel it enter every cell in your body. Then, when you feel deeply relaxed, open your eyes and you will surely see me hovering just in front of you.' Kathleen did as instructed and tried to relax, but she was confused and excited by the melodic voice she was hearing. Her heart was beating too fast to relax. Rick was watching Kathleen with curiosity. He was amazed that she seemed to be taking this seriously.

'Kathleen, please believe in me and try to communicate with us. We need your help. Rick, you should try to open your mind too.'

Kathleen closed her eyes once more and tried again to

relax and commune with nature. She didn't understand what was going on but she decided to go along with the game and see what happened. It helped her relax once she had convinced herself that this was a game and she was back in her childhood. This time when she opened her eyes she saw exactly what she had visualised in her child's mind, but could not comprehend in her adult's mind, a beautiful fairy queen dressed in white damask, hovering a few feet in front of her. She also saw a male fairy and two glowing spheres of light, one purple and one yellow, with a small squirrel at the heart of each. The welcoming committee was there before her and was visible to her; fairies and Pevi alike.

Rick, however, while able to hear Coralie's voice, could not see her form, nor that of Professor Theodore, Doctor Cedric or Edmund. Coralie had already perceived that Rick did not have Kathleen's natural ability to see beings from a parallel dimension. He was currently standing firmly in his logical adult world, so she gently reassured him.

'Rick, I am sorry, but you don't yet have Kathleen's gift to see beings from a different dimension, but please know and believe that we do exist and that Kathleen can see us. You will learn to see us with time and practice. You must first learn to commune with the child buried inside you. You need to learn how to allow that child to enter your consciousness. It came naturally for Kathleen, but you need to work harder. There are four of us here with you. Myself, I am Coralie, the fairies' queen; next to me is my scientific advisor, Professor Theodore, he's also a fairy and finally, two beings called Pevi. One is Edmund, he's the nominated leader of the Pevi in Sevenoaks, and the other is Doctor Cedric, their chief scientist. The Pevi are an ancient race that look similar to your red squirrels, but they are highly intelligent beings with a well-developed social network. Like the fairies they do not dwell entirely in your human dimension. So you have a highly distinguished welcoming committee before you. I feel sorry for you, Rick, sorry that you cannot see us, but you will have to accept that fact for the moment and believe what Kathleen sees and tells you.'

Kathleen and Rick looked at each other, astonished and speechless for a moment.

'Curious as it seems, I do see them,' Kathleen told an incredulous Rick a few moments later. 'The fairy queen is indeed radiant and ethereal. Professor Theodore certainly has the look of a serious scientist to me and the Pevi, Edmund, is a purple sphere of light and there seems to be a small creature at the centre that does look just like a red squirrel. It was him I must have seen last week in the tea rooms and I assumed it was your aura I was looking at. I also see Doctor Cedric who appears as a yellow light surrounding a small squirrel. This is amazing. I now understand what I saw today in the cafe. It was Edmund sitting on one of your shoulders and Doctor Cedric on the other, listening in to our conversation I assume. Rick, you must overcome your highly rational mind and lower your defences. These beings do exist and now we need to understand what they want and why they have chosen to expose themselves to us at this time.'

Kathleen had never before addressed a fairy or a Pevi, so had no idea of the correct protocol to adopt, but she wanted to let them know that she had indeed sensed some presence the week before in the park. She wanted them to know that she did have a special gift, even before she was instructed by Coralie how to open her heart and mind to the fairies' world.

'So we have met before, honourable Leader of the Pevi; last week I believe, in the tea rooms. I didn't realise the true significance of the meeting at that time, or indeed, that I was actually meeting anyone.' She laughed. 'Why have you all decided to make yourselves known to us at this time?'

Kathleen suggested they went to a quiet area in the park where they could talk without being watched or overheard. She rightly sensed that there must be a strong desire for the fairies to communicate with two humans and they must badly need their help or advice about something, but what?

And so the friendship between the two humans, the two fairies and the two Pevi was initiated. It was to be a friendship that would be deep and rewarding for all of them for a long time to come. Rick was unable to see the fairies or the Pevi at this first meeting, but he could hear them and imagine their forms thanks to Kathleen's descriptions. Coralie had told them that creatures that lived in the wild could see them without training, but domestic animals were not sensitive enough to the pull of nature and had long ago lost their natural ability to communicate with fairies.

Rick just kept thinking over and over, *This is surreal, I must be losing my mind*, but he could clearly hear the fairies, even if he couldn't see them, and had to admit to himself that they did exist, though it went against all logic. His disbelief had crumbled to dust. He pledged that he would somehow work on releasing the child within, so he could see them in the future.

The diverse group sat in a quiet glade and listened to each other's stories. Coralie began by explaining how she and Pablo had witnessed Juliet's death in the park on the night of the fairies' fête and felt great sympathy for Kathleen and Rick.

Edmund then got straight to the point and explained the dilemma of the Pevi and their dire need for a source of positive ions. He told the humans how he had overheard their conversations in the park and was excited by the technology that Rick had spoken about. He wondered whether it could be applied to solve their problem. He asked Rick if he would take a sample of the frog pond water and algae to test at BioEnerFuels to see if it was a viable energy source. Doctor Cedric and Professor Theodore agreed that on the face of it the technology seemed an ideal solution to the Pevi's problem, if a low-cost, low-maintenance generator could be created for them, but they were not convinced that Rick had sufficient expertise or seniority in the company to embark on such a project and Rick agreed with this analysis. Rick, however, was fascinated by the idea of helping another race to improve their environment, even if it was not strictly a "third world" problem. He was determined to help them, but he had no idea how he could approach BioEnerFuels'

Chief Scientific Officer with such an outlandish proposition. After all, he had only recently joined the company and they would think him completely crazy if he told them the truth. He would have to invent a convincing story; a red herring to divert them from the real application.

After the serious discussion had concluded, they chatted generally about life in the fairies' and Pevi's worlds; about the fun they had at the annual fairy fête with the deer racing and the frog-baiting competitions. Rick realised that he and Juliet must have witnessed the deer's variety relay race and that would have explained the six-legged, two-headed deer they had witnessed that night. So the mystery was solved. Coralie told Kathleen about the bullfrog and the plans for the pergola and the problems with the tea clipper he wanted them to build, which was a completely unfair and unjustified request.

Edmund told Kathleen about the Pevi's planned expedition to London, Market Harborough and France to meet other Pevi communities and take measurements of their local atmosphere. Kathleen promised to help in any way she could with their travel plans, for which Edmund was immensely grateful as the Pevi were all rather in the dark at the moment about how exactly they would travel to these far-flung communities. The enthusiasm was not lacking, but a detailed itinerary was. Kathleen reassured him that she could easily provide train timetables for all their travels in the UK and France if that would help.

Rick promised to return one evening to collect a sample of pond water and algae for analysis. He would have to wait till BioEnerFuels had some of their own samples to test and he wasn't sure when that would be, but hopefully in the not too distant future. He wanted Coralie or Theodore to show him and Kathleen the exact location of the pond this afternoon, to ensure that everyone was talking about the same place. If the raw materials looked promising, then they would take it from there. There would be no need to explain anything to Dr Macferson at this early stage. Their laboratory tested many samples from sources all over the world in their search for ideal conditions to generate electricity using microbial fuel cells. If the early tests were successful, then they would have to come up with a watertight strategy to ensure that the project was progressed, but he had no idea what that would be at the moment. It would need some exceptionally inventive brain-storming sessions.

When the shadows started to lengthen, the group set out to visit the pond. The fairies and Pevi kept at a discrete distance from the humans as they did not want to involve the bullfrog in their plans at this early stage. If he saw them together with the humans, he would want to know what the hell they were up to. Therefore, to allay any suspicions, Rick and Kathleen pretended to be ordinary visitors to the park (something they would never again be) with no special interest in the pond other than to look for wildlife or interesting plants in its immediate vicinity. When he saw the pond, Rick was fairly optimistic about the quality and quantity of the water, but everything would depend on the outcome of a full laboratory analysis.

The humans bid farewell to their new acquaintances and adjourned to a pub in town, desperately in need of a quick drink and a return to reality. They were in a dreamlike state. What a bizarre afternoon it had turned out to be. They couldn't talk to anyone else about the happenings in the park that afternoon and Rick still hadn't mentioned how charming Kathleen was looking.

19

That night Kathleen lay in bed unable to sleep. Robert was quietly snoring at her side, oblivious to her wakefulness. She was replaying the bizarre events of the afternoon over and over in her mind.

So fairies really do live in the park and they seem to have a well-developed international community, which even includes a Spanish scientific advisor. Of course, everyone has heard of fairies, there are myths and stories going back centuries, but I have never come across anything like the Pevi before.

Kathleen could not get her head around the Pevi and quite how they fitted in, but Edmund and Cedric seemed very pleasant and serious beings, and there had obviously been a long close link between the fairy and Pevi communities over several centuries. Kathleen was pleased that she clearly had some special gift for seeing the fairies and Pevi that Rick, and presumably most other humans, did not naturally seem to possess. Coralie had explained that fairies and Pevi could only be seen when they were in the human universe, which ran parallel to their own, so they decided when they would reveal themselves to humans, which explained part of the puzzle. Apart from fulfilling the Pevi's immediate needs, Kathleen wondered how the acquaintanceships would evolve. She couldn't imagine inviting Coralie and her partner, Pablo, for dinner along with their neighbours, for example. She smiled at the thought of this ridiculous social happening in suburban Sevenoaks.

Then she reflected on her feelings for Rick, her dead-daughter's first and only lover. She had certainly felt a strong chemistry between them in the past, but he hadn't noticed her today, he was engrossed with his new job and the people he had met at work. She had merely been a sounding board for his views this afternoon before the fairies had arrived and changed everything. Still, they had had a pleasant drink in the pub afterwards and he had insisted on walking her home. She didn't know what she wanted of him, but she wanted to be part of his life and now they shared a secret which bound them together and which they could never share with anyone else. No one would ever believe their report about meeting the fairies and Pevi of Knole Park.

She finally fell into a troubled sleep dominated by visions of grotesque warty bullfrogs copulating in filthy weed-infested ponds and slowly devouring pretty young fairies trapped in the deep mud at the edge of the pond.

Kathleen woke the following morning with a clear idea of how to help the fairies in their search for a tea clipper. eBay was the answer. She would logon after breakfast on Monday and see if she could find anything suitable in the online marketplace. Today was Sunday and Robert would be with her all day as they had planned to go to the beach for the day, before September was finally over. She was looking forward to relaxing on the sandy beach at Greatstones and possibly even swimming in the English Channel if the temperature of the seawater was reasonable. The sea was shallow at Greatstones and often warm in September after the tide had risen over the warm sand. She hoped they would have a nice day together and that Robert would try to be cheerful and loving to her. Naturally, they were still both grieving for Juliet, but they also needed to laugh occasionally and start rebuilding their relationship before it was too late. A day on the beach, with fish and chips for lunch, was just what they both needed and today the sun was shining for them.

Unfortunately, things did not work out quite as Kathleen had planned. The sun was soon covered by a thick bank of black cloud and, by the time they arrived at the beach, the rain had started to fall relentlessly. The weather turned blacker, along with Robert's mood. They were home before lunch and spent the afternoon ignoring each other and reading in the lounge. Kathleen kept glancing at the urn containing Juliet's ashes. It was a large ugly plastic container and she hadn't known what to do with it when she had picked it up from the undertakers. She didn't want to put it in the spare room, where Juliet would be alone and cold, so she had brought it into the lounge and put it on the mantelpiece, so Juliet was still at the hub of family life. However, it was not a beautiful tribute to her daughter and she resolved to find a more appropriate resting place for her ashes.

Robert went to bed early, claiming he had a headache and needed to lie down. Kathleen waited until she heard him reach the top of the stairs, then went over and quietly closed the lounge door. She sat looking at the urn containing Juliet's ashes. She wanted to share her secrets with someone.

'Juliet, my lovely daughter,' she whispered, replacing the image of the hideous urn with Juliet's beautiful face in her mind's eye. 'I know you can't hear me, but I still need to share my thoughts with you. I miss you terribly. I feel so alone. Your father is nursing his sorrow in his own private way and I can't blame him for that, but I desperately need some warmth from someone to help me cope with your sudden departure from this world. There is an enormous black hole in my heart, sucking in my spirit. I've met Rick, your boyfriend, on a few occasions and we have had a coffee or glass of wine together and chatted about you. We both miss you and wanted to share our memories. He is a lovely boy, or is he a man? I'm not sure. He's certainly highly intelligent and mature for his age. You chose your first boyfriend wisely. We have become quite close, as friends. I think our mutual love of you has created some unexpected chemistry between us, which is hard for us to deal with. I will try to be strong and sensible for you, but forgive me if I fail. I so need to be held and loved at the moment. Can you understand what I'm saying?'

'The other thing that has happened to draw Rick close to me is that, yesterday, we met some fairies in Knole Park and a race of beings, called Pevi, who are small squirrel-like creatures with brilliant auras. I know it sounds ridiculous and you must think that your mother has gone bonkers, but it's true. Rick and I were both there when it happened. You would love the fairies, they are so delicate and graceful, but the Pevi are even more alluring. It's impossible to describe how they delight you with their cute furry bodies, backlit by their auras, and their fascinating voices. This is now a secret I share with Rick and one that cannot be shared with anyone but you, my darling Juliet. I'll tell you more about them some other time. I'm tired now and am going to bed, to sleep next to Robert. I hope he cuddles me, but, we'll see. So, goodnight darling. Love you.'

Kathleen climbed the stairs to go to bed. She opened the bedroom door quietly. Robert was pretending to be fast asleep, so she undressed and slipped into bed, without disturbing him. She had her own plans for tomorrow and hoped Robert would be more cheerful and attentive after a day at work, away from the house and all its memories. It would be his first day back at work since Juliet died. What a shame their day out together had turned into a dismal day spent reading in the lounge, she had so wanted to connect with him today.

She roused Robert early Monday morning, then took a quick shower and dressed. She made tea and toast for Robert and herself, then, once Robert had left for work, she turned on the computer and started her search for a model boat. It did not take long to find a suitable radio-controlled model boat which was a replica of an old Thames sailing barge. Not a tea clipper, but certainly something rather interesting and unique. She estimated from the description that it was large enough to hold about four frogs. And, the best thing about it was that the seller lived in a village less than an hour's drive south from Sevenoaks, so, hopefully she would be able to take the cash over to his house today and pick up the boat. She offered the asking price and soon received an email from the seller containing details of how to find his house and he said he would be at home all afternoon if that was convenient for her to pop round and collect the boat. Kathleen checked her email and was intrigued to see an email from Rick, sent Sunday evening:

Hi Kathleen,

Wow, what a surreal day we had yesterday. I was so distraught that, unlike you, I could not see the fairies and Pevi and was so overwhelmed by all the strange events that I completely forgot to mention how especially radiant you looked. You always look lovely, but there was a special beauty about you yesterday when you were talking with such animation and enthusiasm to Coralie. I guess I saw a different less serious side to you.

R x

Kathleen was delighted that her efforts had not passed unnoticed and sent Rick an email to his work address to pass on the good news about the boat and thanking him for his compliments.

Kathleen popped into town to pick up some cash and then spent the rest of the morning on household chores, trying to get back to reality. After lunch she changed into clean jeans and drove south in her silver Audi TT, directed faultlessly by the reassuring female voice of her TomTom.

The seller's house was a tastefully converted barn on the edge of a village by Ashdown Forest; close to A.A. Milne's Pooh Bear's hunting ground. The house stood in about two acres of garden, planted copiously with bedding plants, flowering bushes and ornamental trees; a plethora of vibrant colours which contrasted starkly with the mellow greens and browns of the surrounding countryside. The views over the forest were extensive. The bracken was beginning to dry out after the unusually hot summer, turning a dull orange-brown; the sky was a clear blue and the pines were a dark green. *This view is a painter's paradise,* she thought, *which would regularly change its palette with the changing seasons.* She estimated that the barn must be worth a couple of million pounds.

Kathleen pressed the button on the intercom by the black wrought-iron gates and waited. A buzzer sounded and the electric gates glided open, giving her access to the drive. She drove in and parked next to a navy-blue Mercedes Benz SLR sports car. *Nice car*, she thought, *but I prefer my Audi*. The front door opened and a handsome man in his early fifties came out. He wore an old artist's smock that was covered in oil paint and obviously well used. Kathleen smiled at him and then started. He smiled back at her and a glimmer of recognition crossed over his face.

'Kathleen?' he enquired. 'The beautiful wild Kathleen that I knew in my twenties?'

'Chas?' she replied. 'The artist Chas I knew in my teens?'

'Good heavens,' they exclaimed in unison, 'you haven't changed a bit.'

Chas came over to where she was standing and gave her a prolonged, gentle hug.

'What a wonderful coincidence. It had not crossed my mind that the eBay buyer was "that" Kathleen. Obviously, I didn't recognise your surname. You must be married. How are you? Come inside. You will stay a while, won't you? Wow, it must be over twenty years since I last saw you. You look terrific.'

Kathleen followed Chas inside the house. A quick glance around the walls of the lounge confirmed that Chas was still actively painting, and that his technique had matured and taken on a unique style since she had last admired his paintings back in the early eighties. Indeed, the walls of the lounge were decorated with an abundance of his paintings. They were far more abstract than his early works that she could remember. They split into two main themes; landscapes and nudes. The landscapes were full of colour; Chas was bold with his use of extreme colours, pinks, purples, royal blue, scarlet, emerald green and gold. He had a very special interpretation of the nature he saw around him. He had used stones, dried plants, pieces of wood and other materials to build a three-dimensional quality into his art on some paintings. But what really impressed Kathleen were his nudes. They were homage to women in midlife. Some of the models could be called beautiful, but most were women with a lot of character in their faces, women who had lived a full life and not spent all their days being pampered at the beauty therapist. It was almost as if he actively sought out the flaws in his models and somehow made them more attractive because of their imperfections. Again, there was a brave use of colour and texture in his nudes.

'Would you like tea, or a glass of wine? Please take a seat and make yourself at home.'

Kathleen opted for a small glass of wine. Chas vanished into the kitchen and Kathleen took the opportunity to have a closer study of his paintings in the lounge. Several of the landscapes were clearly of the view over the forest from his lounge and there was definitely one rather attractive woman who appeared frequently in his nudes. Kathleen wondered if she was his wife. She bore some resemblance to his girlfriend from the past; the one she had been so jealous of. She could not recall her name.

Chas returned with two glasses of rosé and some gingernut biscuits and watched Kathleen admiring his paintings.

'Your oils are fantastic. I really love this surreal, highly-colourful style that you have developed since I knew you. And by the look of this house, I'm not the only one who loves your work. You must be extremely successful. I can't understand why I haven't seen your paintings in any galleries in Sevenoaks. Don't you have any outlets for your work there?'

Chas explained that he could get much more for his paintings in New York than Sevenoaks and he had a long-standing arrangement with a gallery in Manhattan that sold ninety percent of his work and provided him with more commissions than he could handle. Affluent New Yorkers provided him with photos of a favourite landscape of theirs, often taken on a memorable holiday or just a view from their house, and he applied his unique style to turn it into an artwork for them. And, yes, he was pretty well-off now, thanks to his artistic talent and business acumen.

They chatted about his work, until they had finished their glasses of rosé. Then Kathleen asked about the woman who featured in many of his nudes.

'Yes, she was my wife, but she has gone now. It's not a happy story, perhaps I'll tell you about it sometime. But now, I'm afraid I must excuse myself as I have a visitor arriving in half an hour, the owner of the gallery in Manhattan, and I need to change. Will you promise to come back when I have more time? We have so much to talk about and I would love to see you again and spend a little longer together than is possible today.'

'Of course, I'd love to come back and visit you properly. Perhaps you could show me around your lovely house and garden next time or we could have lunch at a local pub? I noticed a quaint old pub with a thatched roof and whitewashed walls covered with hanging baskets just down the road, but I'm sure you know all the best pubs in the locality. It's been fantastic to meet you again after such a long time. But, I mustn't forget what I came for, the radio-controlled model boat that looks like an ancient Thames barge.'

Chas was curious why she wanted the boat, but she had no intention of entering into any explanations or lies about that at the moment. He refused to accept any payment from her, then they exchanged visit cards and she left with her present for the frogs.

As she drove home with the boat safely stowed in her boot, Kathleen contemplated on the fact that her life was getting more surreal and unpredictable every day. She was still suffering from the shock of losing Juliet, but since then she had become dangerously close to Juliet's boyfriend, had met some real fairies, nearly-invisible small squirrels with glowing auras and now an old flame had materialised out of the blue. She wondered what new adventure would await her tomorrow.

20

Eve had selected two technically-minded Pevi to join her on her short tour of the UK and visit to France, Francis and Eleanor. As well as their technical expertise, they were both fluent-French speakers, like many of the more educated Pevi. Francis and Eleanor were also good company and reliable Pevi, so she felt confident that the trip should prove fun and productive. They were delighted to have been chosen to accompany her.

Their first visit would be to Hyde Park, London, to meet the Pevi community that had returned to settle there again one hundred years after the Great Fire of 1666. From there, they would travel by train from St Pancras station to the market town of Market Harborough in Leicestershire to meet a relatively new community of Pevi who lived along the banks of a side tributary to the Grand Union canal. Finally they would travel to southern France by Eurostar.

Edmund had used his exceptional thought transference powers to contact the Pevi communities that Eve and her team would visit, so everyone would be expecting them. It was the first time any of them had been so far afield, so Edmund was keen that everything went smoothly. Kathleen had kindly put together a complete itinerary for their journey with train and bus times and directions from the stations and bus stops to the Pevi communities. She was proving to be a kind and useful friend for the Pevi and the fairies.

Eve, Eleanor and Francis had packed their electronic measurement equipment, presents for their hosts and some acorn sandwiches into small backpacks the night before. It was now two weeks since the Pevi meeting and they had finalised all their travel plans. They set off for Sevenoaks railway station early on Monday morning, waving goodbye to the Pevi community in Knole Park who had all turned out to cheer them on their way. It was the first Monday in

October and there was a slight chill in the air.

The three Pevi were excited and energised by their adventure, in marked contrast to their human travelling companions. The train to London was packed with commuters, weary from partying too much at the weekend and suffering from severe Monday morning depression. The Pevi sat quietly in the luggage rack eating their sandwiches and watching in horror the sad state of the commuters who were destined to repeat this crowded journey every weekday of their working life. What joy they felt about living their privileged life in the beautiful setting of Knole Park and not being subjected to this daily stress. The train trip reinforced their determination that they must do everything they could to find the source of the problem of the rapidly diminishing positive-ion levels, so the Pevi community could continue its happy relaxed life in the park.

When they arrived at Charing Cross station, they were relieved to be met by Dylan, an exceedingly cool Pevi from the Hyde Park community.

'Hi guys. Good trip? We'll take the number six bus to Hyde Park and you can meet the rest of my team. Follow me closely and don't get lost in the crowd.' With that, Dylan set off at lightning speed, deftly dodging the marching steps of the commuters hurrying to work. Eve, Eleanor and Francis were less accustomed to fast moving crowds and struggled to keep up and avoid being crushed underfoot. Happily, they reached the bus stop without incident, just as the bus arrived, and they jumped on before the first commuter. The bus trip gave them the chance to see a few of the sites in London. Dylan pointed out Trafalgar Square, Piccadilly Circus and the Ritz hotel. The main impact on them was the enormous number of buildings, cars and people they initially saw all around. Everyone was in a hurry. Then, the view changed on the left as the bus passed Green Park and they saw an open green space with trees, but even this was also full of people walking quickly or sitting on benches, soaking up the weak October sunshine.

Too soon, they arrived at their destination and the four Pevi descended from the bus near an entrance into Hyde Park. There was a large group of Pevi eagerly waiting to meet them and welcome them to London. Dylan introduced everyone to each other. The Sevenoaks Pevi had no chance of remembering everyone's name and position in the community, but no one really expected them to. The London Pevi were excited to welcome their country cousins to Hyde Park. They followed their hosts into the park and soon arrived at the Pevi village hidden in the high trees. The views of London were impressive. Dylan pointed out the main sites of interest that they could see from on-high, then, a wonderful buffet lunch was produced for the visitors. Eve presented their gift to Dylan, a packet of wild flower seeds collected in Knole Park. Dylan thought that was really cool. Eleanor was chatting excitedly to everyone, making friends as quickly as possible. Francis had already disappeared with the Hyde Park technical team to carry out the positive-ion tests, keen to get the job done before he relaxed.

Francis soon arrived back at the lunch table and announced the results of his tests. It appeared that the problem of low positive-ion levels was far less extreme in Hyde Park than in Knole Park, so, he concluded it was highly unlikely that the phenomenon was due to general pollution caused by the activities of humans, since this would be higher in London than Sevenoaks. That was good news for the Pevi race as a whole and reassuring for the London community.

The Hyde Park Pevi were generous hosts and before long everyone was sleeping off a large lunch and an excess of acorn wine (fourteen percent alcohol). The afternoon nap was followed by a tour of the park with a stop for pistachio ice cream, which they stole from a local vendor. Hyde Park was so very different from their beloved Knole. There were fewer trees, no bracken and no deer. There was a constant noise from cars and buses in the nearby roads. The flower beds were very formally laid out, with a symmetric mass of colour; pretty, but too artificial for their liking. The lake was enormous compared to the frog pond they were used to and was full of people enjoying themselves in rowing boats. When they returned from their tour, another huge feast was prepared for the evening meal, with entertainment provided by a band of singers and musicians. The Sevenoaks Pevi were overwhelmed by the hospitality of their hosts and the abundance of excellent food and wine on offer. They enjoyed the evening and danced with their hosts, but they were happy to find a wide branch to sleep on when the entertainment finally finished. They slept a deep sleep, but were all visited by nightmares of being trapped in London, surrounded by people and cars in a wild frenzy and being crushed underfoot and under-tyres, unable to escape and return home to the tranquility of Knole Park.

The next morning, Eve, Eleanor and Francis awoke late with thick heads. They washed in the cool water of the Serpentine to refresh themselves, then bid farewell to their new friends and invited everyone to Knole Park in November to see the town's spectacular firework display. Dylan accompanied them on the bus to St Pancras station where they waited for their train for Market Harborough. Their late rising had put them slightly behind schedule, but that was not a problem as there were regular trains to Market Harborough. The Pevi found the architecture of the station superb; built in red brick and with a high glass ceiling supported by pale blue metal rafters. Dylan informed them that the Victorian station had recently been renovated and the impressive Gothic facade was Grade 1 listed. Two statues had been specially commissioned by famous sculptors; one of Sir John Betjeman, and one of a couple embracing, called *The Meeting Place*. The station was now the London terminal for Eurostar, where they would catch their train to France. It was a confusion of sound and colour. There were restaurants, flower stalls and boutiques with goods artistically displayed. There was an enormously long bar selling champagne, which was full of happily chatting holidaymakers and business people. It was far different from their depressing experience at Sevenoaks and Charing Cross stations. They all agreed that they liked St Pancras and were happy to wait forty minutes for the next train, soaking up the atmosphere of the regal station.

The train journey to Market Harborough took just over an hour. The station was near the town centre and again they were met by their hosts at the station, who had been waiting patiently since day break, so were pleased to see them finally arrive. The Pevi community was situated a short walk from the station, which took them through the town centre, around the canal mooring basin and along the banks of the canal. The Sevenoaks Pevi were interested by everything they saw en route. They liked Market Harborough; it was an affluent market town similar to Sevenoaks and also situated in a rural environment. The main street was full of small appealing shops and there was a farmer's market in the central square with stalls piled high with fresh fruit and vegetables, local cheeses, pâté, bread, jams and pickles. They felt quite at home here. Eve was convinced that their measurements here would be key to helping them resolve the ionic problem.

Thirty minutes after leaving the station, they arrived at the small Pevi community by the Grand Union canal. Again, they were welcomed warmly and were fed and watered before they were allowed to make their atmospheric measurements. The food was simpler than the fare provided at Hyde Park and there was, disappointingly, no wine, but the hospitality was warm and genuine. After lunch, Eleanor and Francis ran their atmospheric tests. Here they detected a slightly low level of positive ions, higher than that found in Sevenoaks, but possibly some cause for concern in the longer term. They would need to keep an eye on the situation to make sure it did not deteriorate. The Market Harborough Pevi did not have the equipment needed to run the tests, so had not been aware of this problem. During the discussion that ensued however, it became apparent that they had also observed a mild depression among some of their youngsters in recent months, similar to that seen among the Sevenoaks youngsters, but it had not reached a level to trigger serious concern. Eve reassured them that their problem was a fraction of that found in Sevenoaks and she didn't think they need be too worried for the moment. She agreed to build them their own monitoring equipment in Sevenoaks and bring it to their community in Market Harborough before the end of the year.

The Market Harborough Pevi had no idea what could be causing the positive-ion decrease, though offered a few ideas, mainly related to the effect humans were having on the environment and similar to those ideas already proposed in Sevenoaks by Doctor Cedric. Eve told them about the findings in Hyde Park which seemed to negate the general pollution hypothesis and point to something more specific about the type of environment the Pevi communities of Sevenoaks and Market Harborough lived in, i.e. a small market town in an agricultural area. They spent the rest of the afternoon exploring along the canal path and watching the colourful canal boats chug by.

After an early dinner, Eve, Eleanor and Francis bid farewell to their hosts and returned to the train station to catch a train to St Pancras, where they slept peacefully in the pale blue rafters, safe from the crushing feet of commuters in a hurry to get home. The next day they would travel to France, and have the opportunity to practice their French language skills and see the land their forefathers had travelled through on their journey from the hermit's cave in the French Pyrenees to Knole Park in Sevenoaks.

21

Rick had now been at BioEnerFuels for a fortnight and had learned quite a lot about the functioning of the laboratory equipment. He felt ready to take a sample from the frog pond and see if he could somehow get it tested at the company. He knew the Pevi were undertaking their own research this week and he wanted to have an answer ready for them when they returned in a few days' time. So, at the start of his third week at work, Rick asked Wei all about how to take samples of pond water to test for their efficacy at generating electricity and drinking water. She explained the process, which was quite simple. It just necessitated taking a half-litre sample from a depth of ten centimetres below the water level, using one of their special large pipettes with a wide nozzle to prevent it getting blocked, and then carefully ejecting the sample into a sterile plastic bottle with a screw cap. She showed him where the stocks of disposable pipettes and bottles were kept. One always took at least two samples from different sides of the pond and it was important not to block the pipette with bulky leaves, insects, fish or other matter. What was needed was the water and its microorganisms.

The next moment the phone rang. Wei answered and listened intently to the caller. After she had received the important information and hang up, she related the news to Rick.

'That was our field technician in Sierra Leone. He has completed the collection of ten samples of pond water from five different sites in the country and has just shipped them to the UK via a British Airways flight to Heathrow. We need to arrange for the samples to be collected from customs at Heathrow airport tomorrow morning and brought here to our labs for testing. Perhaps you could go and collect them

146

on your motorbike?' she enquired.

Rick agreed without any hesitation, as he always enjoyed the opportunity to ride his motorbike, even if it was on the busiest section of the M25 motorway and in the morning rush hour. He had two panniers on his bike, which were large enough to hold the samples. Wei prepared all the necessary documents and phoned the customs office at Heathrow to ensure all would be in order for collection tomorrow morning. Then they used *Google Maps* to find the exact location of the customs office at Heathrow.

Rick decided that this evening he would make the trip to Knole Park to collect the two water samples from the frog pond and somehow he would persuade Wei to include them when she tested the Sierra Leone samples. There were several boxes of the special large pipettes, so he did not think that it would be a problem if he took two home with him that evening, along with a couple of plastic bottles. Theoretically, it was stealing, but they were only mass-produced low-cost disposable laboratory items.

For the rest of the day, Rick helped Wei set up the equipment they would need to test the samples. He first got the alpha fuel cells out of the cupboard and set them up on the bench, one for each sample. Wei told him that one of the fuel cells he had selected, labelled "Number two", was malfunctioning. It seemed to work properly and generate electricity and clean water, but did not give the correct digital read-out of the results. So she asked him to replace it in the cupboard and change it for another more reliable machine. She had been intending to get the technical engineers next door to decommission it and see it they could use any of the parts. He then prepared various buffers and solutions needed to calibrate their special equipment and carefully cleaned the glass electrodes with ethanol. Wei prepared a new Oracle database to record all the results. Everything was ready by 5:00 pm, so Wei said goodbye and went home, leaving Rick to lock up the lab. Once she had gone, he placed two large pipettes and sample bottles in his rucksack and set off on his motorbike for Knole Park. Dr Macferson was not in the laboratory today, so he had no fear of being seen taking the items he needed.

The park was quite empty by the time he arrived at 5:50 pm. He parked his motorbike and walked quickly along the path that led to the frog pond. There were a few frogs around, but no humans. The level of the pond water was looking good, but there was some pond weed. He hoped he could pipette out an accurate half-litre sample and the pipette tip would not clog up. He was in luck as he was able to collect both samples perfectly. There was a lot of agitated croaking going on from the frogs, who were uncomfortable with his actions. The bullfrog was making an enormous din, which was clearly frightening the young frogs. Little did they know that he was, in fact, trying to help the creatures who lived in the park, not hurt them. Rick left as soon as he had taken the samples so as not to cause any further distress to the young frogs or, worse, arouse unwanted attention from any park keepers who might be in the vicinity. He rode home and hid the samples in a box in the back of the fridge, hoping his mother would not notice them and ask any awkward questions. He was excited about the tests that he and Wei would perform tomorrow and what could happen in the future if his samples proved interesting.

As he lay in bed that evening, he tried hard to find the child inside him and open his mind to the existence of a parallel magical world that lived in harmony with nature. He tried to recall what he remembered about the wonders of nature from when he was a child.

Yes, I remember the wonder of seeing the first snowdrops pushing their bent heads through the snow in January, he thought to himself. *Even here in Lower Riverend by our front door, there were examples of the magic of nature. Also, in spring, the thrill of seeing the first bluebells flower in the woods down the road and to return a week later and find the whole wood bathed in an iridescent sea of blue light. That was cosmic.* He fell asleep with these images strong in his mind.

His trip to Heathrow the next morning went relatively smoothly. He had got up early hoping to avoid the worst of the rush-hour traffic, but not early enough; the motorway was as busy as always. He located the customs office easily and was able to park close to the entrance. He found the customs officers were surprisingly friendly and helpful; not what he had expected. They were interested in finding out a bit about his company's research and wished him good luck with the analyses. He stopped off at home, to pick up his samples, on the way back and arrived at the labs before midday. He put the Sierra Leone samples and his special samples in the fridge before going for lunch with Wei. They discussed their plan of action over lunch and Rick broached the subject of his special samples. Rick had devised a story which he hoped would appeal to Wei's kind nature.

'I've got a good friend who runs a charity for homeless animals. I saw him for a beer a couple of nights ago. He's a really kind guy and was very interested in the work of BioEnerFuels. He's got a lake in his grounds and he hoped that maybe we could test the water to see if it was an efficient source for the fuel cells. He said it would greatly decrease the charity's costs if he could find an efficient low-cost way of generating electricity to heat and light the kennels. What do you think? I've bought two water samples in today from his lake.'

Wei was perfectly happy to add the additional two samples to the analysis, as Rick had hoped. Apparently, it hardly made any difference to the overall cost and amount of work that was involved. She was an animal lover, so the project appealed to her.

It started to rain heavily after lunch, so they ran back to the labs, laughing and leaping over the puddles that had already formed. They were soaked to the skin when they entered the building, with water dripping from their hair and clothes, much to the secretary's amusement. Janet told them where they could find some clean towels in a cupboard and they dried themselves as best they could, then donned their lab coats and set to work on the analyses. Various procedures were needed before they could actually test the efficiency of the sample to generate electricity and clean water. The process consisted of the following activities:

First, any bulky material was filtered off, such as decaying leaves, insects and aquatic plants, using centrifugation and filter techniques developed at BioEnerFuels. The overall weight of these components was recorded, and they were labelled, and stored in the fridge in case they were needed at a later date. Their main interest was in the results from the chemical analyses on the water and micro-organisms. Each aqueous sample was divided into two equal halves. One half was put back in the fridge and would be tested for its efficacy the next day.

A standard set of chemical and biological analyses was run on the other half, which included:

- Measuring the pH and alkalinity
- Measuring the oxygen and carbon dioxide content
- Measuring the micro-mineral (soil) content
- Measuring the overall micro-vegetation content
- Analysing the percentage of different types of micro-vegetation, algae and other micro-organisms present in the sample and documenting the species present as accurately as possible
- Measuring the total sodium, potassium, sulphur, calcium, fluoride and chloride content.

Rick watched Wei carefully as she prepared the samples for the tests. They had decided that, for consistency, Wei would perform all the tests, so there would be no variation due to changing the analyst, and anyway, Rick was still inexperienced in laboratory work but was proficient at computing, so he was better occupied recording the results that Wei obtained in the database. Because they measured so many properties, they would perform some statistical analyses tomorrow to help elucidate the properties needed to obtain an efficient electricity and clean water production system for their bacterial fuel cell system. However, Wei explained that their statistical analysis would be relatively simplistic as they lacked the expertise for a complex multivariate statistical analysis at BioEnerFuels. They needed to find a suitable consultant or university department who could assist them with this analysis in the near future. Their in-house analyses to date had failed to find any clear relationships between the water properties that they were measuring today and the efficacy of the sample for producing electricity and clean water.

The analyses of the samples' properties were performed quite rapidly using specialised sophisticated digital-readout equipment bought from laboratory equipment suppliers or developed in-house. The time-consuming part of the analysis was the manual identification of the different types of living micro-organisms and algae using a petri dish and microscope. Wei was quite experienced at this, but needed to refer constantly to large manuals of micro-plant species for assistance and verification of her observations. Rick helped her with this, but it was a slow process, and it was after 9:00 pm when they finally completed the first day's studies to her satisfaction. Not unsurprisingly, Rick's two samples had very different characteristics to the Sierra Leone samples, but that did not necessarily mean they would be an unsuitable source of energy for the microbial fuel cell.

The two scientists finally switched off the lights and went home at 10:00 pm, after the lab equipment and electrodes had all been cleaned, dried and put away.

Rick's parents were concerned when he arrived home so late in the evening and scolded him for not phoning to let them know where he was. Olive and Cyril had been worried that he may have had an accident and had tried to call his mobile, but it was switched off. However, when Rick explained that he had been working late and told them about the project, they felt admiration for his conscientiousness and were proud of his commitment and work ethic.

Rick could hardly sleep that night wondering what the

outcome of the key experiments would be tomorrow. He so wanted the results to be positive and successful.

He recalled, *The Pevi are really busy this week; one team is in the middle of their expedition to visit other communities in the UK and France, and another set of teams are out and about exploring the local countryside around Sevenoaks. It would be so exciting if, on their return, I could convey the good news that the pond water is a suitable source for the microbial fuels cell to function efficiently and generate the positive ions the Pevi need so badly.*

'Please let me be their saviour,' he whispered into the night and then once again continued his search for his hidden child and pondered the wonders of nature that he had overlooked in more recent years, being too preoccupied with school, sports and friends.

22

Refreshed by their long sleep in the high rafters of St Pancras station, Eve, Eleanor and Francis woke at 9:30 am Wednesday morning and set about finding the Eurostar train to Paris. They were amazed to see travellers sipping champagne at the Champagne Bar at such an early hour.

Eve commented, 'Goodness me. These humans seem to be even more enthusiastic imbibers than our dear fairy friends in Sevenoaks.'

After a brief reconnaissance of the station forecourt, they found the departure point for Eurostar passengers and passed effortlessly through security, unseen by the X-ray machine. A voice announced the departure of the Paris train and they followed the human passengers up the escalator and onto the platform where the train was waiting. Kathleen had advised them to travel first class as it would be less crowded, so they walked along next to the carriages until they found a half-empty first-class compartment. They installed themselves around a vacant table with four comfy seats and then decided the view was better if they actually sat on the table rather than the chairs. The train slowly pulled out of the station and they sat mesmerised by the passing alternate views of towns and countryside, hardly noticing their hard seat and sore bottoms.

Suddenly, their view went completely black and stayed black. They had passed through tunnels already on their voyage when the train arrived at a hill, but this was something different and far longer. Terrified they clung to each other.

Francis whispered with a trembling voice, 'Is this the end of the World?' They noticed that the human occupants seemed unperturbed, so obviously this was "normal". Kathleen had told them that the train went under the sea after about an hour, so they were expecting to see fishes, seaweed and coral, but all they could see was nothing. It was very curious and disturbing. They wondered whether the sea was so deep and dirty that light could not penetrate to the bottom. After just under half an hour the train suddenly roared into the light again and the three Pevi gave a huge sigh of relief. Perhaps they were not quite as intrepid explorers as they would have liked.

At the Gare du Nord station in Paris, they were once more confronted by a sea of fast moving people. They remained on the train until the rush had died down, then they embarked on their journey across Paris by bus to Gare du Lyon where they boarded a modern TGV train going to Perpignan in the South of France. The countryside changed as they sped south and by the time they reached Lyon it was looking distinctly Mediterranean, very different from the South of England and Northern France. The final leg of the journey took them along the southern coast of France where they saw the sparkling blue waters of the Mediterranean and the large shallow etangs that bordered the coast and which were home to many flamingos. The Pevi were enthralled by the vibrant pink plumage of the birds and their elegant form and grace as they waded and fed in the warm waters of the etangs. They saw wind turbines, dry granite hills, dark majestic cypress trees and endless sandy beaches.

They changed train at Perpignan and took an old local train to Collioure which followed the coastline for part of the trip and provided views of the bays and coves formed where the foothills of the Pyrenees reached the Mediterranean sea. The beaches were not busy this time of year, but there were still quite a few people lying on towels on the sand and swimming in the sea. Colourful parasols shaded them from the sun. The Pevi decided this would be fun and they should find time to spend a few hours on the beach after the important technical studies were finished. The sun was shining through the windows and the temperature climbed slowly in the carriage until it reached the high-twenties and the Pevi left little puddles of sweat on their seats.

They descended from the train at Collioure and were met on the platform by Jean-Claude and Marie.

'Bonjour, mes amis,' shouted Eleanor enthusiastically with a wave of her paw; she was keen to practice her French language skills and impress Eve at the same time.

'Bien venue, welcome,' replied Marie who was keen to practice her English conversation.

Luckily, their hosts had thought to bring small pouches of fresh water for their visitors, to replace that left behind on the train seats. Francis was suffering from the heat in the train and was relieved to be able to quench his thirst and reduce his body temperature. The water was pure and clean, having been tapped from springs high in the mountains behind Collioure. He was keen to be on his way to the Pevi's community in the mountains where the temperatures would be slightly lower. It was the first time any of the three English Pevi had been abroad and they were unprepared for such warm temperatures on the Mediterranean coast. It had been chilly when they left London, but the October sun was hot in Collioure.

'We often have beautifully warm weather in September and October, with temperatures in the mid- to high-twenties,' Marie explained in slow English. 'These are lovely months to visit Collioure. You have come at the right time. This is not hot. Hot happens in July and August, when temperatures can reach the mid-thirties. You would hate it in summer when the tourists are here. It's so busy you can hardly see the sand on the beach for the bodies lying there, soaking up the sun. The restaurants, bars and streets are packed with people from all over Europe, especially the Dutch who bring their caravans and tents. They love the campsites here. We will show you the village tomorrow. Now we will go to our home in the mountains and you can all relax after your long journey.'

Eve was looking forward to the feast that her hosts would no doubt prepare for their English guests tonight. She was pretty sure it would be even more delicious than the excellent buffet they had been served in Hyde Park and hoped she could sample some of the local delicacies from this Catalan region of France. She was also looking forward to getting to know Jean-Claude, her debonair host, a lot better. He was handsome in a rugged way and probably only a few years older than her, though the harsh Mediterranean sun had aged his fur and skin prematurely. Jean-Claude was excited by Eve's voluptuous curves, which were quite unlike those of the French Pevi females who tended to be small and slight of build. Ever the gallant Frenchman, he offered to carry Eve's backpack for her and the five Pevi set off towards the western edge of the village and then followed a small rough track which led up into the mountains.

'The flora here is so different to Sevenoaks,' remarked Eve. 'It's a wonder anything grows in this dry environment on the steep mountain slopes.'

Marie pointed out some of the native trees and plants of the region to the visitors. There were ancient olive trees with their characteristic tortured trunks, grey-green leaves and wonderful green and black fruit that the Pevi chopped up and added to dough to make savoury bread or marinated in oil and herbs to eat with their aperitifs; micocouliers, the branches of which were used by humans to make horse whips; cork oaks with their thick bark that was used to make wine corks; maritime pines which were a source of energy-rich pine nuts for the Pevi, and fig trees that bore large sweet fruits in August which attracted wasps in search of sugary nectar. Also, there were herbs and shrubs with wonderful smells; lavender, sage, juniper, thyme and rosemary, which somehow survived on the meagre stony soil. Marie explained that the most beautiful time was in spring when the mountainside was a mass of colour with yellow, white and pink flowers; cystus, broom, poppies, sedum, lupins and many, many others.

Marie and Eleanor made friends instantly and chatted away in a mix of French and English which they laughingly called "franglais". Eleanor told Marie that there was a market in Sevenoaks on Saturdays where the humans could buy olives from a Frenchman. She had never tasted one, but hoped to get the opportunity here. Francis was too exhausted to talk much and had trouble keeping up with the fitter French Pevi who were used to climbing steep mountain paths in warm temperatures. Even though it was now 6:00 pm in the evening, temperatures were still in the mid-twenties and the sky was cloudless. Eve, being relieved of her backpack, managed to keep up with Jean-Claude and even though she was quite a bit older than Francis, she was less affected by the heat than he was. Eleanor was too busy chatting to notice how strenuous the climb was. It had been a long and exciting day, so the English visitors were relieved when they finally arrived at the Pevi community after a one-hour climb into the mountains behind Collioure. Now, they were exhausted and only wanted to sit in the shade and down a large glass of local red wine with their French hosts.

To Eve's dismay, Marie explained that they had not planned a big party tonight as they knew their guests would be tired after their long journey. They had prepared a small meal of local sheep's cheese, called brebis, cherry tomatoes and multigrain bread, washed down with copious wine and spring water, followed by an early night. Tomorrow they would carry out their technical measurements, spend the afternoon sightseeing in Collioure, and return to the mountains for a party in the evening. Eleanor and Francis agreed this was a splendid idea as they were tired and did not feel like partying tonight. The Pevi all sat around in a large circle in a shady glade enclosed by cork trees and enjoyed their simple fare. The conversation flowed, though a lot of what was said was relatively incomprehensible to the other nationality. Only Eleanor and Marie, and later, Eve and Jean-Claude, seemed to strike up a half-comprehensible discussion between themselves.

Marie told Eleanor about her love of the Pyrenees-Orientales department of France and especially the region around Collioure. She had taken it upon herself to plant the area around the Pevi's home with herbs for cooking and medicinal purposes. Only the herbs which were native to the Mediterranean survived under the harsh dry conditions that prevailed in summer; rosemary and thyme for flavouring nut stews and grilled vegetables and medicinal herbs such as aloe vera and fennel. She had also collected seeds from wild flowers and gardens in Collioure which she then cultivated and planted in moderation around the Pevi's glade.

She explained to Eleanor, 'I have to be prudent with my planting because too much colour would attract human ramblers and we desire privacy and tranquillity above all else. Indeed, we specifically chose our glade to be remote from tracks and paths in the mountains and we never see humans near our home. What is your home in Sevenoaks like?'

Eleanor explained that the situation in Sevenoaks was quite different.

'Knole Park is often busy and full of humans, especially in summer and at weekends when the weather is nice. Like you, we have also chosen the site for our community with great care and the fairies have placed a magical protective cordon around our glade, so the humans never enter or see our home. We live in quite close proximity to humans, but are never threatened by them.' She further explained that they adored their fairy friends who also lived in the park and how they often talked and partied together. Indeed, their community owed a great historical debt to the fairies who had rescued them from London during the Great Fire in the seventeenth century. Marie had never seen a fairy and was enthralled to hear this information and wanted to know more about this special relationship, the magical cordon and the joint parties.

While Eleanor and Marie were chatting about fairies, Jean-Claude was talking to Eve about his past and his contribution to the Pevi community.

'Soon after I was born,' he started, 'my mother was killed by a falling tree during a horrendous storm. My father was devastated by his loss and was left with a baby Pevi to rear. My mother had cared for me one hundred percent and he knew nothing about raising a baby Pevi, but was determined to excel. He was a builder and a very practical male, so he set about teaching me technical skills and knowledge about the environment. The females took turns to look after me and feed me, but from an early age I spent most of my time with my father, learning how to build a shelter in the trees, or find fruits and nuts, and how to classify mushrooms into poisonous or edible categories. I became very knowledgeable at a young age. Sadly, devoted as my father was to me, he greatly missed my mother and was constantly battling depression. Two years after her tragic death, once he saw I was self-sufficient, he went down to Collioure and swam out to sea. He never stopped swimming and we never saw him again. He was presumed drowned and at peace with my mother in the heavens.'

Eve could hardly hold back her tears. What a sad start to life this handsome French Pevi had had. But things had worked out well for him. He became the most accomplished builder in the community, was highly knowledgeable about nature and was voted chief Pevi by the community ten years ago; a position he still held. He had never found a female partner; mainly because he was so busy maintaining the infrastructure of the small houses of the community, hidden high in the trees, or resolving minor disputes between two Pevi. Also, he just wasn't physically attracted to the petite dark French females, but, he explained, he found Eve wonderfully attractive and enticing with her full feminine curves and soft golden fur. He also adored her accent. She spoke an ancient French dialect, with a pronounced English accent, which sounded like poetry to him. He could listen to her talk for hours and her voice carried him away to a romantic ancient past.

So, things were going well for Eve and Jean-Claude. The evening came to a natural close before midnight. The Pevi retired to their small beds and the visitors were shown to clean guest beds high in the trees.

Eleanor and Francis were woken early the next morning

by brilliant sunshine glinting through the canopy of leaves. They had both slept deeply and were confused initially about their whereabouts when they awoke. The trees smelt different to those at home and the bright sunlight was hurting their eyes. They looked around and saw the French Pevi sitting below them in the shade, enjoying a meal of acorns and brebis milk. Marie waved up to them and beckoned them to join her. Francis and Eleanor descended the tree on wobbly legs and sat with their hosts enjoying the balmy morning temperatures and pleasant company. The French and English Pevi were both trying hard to comprehend their new friends and speak slowly and clearly; laughing frequently when perplexed by the language and pronunciation problems. The local Pevi spoke French with a Catalan accent and also used a few Catalan words, which were dissimilar to the ancient French language the English Pevi had learnt from their ancestors. Eve had not yet risen and there was no sign of Jean-Claude either, but no one remarked on this.

After breakfast, Eleanor and Francis gathered up their environmental-monitoring equipment and followed Marie to a large clearing nearby, where they would perform their measurements. There was a light breeze and the morning temperature was pleasant. The local wind, the Tramontana, was not blowing from the cold, high Pyrenees today. The conditions were ideal for taking accurate readings. The results showed that the atmosphere here was ideal and there were no problems of low levels of positive ions. This result was further supported by the fact that all the French Pevi seemed relaxed and of a jovial temperament. Francis and Eleanor had noticed no signs of depression or sulking amongst their youngsters. Though they agreed with each other that this was hardly surprising since the Collioure Pevi were living in such a beautiful part of France with sunny weather most of the year and stunning views of the mountains and rugged coastline where the Pyrenees meet the Mediterranean Sea. Indeed, the French youngsters were remarkably mature and relaxed with adult company compared to their English counterparts, who were frequently non-communicative and ill at ease with adult Pevi.

The Collioure community was delighted that their atmosphere had been found to be healthy, but felt deeply sorry for the problems their visitors were experiencing in the Sevenoaks region of the UK. By now Eve and Jean-Claude had appeared, looking a little sheepish, and were quietly sipping acorn coffee under a large oak tree, slightly remote from the hub of the community. Eve had a glow about her which emitted a brilliance that Eleanor and Francis had never seen before. She was smiling broadly at Jean-Claude, and he back at her, with an expression that suggested they shared a secret. Francis and Eleanor glanced at each other and Eleanor raised one eyebrow, then she winked at Francis. Eve's secret was no longer private.

Marie suggested that the visitors might enjoy a sightseeing tour of their beautiful region, before the big feast planned for tonight. Eleanor and Francis were quick to acquiesce and packed fresh water into their rucksacks before setting off. Jean-Claude filled two pouches with water and placed them both in Eve's rucksack before putting it on his own back. Two female Pevi, Pascale and Patricia, also joined the group, having taken a shine to Francis. The group set off, two, by three, by two; with Marie and Eleanor leading at the front, Francis, Pascale and Patricia behind them, and Eve and Jean-Claude bringing up the rear.

First, they visited the beautiful old village of Collioure with its famous idiosyncratic church tower by the harbour and numerous ancient forts in and around the village. The narrow cobbled backstreets were a rainbow of colour; with vividly-painted houses and colourful flowers planted in tubs or in small holes between the cobbles; scarlet geraniums, white and yellow honeysuckles, orange campsis, and purple, red and pink bougainvillea all blossomed in perfusion and fought for space and sunlight in the narrow streets. The English Pevi were fascinated with the ingenuity of the goods on display in little shops owned by artists and artisans of all sorts. The restaurants around the port were busy with elderly retired people and families with pre-school-age children from all over Europe. French, Spanish, Scandinavian, English and Dutch tourists hovered around the periphery of the full terraces, waiting for diners to finish their meal, pay and free up tables for the next round of diners. The waiters were hurrying to serve everyone and ensure a fast turnaround and maximum profit for lunchtime. It was fun to watch for a while, but a little too hectic for the countryside-loving Pevi.

'It's so hectic,' Eve observed.

'Collioure is always busy and lively. This is nothing,' replied Jean-Claude. 'We are at the end of the tourist season now. You should see the crowds in summer. The only quiet months here are November and early spring.'

They decided to board the little tourist train which departed from the centre of the village and took people on a tour of the vineyards and the old forts that surrounded the village. The train wasn't a real train that ran on rails, but an engine which was driven along the road and pulled six carriages with wooden benches behind. It was painted bright yellow and white, with advertising boards along the sides of the coaches, enticing tourists to sample the delights of the region and visit the local vineyards, restaurants, chateaux and amusement parks. The Pevi sat on top of the roof to get the best views. It was a warm sunny October day, but they had their water supplies to keep them refreshed. The tour gave them magnificent views of the terraced vineyards and different views along the rocky coast towards the Spanish border.

On returning to the centre of the village again, they decided to spend an hour relaxing, by lying on the warm beach and swimming in the azure Mediterranean Sea; something the English Pevi had never experienced in the UK. They had only swum very occasionally in the Knole Park frog pond when the summer temperatures climbed too high for them. The frogs, however, were always unhappy about the intrusion and disliked them venturing into what they considered to be their sovereign territory. The Sevenoaks Pevi had never lain on a warm beach and listened to the sound of the sea and the cry of seagulls in the UK. It was an experience they were to enjoy enormously. They swam exceptionally well, buoyed up by the salty water of the Mediterranean which supported their ultra-light bodies even better than the fresh water of the frog pond. The motion of the waves made them squeal with delight as they frolicked together in the clear sparkling sea. Patricia and Pascale were enjoying splashing Francis and trying to dunk him under the waves, taking pleasure from stealing caresses of his soft fur.

After the swim, they snoozed on a tiny patch of sand safely away from the main beach and the tourists beached there like a school of red, pink and white whales quietly roasting in the afternoon sun. Jean-Claude and Eve lay together holding paws and as the sun warmed their bodies, so their sexual appetite was gently aroused. It was a beautiful moment for Eve, she experienced a silent ecstasy on the beach that she had never imagined possible. The warmth, the sound of the waves, her damp fur drying slowly in the sun, a handsome French Pevi at her side; life could not have been more perfect. She glanced across at Jean-Claude and saw a happy Pevi, relaxed and at peace with himself. He squeezed her paw and they exchanged a smile and a promise for further passion in the high trees tonight. They had made love gently and with a great tenderness last night, respectful of each other's age and lack of sexual experience. It had been a jointly undertaken exploration of their previously suppressed sexuality and they had been sensitive to the fragility of each other's feelings. But, it had been such a wonderful adventure and Eve felt her inner world was finally replete. Jean-Claude was silently musing how to persuade Eve to stay in France and live with him, so making him the happiest Pevi alive.

The other Pevi were also enjoying their afternoon on the beach. Francis found it hard to snooze for too long; he was too excited and took great pleasure in returning to the sea at frequent intervals to splash in the waves. He was invariably joined by Pascale and Patricia and he took delight in their attentions as they fooled around together in the water. Eleanor and Marie had finally stopped talking and were benefitting from a rest, while the sunshine topped-up of their vitamin D levels.

Refreshed by their snooze in the sun, the seven Pevi set off at a good speed up the mountain trail to their home in the foothills behind Collioure. The banquet had been prepared while they were away and was laid out on long flat logs beneath the shady oaks. The Pevi quickly rinsed the salt from their bodies in the clean cool water of the stream that ran next to the Pevi encampment and dried their fur in the low evening sun. The banquet started punctually at 7:00 pm. It consisted of local produce, and included dishes cooked using recipes handed down by their ancestors, and new ideas created by the more inventive cooks: acorn, rosemary and seed bread with cherry tomatoes; fresh sea urchins on sliced artichoke hearts, and grilled freshwater shrimps with coarse sea salt; followed by sweet grapes, dried cherries and the Pevi's favourite brebis cheese served with a rosehip confit. The meal was washed down with an abundance of excellent Collioure rosé and red wines. What a pleasure this was for the English Pevi to experience so many new tastes. They especially enjoyed the sea urchins and brebis cheese...and, of course, the local wine.

A small Pevi band played some folk and blues music during dinner and the Johnny Hallyday classics came later in the evening. They had picked up the words and tunes in the bars and discos of Collioure. These were ideal rhythms for dancing and made the evening go with a real swing till after midnight. Eve and Jean-Claude danced together all evening, their jiving improving substantially as the evening wore on and they got used to their partner's steps. Francis alternated dancing with Eleanor, Pascale and Patricia, not wanting to upset anyone, while Eleanor danced with just about everyone she could; male and female alike.

Everyone slept late the following morning, and breakfast

was a very subdued affair as the adult Pevi nursed their hangovers and tried to refrain from chiding their noisy offspring. Francis and Eleanor sat in conference with Eve who explained that she would prefer to stay here in Collioure than return to Sevenoaks, but needed to be sure that the two younger Pevi were confident of making the return journey alone, without her help. This came as no particular surprise to the two technicians, who were delighted that Eve had finally found love after a life spent as a spinster in Sevenoaks. They hugged her warmly and they all cried at her newfound happiness. It would be tough saying goodbye, but Eleanor and Francis were confident in their ability to travel home without her and knew they would be able to keep in contact via Edmund's remarkable thought transference skills. Hopefully, they would return to spend some more time with their Collioure friends, once their problem of the deteriorating atmosphere had been resolved at home.

So, Eleanor and Francis set off for the train station in Collioure accompanied by Eve, Jean-Claude, Marie, Patricia and Pascale. Their journey would be over tomorrow and then they would start to analyse the results of their findings with Doctor Cedric and Edmund. They wondered how the local research expeditions had gone around Sevenoaks and if there was now a clear protagonist.

23

Today's the big day, thought Rick. *Today I will know whether or not the frog pond is a suitable energy source for BioEnerFuels' fuel cell.*

Rick was first to arrive in the labs at 8:00 am, eager to get started. To his surprise, Dr Macferson arrived soon after him. She told him that she intended to don a lab coat today and assist with the analysis. Specifically, she wanted to double-check Wei's species analysis, as she was far more experienced at this process, and her intuition told her that these results could well be the key to understanding what was needed for an effective fuel source. Accurate, validated results were vital to the analysis. Rick felt slightly nervous about the two additional samples that he had persuaded Wei to include and what Dr Macferson would say if, or more probably when, she discovered them.

Wei arrived just before 8:30 am, quickly donned her lab coat, and they were ready to start the final efficacy analyses and hopefully find out more about the optimal conditions needed for the operation of the fuel cell.

Dr Macferson explained the importance of the Sierra Leone samples to Rick and Wei, 'Our field technicians have already taken many samples from different countries in Africa. Some have proved efficacious, others not, for reasons as yet unknown to us. However, the Sierra Leone samples have consistently been found to have a statistically-significant higher probability of success than samples from other regions in Africa. We obviously are excited to find out why this is and hence we have recently increased the number of chemical analyses that we carry out on the samples to try to pinpoint the vital difference. I have a slight inclination that it may be down to the presence of certain micro-fauna in the pond water and so I've started to culture three of the potentially interesting fauna in large vats. You've no doubt seen them next door. However, many samples which also contain these micro-fauna are inactive, so I can't say that the way forward is clear.'

BioEnerFuels had built twenty alpha versions of their patented microbial fuel cell, which they used to perform the in-house analyses in the laboratory. These cells were cubic and measured twenty centimetres in each dimension. A more sophisticated and robust beta version was currently under development in their engineering laboratory next door. This version would be larger and capable of running for several months under harsh environmental conditions without the need for any human intervention. The results of the data analysis on the different samples would influence the final design of the machine and its operating software. Today, Rick and Wei would undertake the analyses using the alpha versions of the fuel cell, while Dr Macferson verified the accuracy of Wei's species analysis of yesterday afternoon.

Wei and Rick had planned to analyse one sample each from each pair of different samples from a specific lake. Thus all locations would have been tested once by Wei and once by Rick. It would be a long, but enjoyable day. Wei had finished setting up all her experiments to measure the electricity generated by each sample by coffee time and Rick completed the set up of his tests by the end of the morning. They would leave the experiments to run overnight for exactly twenty-four hours and then read off the amount of electricity generated and measure the purity of the water.

Rick knew that the amount of electricity (i.e. electrons) generated was equivalent to the amount of positive ions generated, so it was not necessary to measure directly the amount of positive ions formed. BioEnerFuels was not interested in the positive ions, but he and the Pevi were. So, he was hoping for a high electricity read-out from his samples tomorrow. He had hoped for a final result today, but now was disappointed to realise that he would have to wait until tomorrow. He had not been told that the experiment would run for twenty-four hours before the final measurements were done. The tension he felt was electric.

Dr Macferson also finished her studies by lunchtime and confirmed that she agreed with the majority of Wei's species classifications. This was a good outcome as she knew it was not scientifically feasible to expect one hundred percent agreement.

After a light lunch in the on-site restaurant, they wrote up the details of the experimental design in their electronic laboratory notebooks and prepared the equipment and solutions for the water purity measurements that they would make tomorrow.

Wei, Rick and Josephine Macferson retired to the local pub for a quick pint after work to celebrate the successful setting-up of all the experiments. Sitting, relaxed with their pints, Dr Macferson asked Wei where the extra two samples had come from, as she was only expecting ten samples from five different sites in Sierra Leone. Rick immediately panicked, but Wei remained calm and explained about Rick's friend with the animal sanctuary charity and large pond. She was sure that Dr Macferson would not mind, but she was wrong, Dr Macferson was not happy about the deception.

'We are specifically funded to explore sites in Africa where we can generate electricity efficiently and cheaply as well as providing clean drinking water for the local villagers. We are not an animal charity!' she explained indignantly.

Wei immediately decided to take the blame for the deception as she had been with BioEnerFuels longer than Rick and was now a useful and respected employee and scientist, while he was still very much the "new boy on the block". She apologised that she had agreed with Rick's plan and explained that it was her error of judgement. Rick had not appreciated the implications of his actions, he had simply wanted to help a friend and test the technology outside Africa. It was purely an error of judgement, not an intentional deception and misappropriation of equipment. Wei and Rick both apologised profusely and the matter was dropped.

However, the evening ended on a low rather than a high note and they soon downed their pints, left the pub and went home.

Rick sent Kathleen a quick email when he got home, explaining the current difficult situation, but how he hoped to have a final result from the experiments tomorrow. He soon got a reply with a photo attached of the Thames barge that Kathleen had procured and an invitation to meet Saturday morning in Knole Park by Rick and Juliet's tree to discuss the results of his experimental analysis and to present the barge to Coralie. Kathleen would get an invitation to Coralie tomorrow morning. Kathleen wished Rick luck with his analysis of results tomorrow.

That night Rick dreamt that he was making love to Kathleen in the shallow waves on a deserted tropical beach under a black star-studded sky. It was a vivid electric experience. He could feel the warm sand beneath them and taste the salt crystals on her skin. There was music wafting over the sea from a Caribbean band playing steel drums somewhere in the distance. He woke early bathed in sweat and took a long slow shower, recalling the minute details of his dream with great pleasure.

He dressed quickly, grabbed a banana and black coffee for breakfast, then left for work and was again first to arrive in the labs. Wei arrived soon after him, quickly followed by the secretary who popped her head around the lab door and informed them that Dr Macferson had been summoned to London at short notice to meet their stockbroker and give a presentation on the company to a new potential investor, so she would not be in the office today. Rick felt a surge of relief, as now he could look at all the results from all of the experiments without feeling guilty. Wei was also relieved as, after all, she had supported Rick's plan to help his charitable friend.

Wei and Rick carefully recorded the electricity readings and took samples of the "pure" water generated throughout the morning, being careful to ensure that each sample had been left to run for exactly twenty-four hours. Each pair of samples had given very similar electricity readings, which was the result that they wanted. However, Rick's frog pond water had failed to provide an interesting result, unlike two of the Sierra Leone locations.

They went to lunch together and chatted about the results so far. Wei was excited about the amount of electricity generated by the samples from two of the Sierra Leone locations, while Rick was feeling disappointed that the electricity reading generated by his special samples was low. Wei wolfed down her spaghetti bolognaise, eating and talking animatedly at the same time.

'This is the exciting result that we had been looking for. If the water purity is good for these samples, then we'll have something to really shout about to the shareholders.' Rick toyed with his spaghetti and left most of it untouched. His mind was on other things; he was already wondering what he would say to the Pevi on Saturday.

After lunch, Rick and Wei each measured the purity of the water generated by all the twelve samples. They were happy that their results agreed with each other, so they would not have to repeat any measurements. They worked well together and had produced accurate reproducible results which would please Dr Macferson.

Now they just had the computational and statistical analyses to undertake and hopefully these would give them a clearer understanding of why some samples worked better than others.

After a strong coffee to reinvigorate their brain cells, Wei and Rick sat down together at the computer terminal and began the computational and statistical analyses of all the results. The moment of truth had finally arrived. The computational analysis would provide a single number, describing the overall efficacy of a sample for producing clean water and electricity, on a scale of zero to one hundred. It did, indeed, confirm what they had already observed; that four of the Sierra Leone samples from two different locations were exceptionally effective at producing electricity and clean water at a level which warranted on-site testing of their beta fuel cell. This was by far the company's most exciting finding to date and one that prompted Wei to immediately text the result to Dr Macferson. Two of the samples from a different location had also shown some promise, but were not effective enough to warrant installation of a beta fuel cell on-site. The other four Sierra Leone samples were inactive. Then they came to Rick's special samples. Two nights ago Rick had been lying in bed dreaming of being the Pevi's saviour. He imagined himself as an angelic scientist in a shining white lab coat riding his motorbike into Knole Park bearing the good news about the effectiveness of the frog pond water to generate positive ions using BioEnerFuel's technology. And now their computational score confirmed the observations he had made personally that morning, that his pond samples were an unpromising fuel source for the microbial fuel cell. The electricity generated was only one-hundredth that of the best Sierra Leone sample and the purity of the "clean" water was not especially high. So that was that; the end of his personal crusade to help the gentle Pevi.

The more interesting statistical analyses would hopefully give them an idea why a particular sample was successful. Was it because the water had a specific pH or oxygen content? Or was Dr Macferson's hypothesis about the presence of certain micro-fauna correct? Wei explained that she was not very mathematically minded, but understood the basic operations and calculations that needed to be performed to decide if the sample was an effective source for their fuel cells. Rick had taken a one-term course of statistics at school and had achieved an A grade, so he probably had a better understanding of all the terminology than Wei.

As had happened in the past, the statistical analyses failed to find any significant relationships. None of the individual chemical parameters they had measured two days ago or the presence or absence of certain micro-organisms appeared to be correlated with efficacy. So, despite the phenomenal results from two locations, they were still no further forward in their actual understanding of what made a sample of water an efficient fuel for the microbial fuel cell. Wei repeated her theory that they needed a more sophisticated approach to data analysis, but lacked the expertise in-house. She would remind Dr Macferson tomorrow of the urgent requirement to find a consultant to help them.

The day ended with the young scientists positioned at two extremes of the emotional spectra; Wei on a mega high following the two phenomenal Sierra Leone results and Rick feeling depressed and useless. Saturday morning he would have to go and meet Kathleen, the fairies and the Pevi in the park and tell them about the disappointing outcome. He hated being the harbinger of bad news and it would be devastating news for the Pevi.

Dr Macferson's funding meeting had gone exceptionally well, mainly due to the arrival of Wei's enthusiastic text message about the two highly promising locations in Sierra Leone. The potential new investor had been very impressed with the news and was definitely keen to take a part of the company and support its research efforts. The company's future was looking more and more financially secure. Dr Macferson was well aware that the biggest hurdle for any small biotechnology company was to find sufficient funding to allow it to develop its technology to a stage where it could produce a marketable product, and now the immediate future was looking rosy for BioEnerFuels on all counts.

She was now spending more time talking to businessmen in the City of London than doing scientific research and she knew that would never change. In fact, she actually liked the fund-raising aspects of her position, as Chief Scientific Officer of a small biotech, more than she could ever have imagined. Two years ago she was a professor at a university who spent her days doing ground-breaking research and managing a small team of post-doctoral scientists and PhD students. Then they had developed a fuel cell sufficiently powerful to warrant starting a small biotechnology company to exploit the technology. She had always thought of herself as a true academic and never dreamed that one day she would be spending her days talking to stockbrokers in the City of London, and being responsible for finding the funds to enable BioEnerFuels to continue its research and development program.

24

Immediately after Eve, Eleanor and Francis had departed on their tour, the chief Pevi scientist, Dr Cedric, organised four small groups of Pevi to explore the locality around Sevenoaks to describe the industry and crops they found in the region. The groups were called Pevi North, Pevi South, Pevi East and Pevi West. Cedric led Pevi North, Edmund led Pevi South, his wife, Laura, led Pevi East and her friend, Gwyn, a talented, but serious-minded young adult, led Pevi West. Each group consisted of three Pevi and they were instructed to spend two days exploring in their assigned direction and report back with their findings by 6:00 pm on the second day, Tuesday. They would spend one night camping in the countryside.

There was much excitement in the Pevi community about the action they were taking and everyone hoped for a clear outcome following the expeditions. The groups packed their rucksacks with provisions for two days, paper and pencils for taking notes, and a warm blanket to sleep under during their night away. They set off in their assigned directions, all eager to be part of the group that found the answer to the atmospheric deterioration. Meanwhile, the Pevi who remained behind began preparations for a magnificent feast to celebrate the return of the expedition parties.

Edmund had asked Coralie to keep an eye on the Pevi community in his absence as all the leading lights of the Sevenoaks Pevi were part of the expedition parties. The Pevi left at home lacked a dependable leader should there be any unforeseen problems. Coralie decided that the best way to look after them was to suggest she helped with the preparations for the feast, so in this way she could keep in close proximity to the Pevi without it being too obvious that she was keeping an eye on them. Coralie was a skilful diplomat who could be relied on to find a solution that made everyone feel special and happy. In practice, the adolescent Pevi were highly pleased to be left without their leaders for a couple of days so they could prove their independence and reliability in a power vacuum. Indeed, the preparations for the feast went exceptionally well and all the Pevi pulled their weight with the cooking and scavenging for the meal, or with the creation of decorations and arrangements of flowers for the long log tables. Everyone hoped that it would be a wonderful feast and an appropriate welcoming home party for their intrepid explorers. They would hold another feast a few days later to celebrate the return of Eve, Eleanor and Francis.

The next afternoon the groups started arriving home. The first to arrive, at 5:00 pm, was Edmund's group who had taken copious notes about land use to the south of Sevenoaks. They were soon followed by Laura's group with information from the east and, just before the 6:00 pm deadline, Cedric's group arrived bearing information from the north. Coralie went home once the leaders had returned and promised to return the next day with Professor Theodore for the discussion and analysis of the group's findings. 6:00 pm came and went, but there was no news from Gwyn's group. At 8:00 pm, when the celebrations were scheduled to start, there was still no news. Everyone was now very agitated. Gwyn was the youngest and least experienced leader, but she was one hundred percent dependable. There must have been a serious problem for her to be so late. Edmund tried to contact her mind, but was confronted with visions of fog. Things were looking very serious. At 8:30 pm Edmund arranged a search party to go west and look for Gwyn's group, with strict instructions to keep in contact every thirty minutes via thought transference. The food and drink on the beautifully laid tables were cleared away and replaced by simple fare.

Just before midnight, the search party reported to Edmund that they had found Gwyn's group of three Pevi in a bad state on the edge of a field of yellow flowers, still covered by their sleeping blankets. It looked like they had set-up camp for the previous night and never woken up. They were alive, but all three were in a coma. The search party was returning with them at full speed and would also bring a bunch of the flowers from the field. They were suspicious that these flowers may have caused the Pevi to fall into a coma. Edmund immediately set off for the fairy palace to wake Coralie and request her help.

The Pevi search party arrived back home completely exhausted at 2:00 am Wednesday morning. They had been running flat-out for over five hours and for two of those hours they had been carrying their sick companions. Coralie examined the yellow flowers and declared them to be rapeseed, a relatively recently introduced crop to the UK, that had been cultivated in increasing amounts over the last couple of decades by farmers who grew it to feed their animals and to make rapeseed oil. She had no idea that it was toxic to Pevi. It had no major ill-effect on humans or fairies, as far as she was aware, though some people found the pollen and smell unpleasant and acrid. Personally, she hated the vivid unnatural yellow colour that now covered a lot of farmland and thought it spoilt the natural mellow yellows and greens of the beautiful English countryside. It cried out "Look at me! I am more colourful than the boring wheat, oats and barley you cultivate. I will spread and invade your hedgerows and roundabouts. Above all, I will be noticed."

Normally, rapeseed flowers in the late spring, so Coralie was confused as to why it was in flower in early October. Unfortunately, she knew of no specific antidote to rapeseed poisoning and could only recommend that the sick Pevi were kept warm and in the fresh air. She also gave them a shot of essence of foxglove, which contains digitalis, to make their hearts beat faster.

Edmund and Laura spent the rest of the night sitting next to their three patients, watching their shallow breathing and checking their heart beats every so often. Laura had nurtured Gwyn for a couple of months last year, when she was agoraphobic, and felt a strong bond of attachment to the young adult Pevi who lay before her. Gwyn had played a more and more active role in the Pevi community since her recovery. Her illness had had the upshot of making her stronger and more determined to make a success of her life and not fall back into a state of weakness and dependency on others. She could well become their next leader when Edmund retired. She had the intellect, energy, a balanced view on life and would deal fairly in cases of dispute. Gwyn was important to the development of the community over the next decade.

The next morning, two of the sick Pevi were breathing more strongly and had come out of their comas. The danger was over for them and they were on the route to recovery. Gwyn, however, was still very limp and in a coma, her yellow aura was barely visible. The entire Pevi community was in a state of shock and moved quietly around, talking in hushed voices. Once a Pevi lost its aura there was little chance of recovery and everyone could see how weak Gwyn's aura had become. Coralie was beside herself with worry and racked her brain in vain for any ideas for medicaments that she could administer. Gwyn's chest no longer rose and fell with her almost imperceptible weak breaths. Coralie feared the worst. By midday, Gwyn had died without coming out of her coma. Her aura had dissipated into the ether along with her soul.

The food that had been prepared for the feast the night before was put out for the birds. No one felt like eating. The Pevi all retired to bed early and reminisced in private about the qualities of Gwyn and the effect her death would have on their community. They looked at the twinkling stars in the night sky and wondered which one was her.

The two sick Pevi had fully recovered by Friday morning. They explained to Coralie, Edmund and Cedric how they had all felt exhausted at the end of the first day and had decided to sleep early and set up camp on the edge of a field of yellow flowers. In retrospect, it had been a seriously unlucky decision to sleep so close to the rapeseed that was apparently highly toxic to the Pevi. They speculated that the pollen had three effects on their metabolism. The first was the problem that the pollen neutralised positive ions in the air which weakened their immune system, the second was it made them tired, and the third effect was that the pollen itself was toxic to the Pevi.

Coralie was keen to visit the fields as soon as possible to see if she could find any clue as to why the rapeseed was flowering so late in the year. Edmund was determined to accompany her despite the possible dangers to his health, so they set off together after lunch to find the field where the Pevi West team had slept. They soon found a region where there were three fields of rapeseed in flower and Edmund noticed there was a Portacabin in the far corner of one of the fields. They quickly crossed the field, Edmund holding his breath to prevent him inhaling too much of the toxic pollen, and peered through the window of the Portacabin. There was no one inside, but the door was firmly locked. Coralie picked up a piece of flint lying in the field and hurled it at the window with all her strength. The window shattered and they entered the building through the broken window and went over to a grey metal desk covered in papers. Coralie divided up the pile of papers equally between Edmund and herself and they sat down and started to read the contents.

An hour later they had read all the relevant information and the results were clear. This field and a few others in the vicinity were being exploited by a biotechnology company, called Genrapmod, to develop a genetically-modified form of rapeseed that flowered twice a year, so potentially doubling the rate of production of the oil. This would clearly be a valuable asset to farmers. The project was in its first year and at the moment all the trials were being conducted in an area to the west of Sevenoaks. This was unfortunately the direction the predominant winds came from, so the pollen was blown regularly towards Knole Park.

'So now we know why this plant has suddenly become a

problem to the Pevi. When it flowered only once a year, the level of pollen was probably not a problem for you; it was below critical levels,' Coralie hypothesised, 'but now, it is flowering twice a year, it is effecting the health of the Pevi. Sevenoaks is getting double the amount of pollution this year because of this field trial.'

'So what can we do, if anything?' enquired Edmund.

'We must try to ensure that this trial has a negative outcome; possibly that the crop dies prematurely, before being harvested.' Coralie was convinced that this was their only hope.

'How can we do that?' Edmund was beginning to feel a little faint and unsteady on his paws. He swayed slightly.

Coralie regarded him with concern and replied, 'I don't know at the moment. Let's get you back to the park and discuss our options there, before you have a problem with the toxic pollen and fall into a coma. I suspect that the farmers grow the normal rapeseed around Market Harborough also, but the Pevi there are only subjected to its pollen once a year and so the problem is far less severe than in Sevenoaks. How unlucky that they chose this site so close to our park. We must work out a way to disrupt and terminate this trial. Perhaps Kathleen and Rick can help us. Don't forget they are coming to meet us tomorrow to tell us all about the results of the water analysis at Rick's company. We can ask their advice then.'

They set off quickly away from the toxic field. Coralie held Edmund's paw firmly as she flew through the air and guided him back towards Knole Park.

Eleanor and Francis arrived home later that afternoon full of stories about their travels and the Pevi they had met in London, Market Harborough and Collioure. Everyone asked lots of questions and especially wanted to know all about the romance between Jean-Claude and Eve. The celebrations for their return were held as planned that evening, but the feast was now held in honour of Gwyn who had bravely died in search of the atmospheric pollutant and now, thanks to her, the finger of guilt was squarely pointed at the cultivation of rapeseed around Sevenoaks and Market Harborough. There was no rapeseed cultivation in central London or Collioure, so that was consistent with this observation. The strange thing had been that the rapeseed was flowering in October in Sevenoaks, but now they knew about the field trial nearby, so that was one more piece of the puzzle that supported their hypothesis. The Pevi believed in reincarnation and were sure that Gwyn's soul would be reborn and she would reappear in their lives at some date in the future. So they mourned the loss of a brave and reliable Pevi, but also knew her absence would be temporary.

So their theory that rapeseed flowers were causing the decrease in positive ions and making the atmosphere toxic to the Pevi was pretty much confirmed. There was nothing they could do about the human race's desire to grow these obnoxious plants, but at least the source of the problem had been identified. They may have to move away from Sevenoaks in the longer term unless a solution could be found, but importantly, they now knew they had to avoid moving to a region where rapeseed was grown in profusion.

25

It was a chilly morning. The sun was hiding behind menacing dark clouds when Rick and Kathleen met Coralie in the park on Saturday as arranged. Professor Theodore, Doctor Cedric and Edmund had also joined the meeting, eager to hear their news. Kathleen was carrying a heavy parcel and Rick was carrying a heavy heart. He was annoyed that, unlike Kathleen, he had not been able to see the fairies or Pevi when they had first met. Since then he had been diligently practising relaxation techniques and trying to feel at one with nature whenever he got the opportunity. He certainly felt that he was in closer contact with the child side of his personality. He felt more confident and relaxed than at their first meeting and had come to terms with the fact that he firmly believed in the existence of these beings.

He asked Coralie to help him try to see the fairies and Pevi. She sensed that he was undoubtedly more receptive to their presence this time and repeated the instructions that she had given Kathleen at their first meeting and waited for Rick's response. He closed his eyes, repeated her words to himself and concentrated on his inner child. With his mind's eye, he visualised all the wonders of nature in the park and imagined the fairies and Pevi picnicking together beneath the trees, surrounded by long feathery grass, encircled by flying goldfinches, and with a musical accompaniment from a skylark. He took a deep breath and opened his eyes, praying to see what Kathleen had been able to see so easily. And, there before him, he saw a most beautiful vision of two fairies and two Pevi attentively watching him with love and hope in their eyes.

The feeling of elation brought tears to his eyes and he cried with happiness and wonder. He could now see the world that Kathleen saw. Kathleen felt his strong emotion and realised that he had achieved his aspiration. Instinctively, she took his face in her hands and kissed away his tears. It was an act of great tenderness that left them both stunned and embarrassed for a moment.

Rick could now see with his own eyes what he had been told by Kathleen, that the Pevi were "so, so very cute, that you want to put one in your pocket and take it home with you; to love it forever and never, ever let it go." He had already been enchanted by their gentle voices, but now the picture was complete. He felt even more upset about the news he was about to convey.

Rick perceived that Edmund and Cedric had long faces. They were still mourning the recent death of Gwyn and explained the tragic series of events to Kathleen and Rick, asking for their help in stopping the rapeseed field trial.

Kathleen volunteered, 'I'll do some research on the web to find out more about rapeseed and take a look at the site to see what I can find out. Then we can get together to decide whether or not anything can realistically be done to limit the damage. The sad news about Gwyn has certainly given a real sense of urgency to your problem. You can be assured that Rick and I will do our utmost to help you.'

The fairies were highly intrigued to discover the content of Kathleen's parcel. They wondered if it could it be the fantastic machine from BioEnerFuels that would save the Pevi. However, by this time Kathleen had heard Rick's news and they had decided that he should talk first about the studies at BioEnerfuels, then, to help alleviate everyone's disappointment, Kathleen would present Coralie with the remote-controlled Thames sailing barge for the young frogs. Now she had heard the news about Gwyn and the rapeseed, she was even more relieved that she could present the boat at the end of the meeting to raise the group's mood.

Rick opened the scientific discussion by explaining what had been going on in his laboratory over the past few days, telling everyone about the analyses they had undertaken, and the excellent news about the Sierra Leone samples, compared to the disappointing results from the frog pond. He also mentioned that he had got into deep trouble with the Chief Scientific Officer for illicitly testing the two additional samples and how Wei had bravely defended his actions. The meeting went quiet as everyone reflected on the impact of the negative results. Subconsciously, everyone had pinned their hopes on a positive and joyous outcome to the laboratory analyses. Now they had to revisit the idea of a relocation of the Sevenoaks Pevi community to another part of the UK or Europe, away from their beloved fairies.

Only Professor Theodore refused to accept the outcome of the experiments as final. He was an atypical fairy with an analytical and enquiring mind. His scientific brain caused him to question every analysis that Rick and his colleagues had undertaken and he wanted full explanations of exactly how the results had been calculated. Rick was unable to answer many of the questions in sufficient depth because he was still a trainee at work and lacked detailed knowledge of many procedures. Theodore seemed especially interested in the data analysis and the exact statistical methods that had been applied. To him, they seemed naïve and rather simplistic. He himself had sat in on many a lecture on mathematics and multivariate statistics in his youth at the University of Madrid in Spain and, from what he could ascertain, his expertise in this field far exceeded that of Rick or any of his colleagues at BioEnerFuels. Rick thought it was a great shame that he could not introduce Theodore to the company, as a potential statistical consultant, as his passion for the field was obvious. But, he knew he could never muster the courage to introduce Theodore to Dr Macferson since he suspected she would be unable to see him.

It was Kathleen who made the sensible suggestion that Theodore should accompany Rick to the labs immediately after their meeting had finished, and then he could see at first hand what had, or had not, been done. This would relieve his scientific frustration and reassure everyone that the scientists at BioEnerFuels were true experts in their field and knew what they were doing. Rick was sure that this would be possible, because as far as he knew, no one was working this weekend. Rick could take him on his motorbike, and there was no reason to assume that any other humans could see him if he did not want to be seen. If anyone turned up at the labs, they would have sufficient time to find a safe hiding place for the professor if necessary. There was very little chance that anything could go wrong. So it was agreed that Theodore would accompany Rick to the labs, to reassure himself that nothing had been overlooked. He was quite excited about the trip.

'OK, now that's sorted, will you please tell us what's in the mysterious parcel you are carrying?' requested Coralie impatiently.

'A present,' replied Kathleen, looking rather proud of herself, 'for the fairies to give to the frogs. I hope you like it and it serves both your and their needs.'

'May I open it now?' asked Coralie excitedly.

'With pleasure.'

Theodore, Cedric and Edmund crowded around Coralie as she carefully unwrapped the brown paper from the heavy parcel placed at Kathleen's feet. Rick also watched with interest as the paper was removed. He had only seen a photo of the barge that Kathleen had emailed him, but not the real thing. Inside, Coralie found the model Thames sailing barge and remote control unit.

'It's fantastic; it's perfect. You are so clever Kathleen, where did you find such a beautiful wooden replica of an old barge with canvas sails. It's even got a remote control so they can sail when there is no wind? It is so authentic. The frogs will love this; that is if they are clever enough to learn how to use it properly. I know; I have just the solution. We'll send Zak to give them lessons. He has done some sailing in the English Channel in the past and will enjoy teaching the young frogs. Perhaps it will keep him out of trouble for a few hours,' Coralie enthused as she flew up from the ground and placed a big kiss on Kathleen's cheek. She was genuinely overawed by Kathleen's perfect present.

Edmund felt slightly put out and pointed out to Coralie that the Pevi also had significant sailing skills, their ancestors having crossed the mighty Atlantic Ocean with Christopher Columbus. However, he conceded that the frogs were unable to see the Pevi very clearly and would never take any instructions seriously that were given by a small squirrel-like creature with a gentle voice, so it was probably preferable for the fairies to provide tuition. In reality, his comments were meant as a light-hearted rebuttal of Coralie, intended to raise the atmosphere a few degrees, despite his major disappointment that evening, and everyone laughed with appreciation.

Kathleen offered to carry the boat back to Coralie's palace where it could be stored for the moment, before being taken down to the frog pond once Coralie was ready to present it to the bullfrog. Coralie gladly accepted her offer and they set off together for her palace. Kathleen was excited at the thought of seeing a real fairy palace and Coralie agreed to deactivate the magic cordon for a few minutes to allow Kathleen to see her home, on the strict understanding that she kept the location completely secret.

The sky was looking threatening and Rick was keen to set off to the science park as soon as possible, so Theodore could start his analysis. He would have liked to have accompanied Kathleen to see the fairy palace, but he knew there would be other occasions when he could see it. He was also unsure how to react to Kathleen's kisses earlier. They had been soft and tender, but he was unsure what exactly they signified: friendship or love? Their relationship was becoming quite complex. He sometimes found her difficult to read, so he preferred to take his leave and avoid making any embarrassing mistakes.

Rick set off to the science park at the end of the morning with Theodore riding pillion on his motorbike, clinging tightly to his leather jacket. Theodore had crossed back into the fairies' parallel time frame for the trip to ensure there could be no unauthorised sightings of him by humans. He found it was a bit cold on the back of the motorbike, but the journey only took fifty minutes and luckily the rain held off. He was looking forward to seeing the results of the experiments at first hand and trying some of his own statistical analyses using the software available.

26

As Rick had predicted, the labs were quiet, no one was working today. The security man had waved him through the gates, completely unable to see Theodore riding pillion. Rick logged on to the computer and opened the database of results and the statistical software program to show Theodore. Theodore examined the database and was pleased that everything seemed very orderly and he could easily understand the information it contained. He was also impressed by the functionality of the statistical software program; it contained algorithms for simple statistical analyses, complex multivariate analyses and even a few neural network programs. Everything he needed was there. Rick explained that they only used the simple univariate methods, as no one had experience of the more complex algorithms. Their analyses had failed to identify the important factors and Dr Macferson was currently trying to find a consultant with appropriate statistical expertise who could assist them.

Rick showed Theodore the results of their simple analyses, and it was clear that there was no single factor alone that was responsible for the success of some samples over others.

'This is definitely a multivariate problem,' Theodore explained. 'That's to say, there is a combination of factors that are important, not just a single property, and the trick is to find out which combination is important out of the multiple possibilities. All the algorithms I need are here in your software program, so I just need some time to undertake a succession of data analyses to find the key. I'm sure there must be a solution and I'm glad that you and Wei have measured a variety of chemical and biological properties for each sample. I'm feeling cold after the ride on the back of your motorbike, so why don't you make yourself useful and get us both a coffee, while I get stuck in to the analysis. Can you find a small cup for me? One that is not too heavy to lift. There's nothing I enjoy more than solving a hidden relationship. I am going to enjoy myself for a while.'

Rick went off to get coffee, leaving Theodore to start his data analysis. He found a small Pyrex beaker in one of the cupboards, it didn't have a handle, but it was about right for a fairy-sized cup of coffee.

Two hours later, Theodore had completed his analysis to his complete satisfaction. He had generated a pile of computer printout; 2D graphs, 3D graphs, histograms, equations and predictions.

'Come on, Rick, let's go. I have everything we need. We can discuss the results back in the park with Kathleen, Coralie, Cedric and Edmund. Just one question before we go. Do you have a sample of the micro-organism called MFWS2 that we can take with us and can you confirm that it is *definitely* not dangerous for the environment?'

Rick explained that it was a micro-organism that resembled a minute freshwater shrimp and it was definitely completely safe according to Dr Macferson. It was found in several samples they had tested from Africa and the UK. He would get a small sample from the culture they were growing in the fridge.

Just before they left the laboratory, Rick phoned Kathleen to arrange another meeting and an hour later Rick and Theodore joined Cedric, Coralie, Edmund and Kathleen who were seated together in the fairies' secret dancing glade in the park, waiting expectantly for the news. Rick was grinning broadly as he sat down on a log next to Kathleen. Theodore took centre stage and insisted that everyone had a glass of bubbly fermented myrtle juice before he would say anything. He was clearly excited about the results of his complex analysis. The humans found the glasses a trifle small for their liking, but the fairy "champagne" tasted delicious and it was quite strong. Only when everyone had finished their second glass of bubbly, and was feeling a little merry, did Theodore concede to begin his lecture.

'Well, I've not had so much fun for ages. There's nothing like a good data analysis to raise my spirits. It's like a detective story, you need to try and uncover the relevant facts and relationships hidden in the data. So, first of all, I was delighted to be able to understand quickly what all the data meant. Rick and Wei had created a very precise and straightforward method to display and store the data from all their samples, so I didn't need to waste a lot of time trying to understand everything. They had also undertaken a straightforward, but accurate, data analysis, looking at each individual property that they measure and all combinations of two properties, to see if they could determine what factors were essential for a successful or an unsuccessful sample. In this case however, the reason why some samples worked and others didn't was due to a far more complex model. One that could only be detected by applying multivariate statistical analyses. Yes, I have discovered the key to why some samples are successful and others not.' At this point he surveyed his audience and waited for their acclaim. Only after they had pleaded with him to divulge his results did he continue his lecture.

'A successful sample needs to have the following four properties: a chlorine level of about 0.2 units; a pH between 6.6 and 6.8, i.e. very slightly acidic; a high oxygen content, and, finally, it must contain a micro-organism called MFWS2.'

'That's all there is to it. These are the most important factors for success. Quite why this micro-organism is important is hard to tell. Perhaps it only occurs under these specific environmental conditions, or maybe it helps maintain this balance of properties in the pond water. Anyway, I am convinced that this is an accurate significant analysis and I can now show you my graphs and predictions that support the result.'

Everyone crowded round to look at his graphs and equations. It was clearly apparent that the frog pond samples fell outside the region on the plots where the active samples clustered. The pond water just didn't have the correct properties.

'So can we do anything to alter the properties of the frog pond?' enquired Kathleen.

'The pond water is too acidic, has too low a level of chlorine and does not contain MFWS2; but the oxygen content is perfect because it is fed by a spring and constantly moves which helps the dissolution of oxygen in the water. Rick and I have brought a sample of the MFWS2 organism which we can add to the pond water, but I don't know what to do about the pH and chlorine level.'

'But I do!' exclaimed Kathleen.

Edmund looked at her with hope in his eyes. 'Tell us, tell us,' he pleaded.

'I have a swimming pool in my garden, so I'm completely at ease measuring and altering the chlorine and pH level. I check them every week. I have a small hand-held machine with digital read-out. I just dip a special test strip into the water and place it on the machine and get an immediate read-out of the pH, chlorine and alkalinity. I then add the correct amount of chemicals to adjust the levels. I have pH plus and pH minus chemicals to adjust the pH level and chlorine tablets. It's very straightforward. I can do it for you once a week, or teach someone here to do it. So I believe we can easily alter the properties of the pond water to make it a successful source for BioEnerFuels' fuel cell and so be able to generate positive ions for the Pevi. But, once we have altered the water's properties, we still need Rick to test another sample at the labs to confirm the theory and, of course, the other problem is how we get hold of one of their fuel cells. I'm very wary about telling the truth to Dr Macferson; the fewer people who know about the fairies and Pevi the better as far as I'm concerned. It's important you keep your privacy and your existence secret, and I don't want Rick to jeopardise his job by telling fantastic stories about fairies and Pevi living in Knole Park in Sevenoaks. Rick, any ideas?'

Rick explained that he had three dilemmas. The first was how to tell Wei and Dr Macferson about Theodore's analysis, which was obviously a serious breach of company confidentiality, but the results were spectacular and vital for the fuel cell project. The second was how to retest the pond water, once it had been optimised, without getting sacked. The third was how to acquire a microbial fuel cell for installation at the frog pond.

Theodore proposed that he explained his analysis to Rick in more technical detail. Rick could pretend that he had been teaching himself multivariate statistics at home and had come in on Saturday to try out his new skills and had undertaken the analysis himself using a statistical textbook and the software manual. That should work and solve the first dilemma. Theodore further proposed Rick suggested to Dr Macferson that, to test his statistical hypothesis, he could alter the pond water in his friend's pond so that it conformed to the results of his study and retest it. If the modified water was transformed into a good source for the fuel cell, then Rick's theory would have been irrevocably proved, and this would be a fantastic step forward for BioEnerFuels' future research. Everyone thought this was a good plan. How to obtain a working fuel cell was more difficult to solve at the moment, but perhaps an opportunity would arrive in the not too distant future.

So a plan of action was agreed. First Kathleen would use her swimming pool expertise to alter the pH and chlorine levels in the frog pond. Once she had got the water stabilised in the correct range, Rick would add the sample of MFWS2. They would then wait a couple of days to allow the MFWS2 to multiply and Rick would then take a new set of samples to analyse in the labs. Kathleen immediately set off for home to get the pool chemicals and measurement machine she needed. She estimated that the frog pond held a smaller amount of water than her pool, probably about half the volume, so she did some mental calculations to determine how much pH plus and chlorine she would need to add to optimise the values of these properties. Luckily, Robert was playing golf this afternoon, so she would not bump into him and have to explain her actions.

Late that afternoon the chemical properties of the pond water had been optimised by Kathleen, and Rick added the sample of MFWS2 that they had stolen from the labs. The frogs were curious about what was going on and Coralie explained that the owners of the park had brought in some ecology experts to improve the quality of water in the pond, for the benefit of the frogs, the plants and other wildlife that lived in and around the pond. That reassured them.

So far, so good, she thought.

Kathleen was keen to get home to Robert as she had been out almost all day and it was Saturday, so she really had no excuse for her absence. He would be home by now, wondering where she was. She hoped he had won at golf. They were going to dinner with friends tonight and she wanted him to be in a good mood. This, she realised, was now pretty unlikely and it was her fault for being late home because, at the moment, she cared more about the Pevi's health than her home life.

27

Kathleen began her online investigation into the properties of rapeseed Monday morning. She visited the Wikipedia website and discovered that rapeseed was grown primarily for its oil and that Europe was a major producer of the oil. Apparently, the UK had produced more than one million metric tons of the oil in 2000, which seemed quite a lot to her.

Historically, the oil was produced as early as the nineteenth century as a lubricant for engines. The early varieties were bitter to taste because of high levels of chemicals called "glucosinolates", so were not useful for animal feed. However, as a result of genetic engineering, newer varieties have been developed that contain fewer of these chemicals, making the oil palatable for humans and animals.

Nowadays, rapeseed is a valuable cash crop used for animal feed, vegetable oil for human consumption and biodiesel. Currently, about two-thirds of rapeseed oil is used for biodiesel in Europe and this is likely to rise over time as more and better engines are developed that can run on biodiesel. When rapeseed is processed to extract the oil, it produces a high-protein by-product which is used as animal feed. Livestock are even allowed to graze directly on the rapeseed plant on certain farms. It is also a useful crop to provide cover for the soil in winter and limit nitrogen run-off and soil erosion. The plant can be ploughed back into the soil in winter, so increasing its fertility.

Well, this explains the importance of this field trial that is designed to genetically engineer rapeseed which has two harvests a year. The economic implications must be enormous, she realised. *This really is a useful crop, but, like Coralie, I hate the smell, the gaudy colour and the way it spreads to invade hedgerows and roundabouts, ruining the subtle colours of our English countryside.*

But there were also downsides with the crop, she

discovered. Rapeseed pollen contained known allergens and had been implicated in asthma, though this was unproven. This could be useful ammunition, she surmised, if she needed to launch a protest group to get the field trial stopped.

Kathleen also found a list of animal pests and diseases that attack rapeseed, which she decided could be useful information if she wanted to find a way to sabotage the trial directly and cause a negative outcome. However, she had not yet decided whether or not to intervene on behalf of the Pevi and if so, just how to intervene. This was a problem she had not yet resolved. Obviously, she could not and did not want to interfere with the advancement of science and rapeseed was clearly making a valuable contribution to the planet's future. On the other hand, she was fascinated by the delightful Pevi and wanted them to be able to remain in Knole Park, on her doorstep.

She decided to drive out to the field trial site and take a look around for herself. She donned a raincoat before leaving home because the dark clouds in the sky looked menacing, grabbed her handbag and jumped into her Audi. She soon found the site of the field trial and parked in a lay-by nearby. The first few drops of rain fell as she got out of her car, but undeterred, she fastened her raincoat tightly and went to investigate the field of rapeseed. She noticed a light shining from the Portacabin at the far side of the field so decided to go and have a chat with whoever was there. The heavens opened at that moment and she was drenched by the time she reached the Portacabin. The door opened before she had time to knock and a man's head pocked out.

'Hello. Can I help you? You better come inside quickly, you look absolutely drenched.'

He spoke with an educated accent and Kathleen judged that the man was of a similar age to herself. Not good looking, she observed, but he had a nice lopsided smile and perfect white teeth that looked far too white to be real. There was a strong smell of fresh coffee emanating from the Portacabin.

'Hello and thank you, I would like to come in out of the

rain for a moment, if I'm not inconveniencing you. My name is Kathleen Morgan and I live just down the road in Sevenoaks. I couldn't help noticing that you have a field of what appears to be rapeseed growing here, but it's flowering now, in October, which is not normal. Normally, it flowers in late spring. I was just curious, so I stopped to have a closer look and got caught in this heavy rain shower. The coffee smells good. You wouldn't have a spare cup would you?'

'Yes of course. It's San Marco, my favourite. How do you take it? Espresso?'

'Perfect, thank you. No sugar,' replied Kathleen, pleased that the man seemed friendly and that she now had the opportunity for a chat with him to discover more about what was going on here.

'I'm Brian, by the way, Dr Brian Burton.'

Brian directed Kathleen to a spare chair on the other side of his desk and then made her an espresso and another one for himself. He sat down behind his desk, opposite her, and smiled warmly. He loved talking about his research and he sensed that he had a receptive ear in Kathleen. She was obviously curious about his experiments and he was happy to tell her about the research now all the patents had been filed and the inventions were protected by law. He believed that it was important that the local community learnt to live alongside genetically-modified crops without panicking that the crops would somehow be deleterious to their health. There was a high level of ignorance among the general unscientific population about genetic engineering. They perceived high levels of peril associated with this science which, in his view, was completely unjustified and based on mass hysteria rather than proof or logic. Someone had broken a window in the Portacabin on Friday and had rearranged his papers. Nothing seemed to be missing, but he was aware that he needed as many friends as he could get in the region if Genrapmod was going to be left in peace.

'So, you have noticed our project here, Kathleen. My company, Genrapmod, is developing a new variety of rapeseed that flowers and makes seeds twice a year, so doubling the annual harvest yield. I'm CEO of Genrapmod by the way. I started the company two years ago with venture capital investment money. It's a wonderful project we are working on that will help relieve the pressure on the limited amount of agricultural land around here. Kent is so densely populated and the population is growing as more northerners move south in search of work and a warmer climate. The pressure on agricultural land is enormous in this region and more and more of the green belt land around London is being built on, so reducing the amount of agricultural land available for planting. This project is very important to the local farming community and to the optimisation of land use to maximise production. I'm very excited to be in charge of this project that will benefit so many farmers here in the UK, but also worldwide. Of course, the other major benefit is that rapeseed exploitation will be good in the longer term for the environment. Rapeseed is fast becoming an important fuel source for transport and this will increase significantly over the next few years, making a huge improvement for the environment by reducing our dependence on fossil fuels.'

Oh hell, thought Kathleen. *This really seems like a worthwhile project. Now I'm in a real dilemma about what to think or do. Shit, shit, shit.*

Kathleen finished her excellent coffee and smiled at Brian.

'Thank you for the coffee and thank you for telling me about your project here. I'm genuinely interested in the application of genetic engineering to crops in order to improve yields and help feed the world's growing population. I think it's a fascinating new science with enormous potential to do good, if properly controlled. There needs to be more public debate and education about this science. I'm not someone who throws their hands up in horror when genetically-modified crops are mentioned. I have a degree in chemistry and used to work in pharmaceutical research several years ago, so I can understand the basics of the techniques involved and the perceived risks. I even read *New Scientist* now and again to keep informed about what's new in the world of science. I guess I'm a semi-informed member of the public. So how's the project going? Is it a success so far? The crop looks healthy, as far as I could tell.'

Brian had no intention of telling her about any of the negative results from the trial and there had been a few areas for concern. He was only prepared to tell the good news. After all, Kathleen may pretend to be an innocent member of the public with an interest in rapeseed, but he didn't know her, and she may possibly be a reporter, or an active member of some radical environment protection group lobbying against genetic engineering.

'Everything is going really well, the outcome is better than we had hoped and there are no negative indications at all,' he lied. 'Now, if you will excuse me, I have to get on with my work. It has been very pleasant meeting you. Thank you for your interest in our project. Goodbye.'

'Goodbye and thanks again for the excellent coffee.'

Kathleen walked back to her car around the, now muddy, field. The rain had stopped, but the downpour had left huge puddles of water in the small path next to the field of rapeseed. She had a second, closer look at the plants and thought how healthy they looked despite the relatively dry summer they had had this year. She was unsurprised that the trial was going well; there was no sign of disease or pests in the plants.

Shit, she thought again. *How can I help the Pevi?*

Brian watched her leave from the window in the Portacabin. He was relieved that she did not take any photographs, or remove any samples from the field. Perhaps she was just an interested member of the public, with no secret issue. She was rather attractive and he hoped their paths would cross again sometime in the not too distant future, when he wasn't so busy with writing his business plan for top-up funding, and planning the company's next few press-releases to keep the venture capitalists interested. He also lived in Sevenoaks, so it was highly likely they would meet again at some point in time.

197

Kathleen sat in her car, looking at the view from the lay-by. She loved the countryside around Sevenoaks. It wasn't awe-inspiring, but it was English, very English, with the low hills of the North Downs and their characteristic chalk soil, the rolling Weald of Kent, the wonderful beech woods, the small fields of crops and pasture land. Her heart was firmly embedded in this county. And, she didn't like rapeseed invading her dream landscape.

She sat a moment longer, reflecting on her meeting with Dr Brian Burton. She felt safe in her car, it was a good place to think. It was her refuge and hers alone. She never let Robert drive it. Her mind wandered over their brief meeting. He hadn't told her anything particularly new, that she didn't know already from the fairies and she hadn't said very much at all. She had probably wasted her time.

As she drove home, she resolved to cook Robert his favourite meal tonight, Dover sole with lemon juice, soy sauce and spring onions, and pick up something special for dessert at Waitrose. All washed down with a nice bottle or two of Pouilly Fumé and end the evening with an early night. She would take trouble with her appearance and wear her favourite short red dress. She hoped he had had a successful day at work and that a nice dinner at home would help him to see her as a woman again.

28

Rick had spent the rest of the weekend reading up about the statistical methods that Theodore had used to determine the key properties for a successful pond water sample. Luckily, his mathematical skills were fairly good and he could just about get his head around the complex methods described in the textbook. The two methods Theodore had specifically told him about, were called non-linear discriminant analysis and non-linear regression. The methods were complimentary to each other, but used different algorithms. They had been applied by Theodore to create a predictive model that could estimate whether a sample would be successful or not. Both methods had identified the same set of important properties for a successful sample; the pH range, chlorine concentration, oxygen content, and presence of MFWS2. Therefore, Theodore was confident in the results.

Monday morning, while Kathleen was visiting the rapeseed field trial, Rick showed the results of the analysis to Wei. She was surprised and very impressed with his level of knowledge and excited by the results. Once he had tested out his story on Wei, he felt confident about tackling Dr Macferson. She also fell for his story and sat down at the computer to reassure herself that as far as she could tell the models were correct. She was pleased at his commitment to the project and that he had worked on Saturday to try out his new skills. He greatly went up in her estimation. She also agreed to his idea of using samples from his friend's pond to test the accuracy of the models and see if they could turn a poor sample into a successful sample.

'What a wonderful experiment that would make,' she concurred. 'That would certainly prove your hypothesis to me.' So they agreed that he should alter the pH and chlorine levels to fit in the optimal range and then add a sample of

MFWS2 to his friend's pond. They would retest the pond water two days later. If everything worked out as the models predicted, it would greatly benefit the fund-raising and speed at which the company's research and development could progress. She should also start to write a new patent on their technology based on Rick's findings.

Rick left the labs early, supposedly to visit his friend's pond and to start its transformation into a successful sample. In reality, he went home for a siesta, which was much needed after such a stressful and busy weekend.

On the way into work on Wednesday morning, Rick took two more samples from the frog pond. The pH and chlorine levels were still correct according to Kathleen's digital instrument and hopefully, the MFWS2 had had sufficient time to populate the pond. He'd have to wait till the results from the formal laboratory analysis were completed on Thursday to confirm that assumption.

Wei retested the samples on Wednesday and confirmed that the levels of all chemicals and other readings were comparable to the previous analysis. The only significant changes were the chlorine level, which had increased slightly, and the pH, which was now slightly higher. Both readings were at the required level for the model to predict a successful result. She also confirmed the presence of MFWS2 micro-organisms. Everything was as he had hoped for. The only question now was whether or not the sample would be successful in practice at generating electricity and clean water. And, more importantly to Rick, whether it would generate the by-product of positive ions, which were of no interest to BioEnerFuels, but of great interest to his friends the Pevi. That they would know tomorrow.

Thursday afternoon, he received the news he had been hoping for. The pond water samples had been converted from an unsuccessful source for the fuel cell into a highly successful source, equivalent to the best Sierra Leone samples.

Hurray, hurray, hurray, he thought.

Rick immediately emailed the news to Kathleen and then went to the pub with Wei and Dr Macferson to celebrate. Dr Macferson was delighted that Rick's statistical analysis had been proven correct and declared that the drinks were on her, and Wei and Rick should take a well-deserved day off work tomorrow. She would begin to write the patent that described the properties required for a successful water sample for their microbial fuel cell. Both Rick and Wei would be cited as co-inventors for their contribution to the development of the chemical and statistical analysis methods that had enabled a definitive description of the water properties required.

BioEnerFuels now had alpha microbial fuel cells which functioned in the lab, a beta version under development for use in the field in Africa, a knowledge of what pond water would work, and how to transform a pond which had the wrong characteristics. Dr Macferson's long-held vision, of poor remote communities in Africa or Asia having access to electricity and clean water, had made an enormous step forward this week. She wished that she had not reprimanded Rick for smuggling in his friend's two samples, but the unexpected outcome had been better than she could have dreamed. What an asset Rick had turned out to be for the company, despite his lack of a scientific degree. His motivation and initiative were worth far more than a certificate of education.

Rick's only problem now, was how to obtain one of the fuel cells to install at the frog pond. He certainly was not going to steal one of their precious machines and risk losing his job, or worst, being accused of being a thief. His mind began working overtime, wondering how he could acquire a machine. The engineering technicians were currently developing a beta version for use in the field and as far as he knew, it was nearly ready for testing. He really wanted one of these, because the alpha models they used in the lab probably weren't robust enough to be left outside for a long period, subject to the elements. He decided to go and chat to the technicians in the next lab the following week. It would be useful to get to know them better anyway. In the meantime, he was looking forward to taking Friday off work and enjoying a well-deserved long weekend.

He phoned Kathleen when he got home and arranged to meet up Saturday morning for coffee in Sevenoaks. They had two important issues to discuss: what to do about the rapeseed field trial and how to obtain a beta fuel cell from BioEnerFuels. Wei was a keen hiker and she had tentatively asked him whether he would like to go for a walk along the North Downs Way on Friday and have lunch in a nice pub en route, but Rick had more important things on his mind and had declined her invitation. He did not want to complicate the good working relationship he had with Wei. He hoped he had not upset her too much, because he valued her friendship and support at work. Anyway, his thoughts and dreams were firmly focussed on his relationship with Kathleen and resolving their immediate future together.

Rick spent the evening sitting in front of the television with his parents. He stared blankly at the screen, seeing, but not registering, the events that passed before his eyes; his mind was elsewhere. His parents, Olive and Cyril, were pleased to have his company for the evening, even if he was a trifle quiet and preoccupied. It was nice to be all together. They were so very proud of his achievements at work this week and delighted that his efforts had been rewarded by Dr Macferson, by giving him Friday off work and including him as an inventor on a new patent application.

29

Rick met Kathleen as planned on Saturday morning. They enjoyed a coffee together in their usual haunt and chatted around their dilemmas concerning the Pevi and the rapeseed, but they failed to find any sure-fire solutions. The chemistry between them was getting stronger each time they met. However, neither of them were brave enough to bring up the important issue concerning their own relationship, it was far simpler to focus on someone else's problems and just enjoy the warm feeling of being together.

Kathleen had been doing some amateur research into psychoanalysis during the week and was keen to present this to Rick. She told him that Robert had been on a management training course two years ago which was based on "Transactional Analysis". She had become interested in the topic and had read the literature he was given on the course. It seemed to her to be a method of understanding people and situations that was highly intuitive, and easy to interpret and apply. She wanted to explain to him how she thought it impacted on their relationship with the fairies and Pevi.

'A transaction is described as *one person saying something to someone else and that second person responding,*' she explained. 'So, Transactional Analysis focuses on the way individuals relate to each other and the stance they take during a discussion or debate. Essentially, people adopt one of three basic states when they communicate: child, adult or parent. There are positive and negative sides to the child and parent states; but the adult is always rational and logical, trying to put the facts forward clearly and unemotionally, and is ready to defuse any potential conflict.'

Rick thought she looked exceptionally alluring when she was being serious and talking about something that interested her. He was watching the way her eyes sparkled as she explained her research and he was finding it hard to concentrate on what she was saying.

'We all see situations in which children can be excited and inquisitive,' she continued. 'This is their positive side and when they contribute new ideas and light-heartedness into a conversation. People with these characteristics can become creative scientists by the way. But the downside is that children can be petulant, illogical and stamp their feet in rage, or possibly worse, just do as they are told without questioning. These are their two negative states.'

'This is interesting, but where is it going?' enquired Rick.

'Just wait. Hang on a moment and you will see,' she replied with a smile. 'So, now we get to parents. Like children, they have a positive side which is caring and supportive, so parents can motivate the person they are talking to or give them confidence. But they can also be disciplinarian and tell people what to do with no explanation. Sort of "I'm older than you, or I'm superior to you, so you have to do as I say". This is their negative state and, obviously, it is very bad in business situations. Do you follow me so far?'

'Yes, I think so. Adults are good communicators, but children and parents can have a positive or negative side. Right?'

'Yes, that's correct. So to continue. Essentially, constructive communication can only occur between two people when they are in certain states, positive states. For example, when two people who are in their adult state communicate, the result is a purely logical discussion. Everyone understands what is going on and no one gets aggressive or has their feelings hurt. When two people are being intimate or having fun together, they tend to be in their positive child states. Like you and Juliet would have communicated, when you were on a date.'

Kathleen had wanted to say, "Like you and me communicate when we are on a date", but had changed her mind at the last moment. She paused to take a sip of her coffee which was now cold because she had been talking so much.

'Similarly, an adult may talk to a positive child or a positive parent and have a constructive discussion without misunderstandings. The problem comes when one, or worse, both of the participants are in a negative state, then this results in a series of negative transactions causing disputes and misunderstandings to happen. Discussions played out at this level are disharmonious and disruptive for industry. Therefore, Robert's firm sent the senior managers on a Transactional Analysis course, so they could better interpret discussions, realise when a discussion was going wrong because someone was responding from a negative state, and take correcting action. I found all this really fascinating and easy to relate to.'

'Sorry, am I boring you? Do you want another coffee?' Rick shook his head to both questions. 'I haven't got to the crux of the matter yet, how it all relates to us and the fairies, but hang on a bit longer and I'll get there.'

'Everyone spends different amounts of time in the various states and, if you can analyse this, it's easier to understand the characters of your staff and help bring out the positive sides of their personalities. Well, in order to see the fairies, I believe we have to enter our positive child state and I found this quite natural, but it was harder for you because I think you spend most of your time in your adult state. I may be older, but I'm not as adult as you,' she said with an ironic smile.

'So basically, you think my predominant characteristic is that I talk and act like an adult,' Rick remarked. 'Could be worse. I admit that I have been practising trying to look at life and nature through a child's eye since we first met the fairies and I failed to see them. Your hypothesis seems to confirm that I have achieved this to some extent and now I can see the fairies, like you. But you also said that the child state was important for scientific innovation. And I'm a scientist. So will I now become a better scientist from having re-awakened my child state?'

'Yes, it's important for scientists to be in touch with their inner child because many talented scientists have their best ideas when in their child states, or so the theory goes. Obviously, they need to have a strong adult component to their personality too, to do a good thorough job, but it is probably the positive child that is the most creative. Who knows, one day you may even get a *Nobel Prize in Chemistry* because our meeting with the fairies may have indirectly made you a better scientist.' Kathleen and Rick both laughed at this notion.

'Then what do I say in my acceptance speech? Who do I thank?' he enquired with a big grin.

'I even have an inkling that the Pevi may be more adult and the fairies are predominantly child personalities, with the exception of Theodore, and possibly Coralie, who don't fit my theory. The fairies, in general, don't take life too seriously and seem to be fun-loving relatively superficial beings; while the Pevi have extensive archives of information and are interested in understanding and solving problems in a structured and intelligent way. It's hard to think of Pevi as adults because of their physical appearance, but hey, appearances can be misleading. Don't quote me on any of this will you?' Kathleen joked.

Rick was mulling over what Kathleen had proposed and how it related personally to him. He saw himself as a logical practical scientist who liked creating things and especially things that would be useful and benefit humanity.

'I suppose you could call me a "practical engineer with visionary intent",' he stated.

'Then you're a PEVI, just as I suspected,' she exclaimed and they both laughed again.

'Wow, that was a long intellectual discussion for a Saturday morning,' Rick observed. 'I think our friendship has just taken on a new dimension. I'm going to be very adult now and say, "hadn't you better be going or you won't be home in time for lunch?" I don't want you to go, by the way. I've really enjoyed hearing about Transactional Analysis, even if it was from an *amateur* psychologist. I will observe my work colleagues more closely next week and see if I can understand them better. May I kiss you goodbye or is it a bit public here?'

'I will imagine a virtual kiss, thank you. It is definitely too public here,' she teased.

They parted at 11:30 am without achieving any clear way forward for the Pevi, but understanding more about each other and their friends in the park. Kathleen went shopping to buy food for lunch and dinner, but while she was on her way to Waitrose, Robert phoned her mobile to say he was going out to play golf and would be home late afternoon. They were short of several basic items in the larder and had nothing special for dinner, so she continued to Waitrose anyway.

Rick went for a walk in the park, hoping to find inspiration about the Pevi's dilemma, but finding none. What he did find, however, as he was about to leave the park and walk home, was a very sick Pevi. He was alerted to the problem by the sound of a tiny weak cry, just as he approached the park gates. Rick stopped and listened carefully. There it was again: a tiny plea for help. He parted the long grass near his feet and thought he saw a weak glow of yellow light, a Pevi in trouble. He carefully picked up the tiny creature and held it gently in his warm hands, hoping his body heat may revive it. *What to do? Phone Kathleen, who will probably still be shopping in Sevenoaks.* He got out his mobile phone and speed-dialled Kathleen. She took an age to answer her phone because she was at the checkout in Waitrose. She promised she would come directly to meet him by the gate and would be there in less than ten minutes.

Rick held the Pevi gently and prayed that it would not die. He wondered if the end was near for all the Pevi. *Have I and Kathleen been too slow in helping to find a solution to their atmospheric problem?* Kathleen arrived eight minutes later, at a run, panting and out of breath. She took Rick directly to the secret location where the fairy palace was built and called urgently for Coralie. Coralie emerged through the front door, bleary-eyed and looking a bit dishevelled; she had obviously been having a much-needed lie-in and had been disturbed by Kathleen's cries for help. She immediately recognised the sick Pevi to be Laura, Edmund's wife, who was usually full of energy and fun. Seeing her so weak, with her aura fading slowly, was very distressing for Coralie.

Coralie took Laura from Rick's hand and carried her into the fairy palace. She laid her gently on a bed of goldfinch feathers in the guest room and brewed a sweet-smelling potion that she hoped would give Laura strength and warm her body. Some fairy magic worked for the Pevi, but this new sickness caused by the rapeseed and low positive-ion concentration was problematic to treat effectively. Coralie had failed to cure Gwyn, though the other sick Pevi in Gwyn's team had revived under her careful administrations. Pablo was summoned and sent to visit the Pevi community to fetch Edmund and verify that this was an isolated incident and the other Pevi were fit and well. He soon returned with a long face. He had arrived at the community and found all the Pevi had taken to their beds suffering from extreme weakness. It would appear that the positive-ion concentration had dropped below a critical level, weakening their immune systems and the rapeseed pollen was now killing them. He urged Coralie quickly to brew more of her magic warming potion and take it to the Pevi post-haste.

Kathleen and Rick stood watching with ever-lengthening faces, wondering how to help. Rick made a brave decision. In his heart, he knew that the Pevi were more important than his job. There was no time to lose. He would go immediately to the labs and steal a fuel cell to generate positive ions for them and give them strength to fight the rapeseed poison. It was Saturday, so hopefully no one would be in the labs. He would work out a plan of action en route. Kathleen drove him home and he leapt on his motorbike that was parked in the front garden, and set off for Sittingbourne at high speed, ignoring the thirty miles an hour speed limit. He soon arrived at the labs, hoping he had not been caught on any speed cameras. The man at the security hut was having his lunch and waved him through; he and his rather distinctive Norton motorbike were now well known by all the security guards on-site. He parked his bike behind the labs, well out of sight of the security guard. He flashed his security card over the card reader and the door unlocked to let him in.

Rick went straight to his lab, opened the big storage cupboard and picked up one of the oldest alpha fuel cells, "Number two", that was due to be decommissioned because it had become unreliable. The digital readout sometimes gave grossly inaccurate readings but, as far as he was aware, the fuel cell itself still functioned properly and produced positive ions, electricity and clean water from pond water. He felt vindicated for his actions by choosing the machine that was now of limited use to BioEnerFuels. He returned to his motorbike and put the machine in his pannier. He breathed a sigh of relief when it just fitted. He had already realised on the way over that he couldn't steal a beta version of the equipment because it would be too big to fit in his pannier. He just hoped that the old alpha model would do the trick and work, at least for a few weeks, in the open air in Knole Park.

He was just about to jump on his bike and leave when Dr Macferson drove up in her BMW 3 series estate car. *Fuck.*

'Hello Rick. You're very keen coming in on a Saturday *again*. I thought you would be spending your long weekend away from the labs. Why have you come in today?'

Rick mentioned something confused about leaving his wallet in the labs and coming in to look for it. His voice was shaky and Dr Macferson knew very well that he was lying.

'Did you find what you were looking for?' she enquired.

'Yes, thank you. Sorry, I must go, I have an appointment. Goodbye.' And with that, he mounted his bike and rode away.

Well, I wonder what he has been up to, thought Dr Macferson. *I'd better take a look around the labs.*

Rick rode straight back to Knole and parked as near the frog pond as he could. He lifted the fuel cell out of his pannier and carried it over to the edge of the pond. A loud chorus of agitated angry croaking started up. Rick knew that once the fuel cell was set up properly and was treating the pond water, it would create sufficient electricity to power itself. In principle, it could run continuously under the correct conditions, until some component or other malfunctioned. It needed power from a small AA battery to get started, but then became self-sufficient.

Rick looked up to the heavens for help and then began setting up the fuel cell, so the water was filtered and then flowed through the system, and the electricity generated was ploughed back into the cell to keep it running. He prized opened the cavity that trapped the positive ions with his pen knife, so allowing the positive ions to escape into the air. Then, he took a deep breath and pressed the start button. To his delight, the fuel cell sprang into life and began slowly taking in water and creating electricity. He had no way to monitor whether or not it was successfully producing positive ions as there was no digital readout for this function on the alpha model; so all he could do was hope for the best. He carefully covered it with some bracken, then run at full speed to the fairy palace hoping to find Kathleen, Laura and Coralie.

Kathleen and Coralie were nowhere to be found. He guessed they were at the Pevi community, helping the sick Pevi, but he didn't know where that was. He wondered whether Laura was still in the palace or whether they had taken her back to the Pevi community to be near Edmund. He couldn't enter the palace which was protected with powerful spells, so that question went unanswered for the moment. For a second he wondered what to do. The blindingly obvious solution he realised was to phone Kathleen's mobile; which he did, and she immediately returned to the palace to find him. Kathleen explained that all the Pevi were being treated in a kind of field hospital by Coralie, but Coralie was very stressed as she was working in the dark and didn't know for sure what herbs and spells were the best to use in this case.

Rick explained, 'I've successfully installed the fuel cell by the pond and it seems to be working OK, much to my relief. What I'd like is to take one of the Pevi to the pond to breathe in the positive ions and see if this restores its strength. What do you think? It's the only sensible plan we have.'

Kathleen led him directly to the Pevi field hospital where they found rows of beds neatly lined up, each containing a sick Pevi. No Pevi had escaped the sickness. The fairies, Zak, Benjie, Chantal and Pablo were there, helping Coralie as best they could. Coralie had found an old nurse's uniform in her dressing-up chest and looked quite the part, just like Florence Nightingale. Zak was endeavouring to keep everyone's spirits up by telling an endless stream of silly knock-knock jokes, often in poor taste considering the gravity of the situation. However, he was also being useful by helping Benjie to find extra blankets to keep the Pevi warm. Chantal and Pablo were busy helping brew and administer Coralie's potions. It was a hive of activity.

Kathleen and Rick conveyed Rick's plan to a frantic Coralie and Pablo. After a moment's discussion, it was decided to carry one of the least sick Pevi to the pond to be a guinea pig, as Coralie was loathe to move any of the really weak ones. Coralie decided that Eleanor was the best candidate and she willingly agreed to try out this experimental therapy.

Carefully, Rick cradled Eleanor in the palm of his hand and carried her the half mile to the pond. By now the frogs were really agitated and were spitting at the new-fangled machine that had been placed next to their watery haven. Rick ignored them and gently lowered Eleanor so she was close to the positive-ion outlet. She closed her eyes and breathed as deeply as she could. Rick felt her gentle breath against his hand. After ten minutes, Rick perceived that her breathing became stronger and her breath seemed slightly warmer to him. She was getting stronger. After fifteen minutes he could see that her soft-yellow aura was brighter.

She spoke to him. 'It works. I don't know how long for,

but it works. I feel stronger already. Thank you, Rick. But now the imperative thing is to bring the sickest Pevi here quickly, before their life force declines any further. Quick, we must hurry back to Coralie's field hospital and bring as many Pevi as we can here, to breathe in the magic of your machine.'

Rick ran back to the field hospital as fast as he dared, fearing that a trip could seriously damage Eleanor who he held in his hand.

As soon as they were within hearing distance of the hospital, Eleanor shouted out, 'Quick, bring the sick Pevi. Rick's machine at the frog pond works. I feel much stronger.'

The fairies all breathed a deep sigh of relief.

'OK,' Kathleen commanded. 'If every fairy and human can take as many Pevi as they can safely carry, we'll try to get everyone cured before it gets dark. Let's go to the frog pond now, with the first wave of patients.'

The rest of the afternoon was spent making several trips between the field hospital and the pond. The number of sick Pevi reduced every hour, until everyone had been treated. The frogs accepted the intrusion to their peace and were proud to help in the end. They were not especially friendly with the Pevi, holding them in some contempt because they were so cute, but they were part of the fauna in the park and as such, had every right to be treated fairly, and with compassion when a crisis arose. The frogs were not so happy about having Kathleen and Rick around, but Coralie explained to them that it was, in fact, the humans who had found the way to save the dying Pevi, and they were their good friends, so this reduced the frogs' anxiety significantly.

All the Pevi had recovered their strength and were more or less back to normal fitness by the end of the afternoon. Coralie declared that the field hospital should be dismantled, and then the humans and fairies would celebrate the return to health of their Pevi friends by sharing a few bottles of elderflower wine. She would not allow the Pevi to partake in the celebrations as they needed to rest and certainly not get drunk this evening. So, Kathleen and Rick enjoyed their first party with the small band of fairies who had helped at the field hospital. They found the elderflower wine delicious, if a trifle sweet for their tastes, and it definitely carried a punch. Kathleen and Rick managed to consume about three small bottles each, before collapsing on the grass, unaware just how potent the wine was.

Rick was roused an hour later by two loud beeps announcing the arrival of an SMS text on Kathleen's mobile. He wondered where he was for a moment and then to his horror realised that Kathleen's hand was resting heavily on his crotch and his flies were undone. Her blouse was in disarray, with the top three buttons open, and her bra was exposed. Rick noticed it was a rather expensive-looking lilac satin with ivory lace trim design; very chic and sexy. He gently moved her hand, trying not to rouse her, and did up his flies, then closed the buttons on her blouse, fumbling badly. He looked at the message on her mobile. The text was from Robert.

Shit, he thought. *It is well past seven in the evening and Kathleen has been out all day. Robert must be wondering where the hell she is.*

She looked so relaxed and mellow lying in the soft long grass. Her hair was in complete disarray and she was clearly dreaming about something pleasant as a smile played upon her lips. Rick wondered if she was dreaming about him. He stroked her soft cheek to wake her gently from her slumber. She opened her eyes and looked at him with longing and curiosity. Her eyes were asking him a question, but he didn't know the answer. Rick thought that she was probably unaware of their intimacy caused by the strong wine. He also remembered nothing of what had or hadn't happened between them, and maybe it was simplest if it remained that way for the time being. He handed her her mobile. Kathleen was still drowsy from the wine, but panicked when she saw the text.

How on earth am I going to explain my absence all day to Robert and the fact that I am feeling decidedly woozy from drinking too much of the fairies' wine? she wondered.

The fairies were also sleeping heavily and Zak was holding hands with Benjie on one side and Chantal on the other. The three of them were smiling and their flickering eye movements told Rick they were deep in dreamland. Coralie and Pablo had disappeared. Rick surmised that they had probably returned to the fairy castle to sleep off the effects of the alcohol, if they had any sense.

Kathleen and Rick quickly bade their farewells to each other and both decided it would be safer to walk home and collect their vehicles tomorrow. Kathleen would explain to Robert that her car had broken down and her mobile battery was flat, so she had been unable to phone him or phone the emergency services for help. It was rather a weak excuse, but it would have to do. She would carry home what food she could from the boot of her car, so at least they could have a nice meal together tonight.

30

Rick spent Sunday quietly at home with his parents. He was tired after all the excitement of the day before and just wanted to chill-out and rest.

He rose later than he intended on Monday morning, which meant he would be slightly late for work, but he wasn't too concerned. After all, people at BioEnerFuels were relatively relaxed about each other's time keeping. He showered and dressed quickly, but forewent breakfast, deciding to pop into the canteen at the science park mid-morning to grab a sandwich and coffee with Wei.

He arrived at the Science Park at 9:30 am and waved cheerfully to the security guy. Today, however, he was greeted with a frown and shake of the head. *Curious*, he thought. His electronic pass failed to open the door of the laboratory building, which alerted him to the fact that something might be wrong. The door soon buzzed and opened, however, and he was let in by the secretary. She didn't say anything to him this morning. When he entered the lab he saw Wei sitting at her desk with red-rimmed eyes. She kept her head down and avoided making eye contact with him. Then he saw the reason for everyone's strange behaviour this morning. Dr Macferson was in her office with a man in a grey pin-striped suit, whom he recognized as BioEnerFuels' lawyer, and two other people, one male and one female. All four had serious expressions. Wei told him they were police inspectors, but still avoided his gaze.

Shit, he thought. *That explains everything*. He had dismissed his brief encounter with Dr Macferson on Saturday and this nightmare scenario had not crossed his mind. He had been so preoccupied with the Pevi's plight that he had actually forgotten about the unfortunate encounter just as he was leaving the labs.

Dr Macferson looked up when Rick entered the lab, then continued her discussion with the lawyer and the police officers for a further ten minutes, before summoning Rick into her office.

'So Rick, I think you have a great deal of explaining to do, if you want to keep your job at BioEnerFuels. We have never before employed a thief at this company.'

The lawyer glanced at her and gave a minute shake of his head to imply that she was out of order to accuse Rick of stealing before he had had a chance to defend himself. The police inspectors stood quietly by.

'Can you explain to me what you were doing in the lab on Saturday and why one of our alpha fuel cells has gone missing? Did you take it and if so, when do you intend to return it?'

Rick's mind was racing. What possible excuse could he give that would be believed? He had been found out to be a thief, and worse, he had no intention of returning the fuel cell that the Pevi's continued existence in Knole Park now depended upon. He visibly paled as the four stern faces glared at him, waiting for a response that was not forthcoming. He decided not to say anything, he needed to think first.

'Well?' enquired a furious Dr Macferson. 'Should we take your silence as an admittance of guilt?'

All faces again turned to Rick. Still he said nothing, but he started shaking perceptively.

After what seemed an age, but was probably only a matter of a few minutes, the female police inspector cautioned Rick and he was led away to their awaiting car and driven to Maidstone police station for further questioning. During the car ride, he felt himself falling into a sea of black swirling feathers which were catching in his throat and choking him. He was being engulfed in a deep pit of depression. He was on the scrapheap at eighteen. His parents had been so proud of his A-level exam results and even prouder when he had been offered his first job. They would be so very disappointed in him now. The tears began to collect in his tear ducts.

'It's OK son. You'll be alright. I'm sure there's a good explanation for what happened,' the male police inspector said reassuringly; patting Rick on the shoulder. He had seen some pretty unsavoury youths in Maidstone during his career in the police force and he was pretty sure that Rick was not a thief. He was willing to assume he was innocent before being proved otherwise. The feel of a reassuring touch caused Rick to lose any self-control he had left and he openly wept in the back of the police car. The police inspector handed him a tissue and looked away, watching the countryside speed past as they approached the edge of Maidstone. The weather was dismal and it had started to rain.

Once inside the police station, Rick was led to a small interview room and given a mug of overly-sweet coffee and a cheese and tomato sandwich by a young police constable in uniform. The two police inspectors returned and asked him if he would like to phone anyone, a solicitor or his parents, for instance. He didn't know any solicitors and certainly didn't want someone he didn't know present at the interview. He also didn't want to call his parents; he wanted to put that moment off indefinitely. There was only one person whom he wanted to talk to and that, of course, was Kathleen. He asked to call his friend, Kathleen, and the police agreed and left him alone for a moment to make the call. Kathleen was horrified when she heard his news and agreed to drive straight to the police station to support him. It would take her about forty minutes. The police officers returned after a few minutes and informed him that they would leave him alone, until his friend arrived, so he could compose himself. They then went off to discuss their interview strategy over a cup of tea.

Rick did some deep breathing and slowly felt the panic release its grip on him. He could think of no suitable set of lies to tell. He decided he would just tell the truth and see what happened. At worst he would be sent to a mental institution; at best to prison.

Meanwhile, back at the labs, Dr Macferson and Wei were

trying to understand why Rick had stolen the alpha fuel cell. A careful check of the electronic entry system had been made earlier which confirmed no one else had been in the labs over the weekend, except for Dr Macferson herself. She had arrived just as Rick was leaving and had been suspicious of his actions. She had checked the equipment and found the number two fuel cell to be missing. They agreed that Rick was definitely the perpetrator of the crime and his reaction when confronted with the crime had confirmed their suspicion.

Dr Macferson was convinced that he must have been bought-out by one of their competitors and that he was essentially an industrial spy, working for another company. She knew the investors would be horrified once they knew that one of the alpha fuel cell models had been stolen by an employee at BioEnerFuels and was now in the hands of a competitor. Dr Macferson may even have to offer her resignation.

Wei, however, was still convinced Rick was not a thief. She was especially confused that he had selected the malfunctioning fuel cell, number two, to steal, because he knew that it was not giving accurate readouts. They both agreed that there must be a clue to his intentions in this fact. Wei wondered if he had given the fuel cell to his friend with the animal charity, but they concurred that was unlikely. If he had wanted one for his friend he would have made some enquiries first and not risked losing his job. In fact, Dr Macferson would probably have agreed to give him an old model, like number two, once the patent had been written and filed on Rick's discovery of the key features needed for an effective water sample. She had been so proud to have him on-board and knew he had a great future with the company. She could not understand why he would risk everything? It didn't add up unless he was in the pay of a competitor and could walk straight into another job.

Dr Macferson declared the working day over for Wei and sent her home, but she stayed on to continue work on the new patent application.

The police allowed Kathleen and Rick to spend ten minutes alone together before the formal interview commenced. Rick told Kathleen that he intended to tell the truth; bizarre as it was. She had not come up with a convincing alternative story on the drive over and agreed to support him fully.

The two police inspectors re-entered the room and sat down at the table, opposite Rick and Kathleen. They placed a carafe of water and four glasses on the table. They turned on the tape recorder and formally introduced themselves as Inspectors Joanna Black and David Fountain and asked Rick and Kathleen to do the same. When they had formally cautioned Rick, the female police inspector set the scene.

'My colleague and I were called to the company, BioEnerFuels, at 8:30 am on the morning of Monday 17th October to investigate the disappearance of a piece of equipment from their laboratory. The equipment in question was a fuel cell, described as an "alpha model number two", which had been developed at the company and was considered to be a valuable piece of intellectual property belonging to the company. It was the subject of several patent applications. The company had raised significant funds to develop the equipment for use in Africa and other third-world countries, as a machine to convert pond water into electricity and drinking water. The Chief Scientific Officer of the company claims that the equipment was stolen sometime between Friday evening, when she left the labs at nine pm, and Saturday afternoon, when she discovered the fuel cell was missing. She saw you, Rick Johnston, leaving the labs on Saturday and you appeared to her to be looking guilty about something. You told her that you had left your wallet at work and had come in to collect it, and then you rushed off quickly on your motorbike with two large panniers attached. We analysed the electronic entry system Monday morning and found that you were the only person, apart from Dr Macferson, who had entered the laboratory during this period. What do you have to say?'

Rick glanced at Kathleen, looking for strength. Her heart bled for him. He closed his eyes in concentration and asked if he might tell his story from start to finish without any interruptions, because he wanted to be sure that the police had heard everything he had to say, before they started to interrogate him. Inspector Black looked at her male colleague, who nodded in acquiescence, and she agreed to Rick's request. She was pleased that he had decided to come clean and tell them everything. She just hoped it would be the full truth.

So Rick began his story.

'Back in August, I met a wonderful girl, Juliet Morgan. She is Kathleen's daughter. We met just as friends a couple of times, then after about a week, we started going out, dating. One evening we went to Knole Park in Sevenoaks to be alone together. We were sitting under our favourite tree as night fell, when Juliet was bitten by a snake, an adder, we assumed. Unfortunately, the bite was fatal, because Juliet was allergic to the venom, and she suffered an anaphylactic shock. I phoned the ambulance, but she died just as help arrived.'

Both police inspectors remembered reading about this tragic event in the local paper. They had not realised that this Rick Johnston sitting before them, was that same Rick whom they had read about at the beginning of September.

Rick took a sip of water and then continued.

'I have since become friendly with Juliet's mother, Kathleen, who is here to support me. We have met several times in Sevenoaks to chat about our love for Juliet and to share our memories. I told her all about my new job at BioEnerFuels and we discussed the technology together in Knole Park. Kathleen has a scientific background, so our discussions were reasonably technical in nature. Then, to our complete astonishment, just as we were discussing the technology one day, a fairy introduced herself to us. Please just listen and don't interrupt me for the moment. In fact, there were two fairies and two other beings present. These other beings were called Pevi. That's a French acronym for

Petit Écureuil Volant Invisible, which translates as a small invisible flying squirrel. We could both hear these creatures talk, but I was unable to see them clearly at first. Kathleen, however, could actually see the fairies and Pevi clearly from this first meeting on, once they had told her the necessary technique to open her eyes to their presence. '

'The Pevi are so enchanting, yet intelligent beings. You can't help falling in love with them. We had to help them,' Kathleen interrupted.

Inspectors Black and Fountain exchanged an incredulous look, but remained silent, wondering what on earth was to come next. Great fairy story so far, but they were intrigued how Rick was going to relate it to the stolen fuel cell.

Rick continued, 'Anyway, the fairy queen, who is called Coralie, explained to us why they had chosen to make their presence known to two humans at that particular time. The Pevi and fairies are good friends, and it turned out that the Pevi race had become vulnerable to infection and allergic reactions, because the level of positive ions in the atmosphere had reduced. They need a certain concentration of positive ions in their bodies for their immune system to function efficiently. They would have to leave their home in Knole Park, unless the level of positive ions could be increased, because they were becoming ill. They had overheard our conversations about the fuel cell technology and wondered whether it could be used to save the Pevi race. I should explain to you that fuel cells are important to humans because they produce electricity and clean water using dirty water as their source. However, a by-product of this reaction is the production of positive ions and it was this that interested the Pevi.'

Fascinating, thought Inspector Fountain. *This guy should write a book.* He was looking forward to relating the story to his young daughters tonight, who would be delighted to think there were fairies in Knole Park. *Ha, ha*, he thought, but something was nagging at his conscience and telling him not to be too cynical. Joanna Black was trying hard to retain her formal composure. She didn't dare look at her colleague, in case it made them both laugh out loud. But, both police inspectors remained silent as they had agreed and waited for Rick to continue.

Rick explained how he had tested the pond water in the park at BioEnerFuels and how Professor Theodore had uncovered the hidden relationship which explained why some samples worked and others didn't. He had lied to Dr Macferson and told her that he had discovered the relationship and they had tested his theory by re-analysing the pond water once he and Kathleen had altered its properties. The retest confirmed the accuracy of Professor Theodore's theory and was a major breakthrough for BioEnerFuels' research.

'Dr Macferson immediately decided to write up the results of the statistical analysis as a patent application, citing herself, Wei and me as the inventors. So, although she doesn't know it, the fairies have had a beneficial impact on the company's future and intellectual property.'

Rick paused again for a sip of water. He had noticed that the police officers seemed to be looking slightly less incredulous and were listening intently to him. He was pleased that they had allowed him to continue his story for so long without interruption. When he started recounting the events of the last two months, he had expected to be told to stop telling such outlandish lies well before he got his far.

So far, so good, he thought.

'The fairies and Pevi were delighted with the results, but we didn't know how to acquire a fuel cell so the Pevi could inhale the life-giving positive ions and, anyway, we didn't know at this stage whether or not this approach would actually benefit the Pevi and allow them to stay in Knole Park. I was loathe to approach Dr Macferson directly as I was sure she would never believe me and would only think me seriously deranged if I told her about the Pevi's needs,' Rick explained.

'We also discovered that a field trial was underway just to the west of Sevenoaks to produce genetically-modified rapeseed that flowered in spring and autumn, potentially giving two crops a year, rather than the normal one. Unfortunately, the rapeseed pollen makes the Pevi seriously ill. It even killed a Pevi who slept overnight in the rapeseed field. The pollen is blown into the Park when the wind is from the west. Last Saturday morning I met Kathleen for coffee in Sevenoaks and then went for a walk in the park. I was wondering how I could approach Dr MacFerson to ask for an old fuel cell. However, just as I was leaving the park I found a sick Pevi and, to cut a long story short, discovered that all the Pevi community were seriously weak with rapeseed pollen poisoning and were unable to defend themselves because of the low level of positive ions in their bodies. It was then that I decided I had no alternative but to act on their behalf and go to BioEnerFuels to steal a fuel cell to save them. In my defence, I should mention that I intentionally chose an old one that I knew was due for decommissioning. Well, I installed it in the frog pond and it worked. The Pevi were all taken to inhale the positive ions that it emitted and they were cured of their sickness. The fuel cell is still there. I hope it will function for a while and protect the Pevi community. I am very proud of my actions; I had no alternative option.'

And so he ended his potted history of the last couple of months and waited for the shit to hit the proverbial fan.

Inspector Fountain spoke first.

'Thank you, Rick. That is certainly an amazing story that you told us. I am sure you realise that we will need to verify how much is the truth and how much is fantasy. Mrs Morgan, do you have anything to add?'

'Only, that everything Rick has told you is the truth, as fantastic as it sounds. I have been as closely involved with all these events as Rick has. I am not mad and nor is he.'

The two police inspectors decided to depart for a few minutes to confer what their next course of action should be. They were both strangely entranced by the remarkable story they had just heard and did not want to dismiss it without further investigation, crazy as it seemed. Inspector Fountain suggested that they should first check the frog pond to see if they could find the fuel cell. Then they could visit the gamekeeper at Knole Park to ask him if there were any rumours about the existence of fairies in the park. After all, he must know the park better than anyone else. They decided not to say anything to their superiors until they had some answers to these questions.

Rick was told he would be allowed home after a few formalities, but must stay in the Sevenoaks neighbourhood until further notice. The police would contact him in the next few days, once they had followed up his statement and made a few further investigations of their own. His jubilation was written all over his face. Kathleen drove him home. She was also amazed that the police had apparently taken his statement seriously. Rick's motorbike was still at BioEnerFuels and he would have to collect it at some point, but that could wait a few days.

31

Inspectors Fountain and Black set off for Knole Park once Rick and Kathleen had left the police station. They had cautioned both Rick and Kathleen to avoid Knole Park, so as not to interfere with any police investigations, until they were contacted again by the police in a few days' time.

They went directly to investigate the frog pond on arrival, but could see nothing that resembled the stolen fuel cell. It was just a normal pond surrounded by bracken and bulrushes. Unbeknown to them, the fairies had created an invisible barrier around the fuel cell and the bullfrog's wooden pergola, hiding them from human eyes. Both officers were slightly disappointed as they had secretly wanted to believe Rick's story.

They next went to visit the gamekeeper who lived in the gatehouse. He was at home and in a chatty mood. He invited them inside his historic, but rather run-down house. The gatehouse had a dingy interior, smelt of damp and was obviously occupied by a single male. There were no pretty curtains at the windows or bunches of flowers on the table. No sign of a female touch. Inspector Black was itching to fling open the windows to let some light and fresh air in. She explained to the gamekeeper that, incredulous as it seemed, they had been instructed by their superior to investigate a report that fairies had been seen in the park. That was all the information they were officially able to give anyone at this stage. She thought it was probably a job for psychics, not police officers, but they had to follow up their orders as it was part of a bigger investigation being undertaken by Maidstone police into stolen property in Kent.

The gamekeeper was intrigued and keen to know more, but the police were adamant that they could not divulge any more information. The gamekeeper had been told all about the fairies by his grandfather who had also held the position of gamekeeper at Knole Park. However, before he revealed anything he wanted reassurance that any information he gave the police today was strictly off the record, and he told them he would deny all knowledge of any fairies in the park if he was forced to make an official statement. He did not want his name connected with any investigations into the paranormal. Inspectors Black and Fountain agreed that all information would remain strictly confidential between the three of them at this stage.

The gamekeeper told the police that his grandfather had worked in the park forty years ago and he had been able to see the fairies who lived there. There was a community of about fifty fairies living in the park at that time. His grandfather had been an intelligent kind person, who had regularly conversed with the fairies and cared about their privacy and basic nutritional requirements. He had ensured that the park was well planted with some of the fairies favourite foods, like elder, hazelnut trees and dandelions. His grandfather had told him about the fairies' many customs and festivities and explained that the deer were their friends. He had also described a race of small squirrels who emitted a pale-yellow glow during the day which turned to blue at night, and that they also lived in close proximity to the fairies.

Unfortunately, his grandfather had been unable to pass on the gift of fairy vision to his grandchild and sadly, he lacked the ability to see them or communicate. However, he had seen regular indications of their presence, such as the neatly manicured circular patches of grass which appeared in early September and somehow reminded him of a dance floor. He had even witnessed the spectacular firefly display, which accompanied the fairies September festivities, on one occasion. This year at the end of August, just before and after the manicured patch of grass had appeared, he had noticed that the spiders in the park were spinning pink webs. This was highly irregular and he had no firm explanation, but he supposed that it was probably something to do with decoration for the fairies' party.

The gamekeeper went on to tell the police inspectors that he had seen the young boy whose girlfriend had died in the park of an adder's bite. He explained that he frequently walked in the park with the dead-girl's mother and the gamekeeper believed that these two people could converse with the fairies. He had often seen them deep in apparent conversation with trees and bushes. Their rather strange activity had alerted him to this paranormal possibility and he suggested that the police officers paid them a visit if they wanted to find someone who could talk to fairies.

He made tea for the police inspectors and invited them back for a chat at any time. Before they left, he reminded them that he had told them nothing and bade them farewell.

The police were genuinely pleased that they now had some evidence to support their intuition that Rick had been telling the truth, if it was indeed a remarkable truth. They agreed that he was just not the criminal type and his close friendship with an elegant educated lady, like Kathleen Morgan, confirmed their suspicions that he was a remarkable boy, not a crook. They needed to contact Rick again to help them find the missing fuel cell. Then they might consider discussing everything with their superiors.

They drove to Rick's house and rang the bell. The door was opened by his mother who was in the middle of baking and had her hands covered in flour. She looked surprised at the sight of the two police inspectors and they realised that he had probably not told his parents about this morning's events.

'Good afternoon, madam. We would like a word with your son, if he's in.'

Rick immediately appeared and shooed his confused mother back into the kitchen.

'What's happened?' he asked.

'We would like you to accompany us to Knole Park because we cannot locate the missing fuel cell.'

'Fine. I'll get my coat.'

Rick climbed into the back of the police car. This time he felt much more relaxed.

When they arrived at the frog pond, Rick couldn't see the fuel cell either and realised that Coralie must have put a magic cordon around it to make it invisible and protect it. However, he knew exactly where he had installed it. He fell to his knees and groped around in the bracken by the side of the pond. He soon detected the cold metal casing of the fuel cell and felt the gentle throb of the motor which pumped in the pond water. He could also feel the slight cool draught caused by the flow of positive ions emanating from the equipment. Yes, it was definitely still there, and working. He asked the two police inspectors to join him on the ground and one at a time he guided their hands to feel the machine.

'Right, we'd better get this back to Dr Macferson,' declared Inspector Black.

'No, wait,' retorted the other inspector. 'What about the Pevi? They may still need it.' Rick could hardly believe his ears. Inspector Fountain was definitely on his side.

But, what about Inspector Black? he wondered.

'Yes, you're right,' replied Inspector Black. 'Let's pay a visit to Dr Macferson and tell her what we have found out today. After all, it is she who has to decide what to do with this fuel cell and whether or not to press charges against Rick. We can drop Rick off at home on the way.' Rick, however, decided he would prefer to pay a visit to Kathleen to discuss the latest events.

The police inspectors arrived at BioEnerFuels, just as the secretary was leaving for home. She showed them into Dr Macferson's office, then left to do her weekly supermarket shop for provisions for her family.

Inspector Fountain asked Dr Macferson to maintain an open mind about what he was about to tell her. He further explained that they had not involved any of their superior officers in the case to date because, quite frankly, they did not want to appear foolish in their eyes. He then went on to explain the bizarre revelations made by Rick during their interview with him, how he had been supported one hundred percent by Kathleen Morgan, his dead-girlfriend's mother, and the outcome from their subsequent investigations this afternoon in Knole Park.

Dr Macferson was flabbergasted. For a start, she had not heard about the tragic death of Rick's girlfriend. He had kept that a secret from his work colleagues. She had noticed that he had been reticent to discuss his personal life with herself and Wei and she now realised why. He must still be hurting from his recent loss. But, she thought the stuff about the fairies and the small squirrels had to be a joke, however, the two police inspectors appeared totally serious.

Do they take me for a complete idiot? she wondered.

'So do I correctly understand that you believe Rick's story about the fairies and their little squirrel compatriots, and the interview with the gamekeeper at Knole supports the theory that fairies do exist and are alive and well in Knole Park? This can't be normal police investigative work! Do you want me to drop all charges against Rick to save the Pevi from extinction and accept the loss of the alpha fuel cell? I can't believe this conversation is happening!'

'Yes, madam. You have it in a nutshell,' replied Inspector Fountain. 'But, before you make any decisions, I suggest you accompany us to Knole Park to "see" the fuel cell in action and meet the gamekeeper, who is a pleasant fellow, if a trifle lonely.'

Dr Macferson reluctantly agreed to their request, but suggested she brought Wei. She would appreciate her view on this nonsense. She phoned Wei's mobile and they arranged to meet at the main entrance to Knole Park in an hour's time.

The gamekeeper was surprised to see the police inspectors back again so soon. He welcomed Wei and Dr Macferson into his home and made tea for everyone. He had bought a ginger cake that afternoon and he shared it with his guests. It had been a while since he had entertained so many people in his home at the same time. He reiterated the information he had given the police earlier that afternoon about his grandfather's psychic powers, and spoke about the strange behaviour he had witnessed when Rick and Kathleen were together in the park. He reaffirmed that he was sure they were conversing with the fairies. Wei was entranced by his stories of the fairies' parties and dancing at midnight with disco lighting provided by fireflies. When they left, he again asked them not to tell the media about their conversation. The existence of the fairies was strictly on a need-to-know basis and he did not expect to see any reports in the press. The scientists and police gave their word of honour that his information would be treated in strictest confidence.

The police inspectors then took Wei and Dr Macferson to the frog pond where they also were able to feel, if not see, the fuel cell and the gentle flow of positive ions. Edmund and Laura were there at the time, breathing deeply on the positive-ion flow, empowering their bodies. They listened with interest to the discussion between the police inspectors and scientists, and managed to piece together the problems that had befallen Rick since he had saved every member of the Pevi community on Saturday with this marvellous piece of equipment.

Dr Macferson was clearly in a dilemma about what to do. Her young colleague and the two police inspectors both accepted Rick's story was true and wanted Dr Macferson to drop all charges against him and leave the fuel cell where it was. The police were exceedingly reticent about taking this prosecution any further because of the extraordinary, and undoubtedly negative, press coverage it would receive. It would be bad news for BioEnerFuels and the Maidstone police force. Whether or not Rick retained his position at BioEnerFuels was not their decision to make.

Dr Macferson decided she needed time alone to think and to decide whether or not to include the company's lawyer in the discussions. He was already aware that the fuel cell had gone missing. She agreed to pay a visit to Maidstone police station the following morning to report her decision. She decided to take a wander around the park and reflect on the events of the afternoon. She did not believe in fairies or Pevi, but was being harassed by Wei and the police to accept this ridiculous story. It was dusk and the park did seem rather magical in the fading light. There was a slight mist rising from the grassy banks and the deer were grazing contentedly on the long damp grass. It was tranquil since the tourists had now all left. She strolled along a wide path that led her down the side of the beautiful manor house. The silhouettes of the tall ancient chimneys were magnificent against the dark grey sky. She decided not to think about her dilemma, just let it stew for a few hours. She had found that difficult decisions often resolved themselves better this way, rather than by trying to over-analyse a problem. Although she was a scientist, she had learnt to value and trust her intuition.

'Shit. What the fuck!' she exclaimed. Professor Theodore was sitting on her shoulder and whispering into her left ear.

'A successful pond water sample needs to have the following four properties; a chlorine level of about 0.2 units, a pH between 6.6 and 6.8, a high oxygen content, and it must contain the micro-organism, MFWS2.'

She ignored the voice in her ear. She was a scientist, there was no one around. She must have been thinking out loud.

But, Theodore was not about to give up easily.

'Hello, I'm Professor Theodore, a fairy with expertise in mathematics and physical sciences. I'm Rick's friend. I believe you are familiar with my analysis of your pond water samples. In fact, I think you should cite me as the inventor on your latest patent application: "Professor Theodore; Mathematician, Physical Scientist and a Fairy". That should raise a few eyebrows at the Patent Office.'

Dr Macferson was forced to reconsider her stance on the existence of fairies. She couldn't see anyone, but she could hear someone and feel his breath on her cheek. She could think of no alternative explanation other than she was being spoken to by a fairy, and one with a sense of humour apparently.

'OK, OK. I would like to confirm that I do now believe in fairies. I have been convinced of your existence for ten full seconds, even though I can't see you. The gamekeeper was such a simple soul. I didn't believe his stories about the fairies' parties in September. But you, Professor, have succeeded in breaking down the barriers to my naturally cynical mind and I've let the fairies in. After all, fairies have been talked about for centuries, so why shouldn't they exist? But Pevi, I'm not so sure. Tell me about them.'

'Oh they exist alright. But they nearly died out completely in Knole Park on Saturday, and it was only the quick thinking of your exceptionally intelligent employee that saved their lives. They need your fuel cell to survive here in the park. Please don't turn your back on them. They told me you were in the park, so I came to find you. I understand that Rick is in big trouble with the police for borrowing the fuel cell. Can't you drop the charges against him now you know the truth? He is not a criminal, but a wonderful caring person who had no alternative other than to react the way he did on Saturday, or watch his friends the Pevi die.'

'It's late and I'm tired. I also realise that it has got quite dark and I shouldn't be here alone in the park. Perhaps you will escort me to my car near the main entrance and en route you can tell me all about these curious Pevi friends of yours. I can't believe I'm really talking to a fucking fairy.'

So Professor Theodore escorted Dr Macferson to her car and described the provenance of the Pevi. He knew the history of their journey from Venezuela to Europe and how the fairies had saved them during the Great Fire of London in 1666. She was unable to see Theodore, but heard him clearly. By the time she reached her car it was quite dark and she was glad to have the fairy's company. She bid him farewell and thanked him for his statistical analysis that had proved highly important for the company's intellectual property, but declined to cite him as inventor on the patent. Then she drove home to relax in a long hot bath and decide her course of action. She had already decided to drop the charges against Rick. There was no alternative.

But, should I reinstate him as a scientist in the company? Can I ever fully trust him in the future? she pondered. That question needed an answer.

32

Dr Macferson arrived at Maidstone police station early the following morning. She was directed to an interview room by the officer manning the reception and was soon joined by Inspectors Black and Fountain. She confirmed that she wished to drop all charges against Rick and she completely understood his motivation for removing the fuel cell. The two inspectors were happy and relieved to hear her decision. Nothing need appear in the newspapers and any official talk of fairies living in Knole Park was negated. A good decision all round. She thanked them for their assistance in resolving the matter and departed.

She told Wei about her decision to drop charges against Rick and reinstate him as an employee when she arrived at work, but said nothing of her encounter with Professor Theodore. She was still wary of publicising her newly-found belief in fairies. She then phoned Rick and told him the good news. She told him to report back to work on Thursday, giving everyone a bit of time to calm down and come to terms with recent events. His motorbike was still parked behind the labs where he had left it on Monday morning.

She phoned the company lawyer and told him that Rick had taken the fuel cell home for the weekend to try to mend it, but had panicked when the police were called because he had not asked for her permission first. He had been acting entirely on his own initiative. He was distraught for the trouble he had caused. He was an excellent employee and was to be cited as an inventor on the company's latest patent application, so Dr Macferson was delighted to have him back on board as he had a potentially great career with BioEnerFuels. The lawyer accepted her explanation. He didn't want to attract any avoidable bad publicity for the company.

33

Kathleen lay awake in bed on Tuesday night, unable to sleep. She was delighted that all charges had been dropped against Rick and he had been reinstated at BioEnerFuels and would go back to work on Thursday. Now Kathleen needed to make some hard decisions herself. She had known for some time that she loved Rick and that he returned her love. But their love was a forbidden love. Juliet's death had brought them together and now they were tied together by their shared knowledge of the fairies and Pevi. She realised she was being selfish by wanting him. He was too young, and she needed to turn off her impulsive childish behaviour and switch into logical adult mode.

She phoned him early Wednesday morning and arranged to meet for lunch in the park. She wanted to be somewhere quiet where they could discuss their relationship without fear of being overheard. She put together a picnic basket containing wine, fruit, quiche and sandwiches and waited anxiously for the clock to chime twelve.

They met at 12:30 pm under Rick and Juliet's tree. They kissed deeply and then sat on the grass beneath the tree. Kathleen remarked that the grass had been cut short, presumably to deter any adders from hiding there. Rick noticed that Kathleen looked nervous.

'Is something wrong?' he enquired. 'I thought you would be happy that everything worked out so well for me yesterday and the police and my boss actually believed our amazing story.'

'Of course I'm delighted about the outcome of the investigation, but I need to talk to you about us, Rick. I've been thinking long and hard about our relationship and where it's going. Since Juliet's death, we have both needed each other and drawn strength from each other. I realised last night that I am in love with you.'

Rick was relieved. 'I love you too, you are everything to me. I've been so frightened that you thought of me as a kid, not worthy of your true love.'

Kathleen continued, 'But I asked myself, "When you look at me, who do you see, Juliet or Kathleen, her mother?" When I look at you, I don't see Juliet's boyfriend. Yes, I see Juliet reflected in your eyes sometimes and you keep her alive for me. But I see Rick Johnston, an independent intelligent man starting out in life, with an excellent career ahead of him and so much to live for.'

'But I do see you, Kathleen, not Juliet, she is gone now. I loved her once, but I love you with a love that is much more profound. We get on so well together, we complement each other. Think back to the challenging discussions we have had and the number of times we have laughed out loud. You are so interesting to be with and so, so beautiful. I have never been happier.'

'I know, I do agree with you. But it can't continue. We cannot become lovers in the full sense of the word. I have to be adult about this, Rick. Much as I would love our relationship to develop and mature, it can't. Ours is a love that our social world shuns, a prohibited love. It is the least accepted of all relationships in our little world, here in Sevenoaks. Love between two people of different races, religions or castes is accepted; as is lesbian and gay love. Love between an older man and a young woman is commonplace, but love between an older woman and a young man, that frightens our society. What will your friends think when they come back from university for the Christmas holidays? What will they say when you meet them in the pub with your current girlfriend on your arm and it's me, Juliet's mother. They will never accept me and my Sevenoaks friends will never accept you as my partner. I am deliriously happy now, but we cannot be happy in the longer term.'

'No you're wrong, why should we worry about what other people think? I haven't seen my friends for a few weeks now and I haven't missed them. I want to be in your company, not theirs. I've changed and so have you. We have a wonderful chemistry between us. You are always happy when we're together; you're not happy at home with Robert. He doesn't appreciate you and love you like I do. Please try to see that we can be happy together, we don't need the rest of the world. I earn a reasonable salary and you could go back to work. We can make it work. I don't want to lose you.'

'This is so hard for me, but I have to be strong and realistic; that doesn't come easily to a natural child like me. I want you to be my friend, I want to continue to see you, but we cannot be lovers. I can't leave Robert, he needs my support at this time, he is very depressed. Please think about your future and consider what I've said. I'm sure you will want a family at some time, kids of your own, and I can't give you that. Do you really want a life being shunned by other people, always feeling a misfit? You have so much to offer the world and I don't think that you will find the freedom you need living with me.'

Kathleen poured them both a large glass of wine and they drank copiously.

After several minutes of quiet reflection, Rick finally said, 'I know, I hear what you are saying, but what I feel for you is so powerful, you have shot a bolt straight through my heart. Part of me knows you are right, the logical analytical part, but I want to continue to enjoy being with you. Are you *really* sure this is what you *really* want?'

'Yes, I'm sure.'

'Do you never want me to make love with you, or to wake up in my arms on a spring morning, with the sunlight streaming in through the window and warming our naked bodies?'

Kathleen was unable to answer these questions truthfully, so remained silent. A tear ran slowly down her cheek. Rick correctly interpreted her silence and admired her strength, but he could not just walk away and never see her again.

He asked, 'Can we leave it that we will continue to see each other and I will try my hardest to see you as a friend again, not as a potential lover? It would tear me apart never to see you again.'

'That would make me very happy,' replied Kathleen. 'That's my preferred solution. Our forbidden love should be gently laid to rest. We will never forget what we so nearly had, but "nearly had" is a much happier ending than "regretted".'

34

Once all the worry about the sick Pevi and the stolen alpha fuel cell had died down, Coralie returned her attention to the matter of the nearly-finished pergola that the fairies were making for the frog community. Benjie and his team of carpenters had finished the construction a couple of weeks ago, but she and Chantal had not yet found time to complete the planting. A display of climbing dog roses, passion flowers and ivy had been selected and she knew where to find them growing in the park. Coralie decided they needed to get the planting finished that week, before it got too cold and wintry. She would then present Kathleen's Thames barge to the bullfrog at the weekend when they had finally finished everything to do with the pergola. They would hold an official handing-over ceremony and she would cut a red ribbon to formally open the pergola. She could then extend the magical perimeter hiding the fuel cell and pergola so it included the boat.

The date for the presentation was set for Saturday 22nd October. She contacted Kathleen, who agreed to rise early and carry the boat to the frog pond before the frogs were awake and depart quickly. Coralie would then wait for the frogs to wake up and present them with the sailing barge and cut the ribbon on the pergola. Everything went to plan on the Saturday morning and the young frogs were delighted with their nautical present and the completed pergola. Even the bullfrog looked genuinely pleased and did not say anything sarcastic or dismissive about the Thames Barge. It was not a tea clipper, but it was far better than anything he had imagined the fairies would come up with. Coralie explained that Zak would give them a sailing lesson the next day, once they had had a chance to explore their new acquisition. Then she left them alone to familiarise themselves with their gift, after she had carefully hidden it from human sight behind a magic screen.

Coralie was eager not to hang around too long at the pond because she and Pablo had planned to spend a lazy day sitting in the park, watching the humans feed the deer, and Chantal was at this very moment preparing them a special picnic to enjoy together. She was one of the best cooks in their community, as well as being an outstanding artist. Coralie and Pablo would share a bottle of wine with their meal and snooze off the after-effects in a secluded glade under dappled sunlight. They had had wonderful weather this summer, but now autumn had well and truly arrived, they would not have many more warm sunny days to enjoy together. The colours in the park were taking on their autumnal hues; the greens, pinks and yellows of summer, giving way to oranges and browns. This weekend was probably one of the last opportunities to enjoy some gentle warmth from the low sun, and they did indeed enjoy an excellent picnic together and afternoon snooze as planned.

Sunday also turned out to be a balmy autumnal day and early Sunday morning, Zak and Benjie went down to the frog pond to survey the completed pergola and the associated planting scheme that Coralie and Chantal had finished on Friday. Zak was planning to give the young frogs their first sailing lesson in the Thames barge that the human, Kathleen, had so cleverly found, and in so doing had saved Coralie and the fairies from embarrassment. The pergola was looking quite grand and the bullfrog was sitting contentedly in the shade. The plants were still a bit on the small side, but that would soon rectify itself.

Four young frogs were lined up expectantly on the small wooden jetty at the base of the Pergola, waiting for Zak to arrive. In unison, they all gave an exaggerated salute, then collapsed in a fit of giggles. Zak planned to teach them the fundamentals of sailing first, followed by a lesson on how to use the remote control. They were keen to learn about reading the wind direction and strength, setting the sails accordingly, and steering with the rudder. The latter proved exceptionally difficult for all the frogs as their natural intuition proved completely opposite to what happened in reality, and they repeatedly careered into the muddy bank amid shrieks of laughter. After a couple of hours of learning and laughing together, Zak declared that the lesson was over and the young frog sailors had achieved a lot during their first lesson. He had enjoyed himself immensely and was looking forward to the next session with his eager students. Benjie had also been kept amused by the antics of the sailing lesson. However, he was yet to be convinced that frogs had sufficient intelligence to learn to sail the barge, let alone use the remote control, despite Zak's sterling efforts to teach them. Their team work had been pitiful.

Benjie had invited Zak to lunch, so they set off together back to Benjie's house, feeling that they had achieved a lot that morning and had left behind a happy group of young frog sailors. On the way, Zak told Benjie about the trick he had played on Chantal last Friday morning; hiding the plants she had carefully selected for the pergola and replacing them with a new set of poisonous and half-dead specimens. She had exited her house Friday morning, ready to take the plants down to the pergola for planting, and had been confronted by a horrific sight of twelve ugly brown plants where her top specimens had been carefully arranged Thursday afternoon. She had cried out in shock and grief.

Zak had been hiding in the bushes, watching her reaction. He had immediately leapt from his hiding place, swept her up in his arms and flew her down to the pergola where, to her delight, she saw the healthy plants already lined up ready for planting. She had punched him hard in the stomach, then repented and kissed him on the cheek; furious at his trick and the shock he had given her, but delighted that he had secretly done the heavy work of carrying all the plants to their final destination.

Benjie sometimes worried about Zak and the tricks he enjoyed playing on his fellow fairies, but on the other hand, what was wrong with the occasional bit of fun at someone else's expense, as long as no one was hurt or seriously insulted?

Later that afternoon, Benjie and Zak were warming

themselves in the low hazy sunshine, watching the antics of a few visitors to the park through half-closed eyes. They were feeling soporific after eating a particularly large Sunday lunch that Benjie had cooked for his best friend. Autumn had been superb this year. There had been a few days of rain in September, but overall it had been a beautiful month in Sevenoaks, with warm breezes and cloudless skies: a classic Indian summer. There had also been some rainy days at the start of October, but this weekend was again sunny and warm.

Tourist-watching on a Sunday afternoon was a pleasant harmless sport which they both enjoyed. They had ensconced themselves in a young oak tree near the main car park, so they could get a good view of all the new arrivals: mostly families with kids in tow; some rich Sevenoaks-types, and some less-affluent noisy Lower Riverend-types. The affluent men were discrete in polo shirts and designer jeans with a fading Mediterranean suntan; the ignorant ones proudly displayed their tattooed pink arms and wore garish tracksuits or baggy shorts. In one family, a whale-like mum was even sunbathing in her bra, while the kids ran riot, trampling plants and dropping litter in the undergrowth, oblivious to the normal codes of behaviour in such an idyllic park. They were not ideal visitors to the park. It seemed to Zak and Benjie, that the entire spectrum of English humanity was represented.

Zak began marking the female humans out of ten for looks, demeanour and dress sense, while Benjie was grading the kids for their obedience, or lack of it. After a while, they tired of this sport and lay quietly in the dappled shade of the oak, half-dozing, half-watching, until a sudden jolt woke them from their semi-slumber. Some idiot had backed his car into their tree after having downed a few too many cans of lager in a town pub at lunchtime. The impact had caused Benjie to fall head-first out of the tree and he was lying concussed on the grass with a deep cut on his forehead. Zak was beside himself with anger. His friend was hurt, and the tree was badly damaged and might not survive. The driver drove the car forward a few inches, and then got out to inspect the damage. Not the damage to the young tree, but the damage to his car!

'Not too bad, just a little dent, nothing that will fail an MOT,' he declared. 'Too many trees in this goddamn park anyway. Come on kids, let's set up our picnic over there.'

Zak leapt down from the tree and forcefully kicked the back tyre of the car in anger.

How could this human be so incompetent and ignorant? He went over to Benjie and realised he had suffered a serious blow to the head and was still unconscious. He returned to the car and kicked the back tyre again, deciding to get his revenge by letting the air out of the tyre. He vowed to cause this family some problems, even if it was the last thing he did. He let the air out of one back tyre, then walked round to the other side of the car and unscrewed the dust cap on the other back tyre and pressed hard on the valve to release the pressure. The exiting air hissed reassuringly as the second tyre slowly deflated and Zak felt vindicated. He was focussing all his attention on the valve, not watching his surroundings. Unfortunately, at that exact moment, the father returned to the car in search of a corkscrew and saw the flat tyre.

'Fuck that!' he exclaimed, and planted an almighty kick squarely on the flat rubber tyre.

'Fuck that!' cried Zak, as he felt the full force of the impact from the man's boot and the life force began to ebb from his body.

Benjie was still out cold and did not see the fatal blow to his best friend. He came around half an hour later, to find Zak's lifeless body lying crumpled in the grass by the car, an expression of agony on his face. Benjie was still concussed and shook his head violently to make himself wake up. He could not believe his eyes. He lifted his friend's body and cradled him in his arms, rocking back and forth, and crying violently. Life had been perfect an hour earlier and now his best friend lay cold in his arms. He was beside himself with grief. He saw Shawn grazing nearby and cried out for help. Hearing Benjie's cries, Shawn ambled over towards the car and then saw the dead fairy. Gently, he picked Benjie up in his mouth and placed him on his back. Then he picked up Zak's body and placed it next to Benjie. Shawn walked carefully back to the fairy palace with his sad burden and left Benjie with Zak's body at the entrance. He said nothing, he did not know the right words to say. He walked slowly away, with a heavy heart.

Benjie knocked softly on the door of the palace and waited. Coralie soon answered and her eyes immediately fell on the lifeless body. Zak had been one of her most favourite fairies. He was always in a good mood and laughed easily. He was helpful and fun, even if he was a bit of a prankster at times. She had often sought him out because he could make her laugh, something that Pablo did not do. She had even had a crush on him when she was younger, but he was in love with someone else at that time, and her admiring glances had been too subtle and had gone unnoticed. Now he was lying here before her on the doorstep of her palace, dead.

'What happened?' she enquired.

'I don't know exactly,' replied Benjie. 'We were dozing in a young oak tree by the car park when a human backed his car into the tree. The impact shook the tree and made me fall from my branch. I must have passed out, because when I came round sometime later, I saw Zak lying next to the car, crushed and motionless. The car had two flat tyres, but I don't know what happened, there was no one around. I just can't believe he is dead. He bought such joy to my life. I will miss him terribly.' Then he broke down in tears again and Coralie held him while he cried into her hair. Pablo soon appeared and cradled them both. It was such a tragedy for the fairy community, and it was the second tragedy that had happened in the park that summer, following close on the death of the human girl, Juliet.

The death of a fairy was rare and Coralie knew she would have rituals to perform. This would be the first time that she had presided over a funeral and subsequent rebirth ceremony since she became queen. But now she felt empty. She mourned for herself and Benjie.

35

Coralie was determined to do something special to recompense Kathleen and Rick for all their efforts to help the Pevi. They had been completely selfless in their devotion to the project and the functioning of the fuel cell appeared to be out-standing; better than anyone could have predicted or dared to imagine.

She wondered, *What can I offer that would come anywhere close to equalling their contribution to the fairy and Pevi society in Knole Park?*

Tomorrow she would be presiding over the rebirth of Zak. To her dismay, the fairies had marginally voted for a randomised rebirth, so Zak would not be reincarnated as his previous lovable character. Zak had played a few too many tricks on a few too many fairies during his life and this had counted against him when the vote had been taken yesterday. She had loved his antics and sense of humour, and he had always been charming and respectful, if slightly mischievous on occasion, with her.

So, the final decision had been taken that Zak had not made a sufficiently positive contribution to the fairy society and therefore, his genetic make-up would be randomised in the hope of producing a nobler fairy upon rebirth. Coralie's role tomorrow, was to extract one of Zak's teeth and pound it to a fine powder with her diamond-encrusted hammer. Zak's body would be buried in the woods by Pablo and Benjie and left for nature to devour. She would then place the tooth dust in a gold casket surrounded by the earth from a pine forest which had been soaked with fermented cow's milk. As tradition dictated, she would then break a fresh quail's egg on top and add a few sage leaves to create a pleasant aroma for the embryonic fairy. Then the party would start and continue for two nights, while the casket cooked slowly in the embers of a bonfire, surrounded by dancing and copulating fairies.

Coralie felt far too distraught at the loss of Zak to think about planning the party, but as always, she valued the fairy traditions and knew she could not shirk her duty. After all, it was not a death, but a rebirth that they would celebrate. The tragic death had occurred two days ago and she had mourned long and hard, crying into her pillow during the night, but being brave during the day to provide leadership to the shocked community. Now she needed to move on and enjoy the celebration of Zak's life and look forward to his reincarnation as another baby fairy.

Maybe I will personally take a close interest in the new fairy's up-bringing, she mused. This idea gave her more courage to face her responsibilities. She went off to find Padraig and Shawn, to ask their help in arranging the collection of wood for the bonfire and provision of ample quantities of booze and food for the two-day celebration of the rebirth. Neither of them had been especially close to Zak, but they knew how to organise a party.

Padraig and Shawn were, as usual, always happy to help Coralie and they loved a good rebirth party. They entered into the arrangements with great gusto. The party would start this evening in the dancing glade at 9:00 pm. The grass in the glade was still quite short from the fête and the protective barrier was still in place, so the fairies would not be seen or heard by any humans in the park.

With that organised, Coralie returned to her palace to rest, she also needed to start thinking about her speech to highlight the joy that Zak had brought to the community during his life. She would make a positive speech even though many fairies did not agree with her interpretation of his character. At least he had an amusing character. His antics mostly brought a brief embarrassment to some older fairies, they were rarely cruel.

Coralie badly needed to release her pent-up emotions, so she sought Pablo when she arrived home. He was playing his guitar on the balcony of their bedroom, overlooking the garden. She crept up behind him and placed a kiss on the nape of his neck. He wriggled with pleasure and she repeated the affectionate act. He laid down his guitar and stood up. He lifted her in his arms and walked over to their bed, where the bedclothes were still rumpled from last night's troubled sleep. Pablo understood Coralie needed to lose herself in passion for a while and he was ready to help. He too felt a need to do something physical to rid his body of tension and sad emotions. They made love with great ardour, breathing in the musty aromas of last night's stale bodies and the fresh scent of each other's sweat and pheromones. Their kisses came in waves, their tongues explored each other's bodies, and their caresses were bold and searching. Coralie came first and then a few moments later, they climaxed in unison. A joint passion for sex had brought them together initially and it kept them together. They both lay exhausted, but relaxed, while their heart rates slowly returned to normal. They slept for an hour, cuddled together in a sweaty embrace.

During her sleep, Coralie dreamt a vivid dream that was to have far-reaching consequences. In this quiet period following her orgasms, she had been able to empty her mind of muddled thoughts and then to subconsciously begin to conjure a plan on how she could thank Kathleen and Rick. The idea was radical, but she had confidence in ideas that came via her dreams. She was an unusually wise fairy who had powers to foresee the future on occasion. The humans may be shocked, but just possibly, they would agree and be delighted.

She awoke completely refreshed and excited by her visionary dream. Now she could start working again, she had the motivation to carry on with her duties. She decided to waste no more time in bed. She would go immediately to visit Kathleen with her preposterous proposition. Pablo could lie there for a while longer, but she had things to put in place.

First she went to her studio and picked up her two prize works of art; the life-sized bejewelled frog with the bewitching eyes, and the sensuous orchid plant, that had been intended as surprise birthday presents for Pablo. She carefully wrapped them in moss, tying each with a coloured ribbon, and packed them in her rucksack. They only just fitted and her rucksack was now very heavy. She realised that she would need help carrying it, so she summoned a passing seagull and hitched a ride to Kathleen's house.

It was a warm afternoon with a gentle breeze, so Kathleen was taking advantage of the clement weather and working in the garden, tending Juliet's favourite bed of euphorbias. It had become rather overgrown with weeds lately and was lacking water. She had neglected the garden recently and all the flower beds were badly in need of some care.

At least Robert found time to mow the lawn at the weekend, so that looks well groomed, she noted with relief.

Coralie arrived on the wings of the seagull and set down her heavy rucksack on the manicured lawn, dismissing her chauffeur.

'Hello, Kathleen. I wanted to thank you for helping the Pevi; your plan was an inspiration and now they are saved from extinction and having to relocate in the short term. They can continue to live with us in Knole Park for as long as Rick's machine functions. You have even made the grumpy bullfrog and his family happy. This is the dream solution that everyone had prayed for. I've brought presents for you and Rick. I hope you like them. They are my most recent and, probably, best-ever artistic creations. This one is for you,' she said handing the bejewelled frog to Kathleen, 'and would you please give this present to Rick?' Kathleen carefully unwrapped her present and found the frog sculpture in her package.

'It's so beautiful,' she exclaimed, 'I will treasure it always. I love the huge ruby eyes; see how they reflect the sunlight; it's almost as if he is watching me. And the brilliant green mosaic body, composed of a myriad of tiny pieces of different coloured ceramic chips. It's a wonderful piece of art. Thank you so much, you have extraordinary talent, Coralie. Can I know what's in the other package?'

Coralie explained that it was also a life-sized sculpture,

but this one was a highly realistic lilac-coloured orchid plant. Kathleen said she would phone Rick immediately and ask him to come round straight after work. Coralie was pleased as she wanted to discuss the next stage of her "thank-you" plan with both of them. Kathleen phoned Rick who set off from work on his motorbike without a moment's hesitation. It was a bit earlier than his usual leaving time, but he was the only person in the lab that day and Kathleen's call sounded important. He would be there in under an hour. Kathleen started to prepare tea and found tiny fairy cakes for everyone. Luckily, Robert was at work, so there would not be any difficult explanations. This would be her and Rick's first meeting since their intense discussion the other day, and Kathleen was determined it would be a meeting between friends, nothing more. She resolved to keep strong and true to her decision.

Rick soon joined them in the garden and opened his present. He too was delighted with the intricate sculpture; it was so realistic and delicate.

'I love the colour of the orchid, Coralie. It reminds me of something special.' Then he realised what it was. He looked at Kathleen and smiled his wry smile. She looked back at him blankly, having no clue what he was referring to. The colour of the orchid's petals was exactly the same as Kathleen's rather chic bra that he had seen a few days ago after the celebration with the fairies in the park. He felt honoured that Coralie had given them her best creations and the orchid's colour would be a constant reminder of the love he had shared briefly with Kathleen.

After some small talk, Coralie plucked up courage to approach phase two of her "thank-you" plan. It was not an easy topic, but she was convinced that it was worth talking about. She started by explaining that Zak had been tragically killed in the park, just like Juliet. No one knew the exact details of what had happened, but the funeral had taken place and now they were planning the rebirth. The rebirth took some explaining and Kathleen and Rick were full of questions and in awe of the process. They wished they could be there, but that was not allowed in fairy tradition. Coralie avoided telling them that Zak was to be reincarnated as a randomised fairy, which she felt was an insult to him. Instead, she just explained the randomised process as if that was the normal procedure. Then she asked the big question.

'Would you like to include a few grains of ash from Juliet's urn in the casket? In that way a small part of Juliet would be reborn as a fairy and she would live in the park with the fairies.'

Rick looked shocked, he was horrified, but Kathleen was intrigued and quietly pondered the proposal. Coralie had to admit, that this was without precedent in her fairy clan, and that she would prefer not to tell any of the fairies about her plan. It would be their secret. There was also the possibility that the addition of human ashes to the casket may even prevent the rebirth process altogether. However, there was a legend that a similar event had taken place several hundred years' ago in an Irish fairy clan and the rebirth had been successful. In fact, it had created a new subspecies of fairy, the very first leprechaun. She explained that the baby fairy would not be a reincarnation of Juliet, since it was Zak's rebirth, but some of Juliet's characteristics may be taken up by the new fairy. She also secretly hoped that if the process worked, then the baby fairy may have improved powers of communication with humans, which she saw as an advantage.

After a short pause, Rick said, 'Definitely, no. That's grotesque.'

Kathleen, however, said 'I don't know.'

Coralie explained that the decision must be made that afternoon as the rebirth would start that evening. She felt it was a wonderful opportunity to pay tribute to Juliet and preserve a small part of her. To have lost her completely at such a young age had been an awful tragedy and this was a chance to let part of her soul live a little longer, albeit in a completely different body. She further explained that in her dream, the baby fairy had been beautiful and had grown to become a great fairy leader with psychic powers.

All three sat in silence, pondering the unthinkable.

Finally, Kathleen spoke, 'Dear Coralie, I want to thank you for this wonderful suggestion. I feel it is definitely a truly unmissable opportunity for me to retain a part of my Juliet. Losing her at such a young age was so hard; I would be delighted if she had the chance to live a little longer, as a fairy. I am sure this is what she would want as well. I have been wondering what to do with her ashes recently. They can't stay on the mantelpiece in the lounge, it's too depressing. I wanted to scatter or bury them somewhere in nature that would be special to Juliet. She always loved Knole Park and I was thinking of making that her final resting place, if the owners would allow it, but now you are offering her the chance to be reborn and actually live there. It will be a fairy tale with a magical ending, just like *Sleeping Beauty*.'

Rick was still unconvinced. He worried what would happen if something went wrong; supposing they created a monster; that would not be a fit way to honour Juliet or Zak. He saw the process as genetic engineering, but completely haphazard, with an unknown outcome. They were playing at being God. Coralie could not counter his arguments because he was right, the outcome was unknown, but her instinct strongly told her that the result would be positive and wonderful. The idea had first come to her in a dream and her dreams were notoriously accurate at predicting the future.

Finally, Rick relented and reluctantly agreed to the idea. He still had strong reservations, but decided he would support Kathleen, because, after all, she had known and lived with Juliet for eighteen years while he was only a recent friend and lover. And so Kathleen went into the house and returned with a small glass jar that contained a few flakes of ash from Juliet's urn. She entrusted this to Coralie, then broke down in tears, overcome with emotion. Coralie kissed her, then Rick, and flew home, leaving the humans to come to terms with their momentous decision.

Later that evening the rebirth party began. There was an

electric feeling of excitement and anticipation generated by the fairies gathered together in the glade. The re-energised Pevi were also present, providing a spectacular display of lights. Coralie initiated the proceedings by paying tribute to Zak. She recounted an impressive list of generous actions that Zak had undertaken during his life and reminded the fairies of some of his more spectacular antics, embarrassing a few of them in the process. Benjie also asked to say a few words of tribute to his recently departed best friend. He ended his speech by asking for volunteers to become his new best friend and was rewarded with a mass of raised hands and cries of "Choose me, choose me".

Coralie ceremoniously placed the casket containing Zak's ground tooth, a few of Juliet's ashes, and the other ingredients required for the process of regeneration into the smouldering ashes of the giant bonfire. She whispered to herself, 'Good luck, Zak and Juliet, make us a beautiful new baby fairy.' Then the party started, and would continue for two nights. Shawn and Padraig had agreed to take turns keeping watch over the bonfire to ensure the ashes stayed warm and Benjie was acting as DJ. Juliet's iPod was coming in useful for the fairies for the second time.

For the next two nights the fairies partied in the glade, sleeping off the previous night's excesses in ever-changing huddles during the day. At the end of the second night, as soon as the sun appeared over the horizon, a surprisingly sober Coralie declared the rebirth festivities over and everyone clustered round the bonfire to watch the ritual opening of the casket.

Coralie removed the warm casket from the ashes. She looked heavenwards and uttered a short prayer. Then, with her heart in her mouth, she opened the casket and peered inside. And there lay a perfect tiny hermaphroditic fairy with the face of an angel...the face of Juliet.

Acknowledgements

I am indebted to the following people for their support and help with this project: my insightful and helpful editor at BubbleCow, Gary Smailes; the staff at Matador Publishers; especially my project manager, Amy Cooke, marketing manager, Sarah Taylor, website designer, Aimee Fry, and ebook manager, Amy Chadwick; friends who kindly read and commented on early drafts, including Andy and Francesca Vinter, Graham Moyes, and Jan and Jon Court; Anna Backerra for her faith in my ability to create a fascinating story; Alan and Suzy Fulton for taking photos of Knole Park for the back cover and my marketing projects; Warren Photographic for providing the photo for the front cover; and my husband, Han van de Waterbeemd, for his invaluable comments and enthusiasm for this project.

Principal Information Resources

Wikipedia (www.wikipedia.org).
Knole Park internet site (www.nationaltrust.org.uk/knole/).
The Transactional Manager by Abe Wagner, published by the Industrial Society, London (1996).

Copyright Acknowledgements

About the Author

V S Rose was born in Bromley, Kent in the UK. She worked in the pharmaceutical and biotechnology industry for thirty-five years and was a founding director of BioFocus plc, one of the first ever chemistry out-sourcing companies in the World. She received a PhD in computer-aided drug discovery in 1993 from the University of Reading. She lived in Sevenoaks from 1998-2002 and now lives with her second husband in the South of France, near Collioure, close to the Mediterranean Sea and the Pyrenees. She is an avid reader, enjoying many contemporary authors of diverse styles, including Haruki Murakami, Margaret Atwood, Alexander McCall Smith, Carlos Ruis Zafon, Joanne Harris, Ian McEwan, Kate Mosse, J.K. Rowling, Philip Pullman, C. J. Sansom and many others. Night of the Fête is her first novel.